IN QUIET PLACES

A Paperback Original
First published 1989 by
Poolbeg Press Ltd.
Knocksedan House,
Swords, Co. Dublin, Ireland.

Roy McFadden's tribute to Michael McLaverty, "Letter to an Irish Novelist", quoted in the Introduction, was first published in *Flowers for a Lady*, by Routledge, London, in 1945. Epigraph from B. Kiely: "Michael McLaverty: The Thorn in the Writer," *Hibernia*, 34, 17 July 1970. "The Child on the Swing" by Alexander Henderson is from *The Tunnelled Fire*, Martin Secker and Warburg, London. Some of Michael McLaverty's essays reproduced here were first published in *The P.E.N. in Ulster, Forecast* (Catholic Literary Foundation, Wisconsin) and *The Belfast Telegraph*.

ISBN 1 85371 040 7

Cover design by Steven Hope
Cover photograph courtesy of the McLaverty family.
Typeset by Print-Forme,
62 Santry Close, Dublin 9.
Printed by The Guernsey Press Ltd.,
Vale, Guernsey, Channel Islands.

IN QUIET PLACES

MICHAEL McLAVERTY

"Because of environment and choice his concern has been with man's lot in quiet places."

Benedict Kiely

POOLBEG

*In memory of my brother, Séamus Hillan**

* Editor's dedication

Acknowledgments

The editor wishes to express her grateful appreciation to Michael McLaverty and his family, for their unfailing help and support during the preparation of this book; to Professor John Cronin, of the English Department in Queen's University, Belfast, who supervised the doctoral thesis from which the project grew, and who helped greatly in the organisation of the material; and to the Institute of Irish Studies, Queen's University, Belfast, whose award of a Junior Fellowship (1986-1989) enabled the editor to bring the work to completion.

The assistance of the Arts Council (Northern Ireland) in the publication of this book is gratefully acknowledged.

Grateful acknowledgement is due to copyright holders for passages from the works of writers other than Michael McLaverty quoted in this book.

Contents

A Note on the Text

In Michael McLaverty's letters, no salutations or closing words are reproduced, in order to avoid repetition. The name of a correspondent is given only with the first of a series of letters; the absence of a name indicates another exchange with the same person. Michael McLaverty's address is given as Knock (where he lived until the early Forties), Belfast (where the McLaverty family moved at that time), or Strangford, where they have a holiday home.

[...] denotes a phrase illegible in manuscript.

Introduction

If you ignore the adolescent dream,
The raised fists of the mob, the tumbled bed,
It is because, knowing your pattern's form,
You choose the threads. Even this country fails
To blow your petalled purpose into grass,
Or drown you in a puddle's politics.*

Roy McFadden's poetic tribute to his friend, published first in 1945, catches much of the essential spirit of Michael McLaverty. Reserved to the point of shyness, McLaverty has consistently resisted fashionable trends in literature, so that, at whatever cost to his popularity, he has refused to make literary capital of political or sexual matters. This is not to suggest that he has been unaware of developments in literature over the past sixty years. In his many letters and articles, published here for the first time, he sets down with humour, and a finely developed critical sense, his views on literary and moral questions. That these writings have lain, virtually untouched, since the time of writing, is due largely to the writer's reticence. When asked, in the last few years, why he had stayed so far out of the limelight, his reply has always been the same: "I never wanted to put myself forward."

   To those who know his work, this book should afford much pleasure, as work unpublished for up to fifty years reaches, at last, a wider public. Those who know him only by repute, or by

* Roy McFadden, "Letter to an Irish Novelist", *Flowers For A Lady*, London, 1945.

1

such much-anthologised and justly famous stories as 'The Poteen Maker," or "The Wild Duck's Nest," may find revelation in the range of his writings; for the McLaverty of this book is not only novelist and writer of short stories, but literary critic and faithful correspondent with such friends and fellow writers as Daniel Corkery and John McGahern.

Here can be found the early version of "The Wild Duck's Nest," with a starkly different ending from that with which readers are familiar. Here, too, is the short story, "Leavetaking," which became Chapter Three of McLaverty's famous first novel, *Call My Brother Back*, and an early, more colloquial version of "Aunt Suzanne". In all, an astonishing eighteen stories were written in the years 1932-1939, during which time the author, married, with a young family, was also fully occupied with the teaching of schoolchildren. Nine of these stories appear here for the first time since their publication in the Thirties. They are not practice pieces. When they were published, they attracted the interest of, among others, the American anthologist Edward J. O'Brien, and John Middleton Murry. It was Murry, indeed, who persuaded McLaverty to change the ending of "The Wild Duck's Nest," because he believed that the original ending, in which the duck drops her egg when she flies upward in panic at the sound of the boy's footsteps, lacked "general truth," a phrase much used in later years by McLaverty himself. These nine stories are the early writings of one of the finest exponents of the short story form which this country has produced, showing his search for a voice and the discovery of his first subject—the people of the islands and of the city.

Later, in the Forties, he would turn his attention to those who, in Thoreau's phrase, "lead lives of quiet desperation." Much of his correspondence of this decade reflects this concern; and in those letters, as in his critical work of the Forties, which deals with such writers as Gerard Manley Hopkins and François Mauriac, there begins to emerge a growing concern with the moral responsibility of the writer. To read these is to understand his turning away, in the spirit of Hopkins, from what was, to him, the relatively straightforward discipline of the short story form, to a determined Mauriac-like devotion to the production of the moral novel. There is some irony in the fact that McLaverty took this decision just after he had entered what seemed a new phase in his writing, with the publication, in David Marcus's journal, *Irish Writing*, in 1948, of the strong and subtle story "Six Weeks On and Two Ashore." This was the first, and, with the exception of the later story, "After Forty Years," the only one of his stories to deal, however obliquely and delicately, with sexual matters. He would not write on this subject again; and there is further irony in the fact that, two years later, his contemporary, Francis McManus, would deal directly and powerfully with Irish attitudes to sexuality in his novel, *The Fire in the Dust*. By 1950, McLaverty was writing the novel which would be published in 1951 as *Truth in the Night*, a novel with a heroine strongly reminiscent of Mauriac's tormented women. Sexuality, as opposed to love, appears here, and in the later novels, as a snare and a delusion: the author would not risk the corruption of his readers by any further explorations of the kind so powerfully begun in "Six Weeks On and Two Ashore." He has been known, however, to make, in recent years, the wry comment that those who maintain that he cannot write about sex should read that story.

Readers, understandably, wanted more short stories, but were to be given only seven more over the next fifty years. The letters and critical articles of the Fifties and early Sixties reflect the author's deep struggle to produce a novel which would satisfy him, while at the same time demonstrating his growing concern with the encouragement of young writers, among them Séamus Heaney and John McGahern, both of whom speak of him with immense respect and deep affection. Yet, the way that these younger writers could go was not open to McLaverty. His deep sense that he must write nothing to shock the moral sensibility of his public caused him, in effect, to withdraw from the world of letters in 1965. In this year, it became clear that his last novel, *The Brightening Day*, had received a cool reception from critics and, a greater blow to him, from the reading public. The novel had cost him much effort, and he had deliberately changed its plot from that which had occurred to him in the early Fifties. In the original plan, the hero of the novel was to have had an ill-advised affair with a married woman, and to have fled his hometown in the wake of the scandal. Given the strong moral imperative under which McLaverty laboured from the late Forties onward, it was always unlikely that this story could go ahead as originally conceived. In the end the young man was unjustly accused of having had the scandalous affair, but was, in fact, innocent. *The Brightening Day* came out in the very year that John McGahern's second novel, *The Dark*, appeared, and, for McLaverty, it was a time to stop. He had been one of the first—perhaps the very first—to recognise McGahern's gift, but now, while he applauded his friend's success, and acknowledged the power of his writing, he withdrew, puzzled and uncomprehending, from a growing realisation that the public did not, as he did, recoil from McGahern's subject matter in *The Dark*.

McLaverty did not write any more novels. Although retired from full-time teaching, he continued to teach and lecture on a part-time basis. He made notes for future novels, and produced one or two late stories, but the letters and writings of this time show a man sadly resigned to the fact that the world had grown strange to him.

It would be too simple to say that he was born out of his time. It may be more accurate to say that he has lived his life out of his time, or at any rate, out of its prevailing concerns and preoccupations, remaining true only to the promptings of his intellectual and moral sense of right and wrong. It has never concerned him that his novels have not been runaway bestsellers; but he would have been bitterly ashamed to produce a popular novel against his conscience. Therefore, he has stayed out of the glare of publicity, writing, in Benedict Kiely's happy phrase, of "man's lot in quiet places," and content that a handful of friends should know the reason for his reticence.

In recent years, he has several times made notes for his autobiography, and has been saddened that he has not completed it. This collection, which ends with two autobiographical fragments, represents, in effect, the life story of Michael McLaverty, as told by himself.

Sophia Hillan King
10 April 1989

The Green Field

Irish Monthly, August 1932

It was a warm afternoon in summer, Maura Murphy, a slim fair-haired, girlish figure, stood in the porch of her small one-roomed island school overlooking the sea and the mainland. Behind her the children, oppressed by the heat of the day, fidgeted on long forms. Maura was bored, and with her hands clasped behind her back she idly regarded the blue sea and the grey land. The sun shone full on her face and threw a dark shadow into the white porch.

She watched the sea and the dark mountains of the mainland, with their elfin-like houses resembling scraps of white paper blown against a black hoarding. The sea winked and blinked with frivolous fairy-lights and, far-off, fishing curraghs wriggled like upturned beetles. Maura shaded her eyes as she gazed at the landscape of the island; little drills of potatoes spiralled around grey rocks and thin patches of corn gleamed like green islets in a grey sea. Man and women were in the turf-bogs and flashes of flaming-red petticoats, bare legs, and white frieze trousers symbolised industry and movement.

Maura sighed and mechanically looked to her left at a small green field within a stone's-throw of the school. A rough limestone road swept past one side of it, licking its unmortared stone wall. The grey of the surrounding country enhanced the greenness of the field and made it as conspicuous as an oasis. At one end of the field a few geese slept with their necks tucked under their wings, and a brown heifer lay lazily beside them swishing flies with its tail. Maura looked longingly at the field, and a quiet smile suggested inward happiness. Someone shouted in the school, and the teacher entered, her light-blue eyes restless, trying to detect the source of the noise. She tried to adopt an expression of gravity, but the children's faces intimated a failure. A donkey with creels of turf passed the large, low windows, and all eyes followed it. Maura rapped the desk with a sally-rod, and drew her pupils to attention. There was silence but for a clock ticking on the teacher's desk and a bee buzzing around a jam-jar of flowers.

The school-day being finished, Maura hummed a tune as she put her books in her desk, locked the porch door and set off for her home. She stood for a while looking over the breast-high fence that separated the green field from the road. It was flat and without rocks. A rabbit, unperturbed, sat on the far side nibbling grass. Maura moved. The rabbit cocked its ears, sat motionlessly on its hind legs, with large eyes staring at the disturber. She smiled, clapped her hands, and the rabbit disappeared with a flash of its tail into a fuchsia-hedge. Someone whistled to a dog, and, looking towards the direction of the sound, she saw Frank King, the owner of the field. Somehow Frank always managed to be working near the road when Maura was passing.

He was sharpening a knife on a flint stone, and his red face, blue jersey, and black hair formed a pleasing picture against the white background of his little cabin.

"It's the warm day that's in it, thank God," he said as Maura drew near.

"It is indeed, Frank. I see you are working as hard as usual."

"There's nothing like it when a body's able. It's the easy job you have yourself," continued Frank, good-humouredly.

Maura laughed and swayed to and fro light-heartedly.

"It's not so easy as it looks," she replied.

Frank blinked his eyes and tried to remove with his forefinger a fly that was embedded in his right eye.

"Don't rub it! Wait a minute and I'll remove it," said Maura, fumbling in her bag for a handkerchief.

Frank stooped and the girl leaned forward. She pulled down the lid gently. The young man thrilled as he felt her soft, gentle hand cool against his cheek.

"It's out now; it was only a midge," she said, withdrawing to her former position.

"You're the great girl, Maura. It's a lady doctor you should have been. There's Brigid inside there and it would have taken a day's poking at my eye before she could have got it out. She's as awkward as a seal out of water."

Brigid—Frank's sister, an elderly woman of forty—was standing in the shadow of the doorway. When she heard her name mentioned she pretended to be working around the dresser. When she saw Maura going away, she came and stood in the doorway, rubbing her hands on a sack tied round her waist.

Frank bent forward, placed his elbows on the stone fence, and, resting his chin on his hands, watched Maura swing over the crest of the road. He sighed, turned to go into the house, and encountered the sharp eyes of Brigid.

"Well! What kind of a carry-on is this, with your flattering talk to that hussy?"

"She's a good girl, Brigid," replied Frank sincerely, "as good, aye, and better than any's in Innisdall."

"It's the fine wife she'd make ye," said Brigid sarcastically. "She couldn't turn a griddle of bread or milk a cow. And her face as white as an egg with the powder, and her lips as red as the comb of a laying hen."

"If they are red it's from the walking she does be puttin' in and the mellow breezes that blow from the West, and I don't know what Maura done to you that you're so down on her,"

"Now, Frank, she wouldn't be makin' a good wife for ye."

"Nonsense, woman; what with me at the fishing and she teaching in the school we'd be millionaires in no time," said Frank, rubbing his hands on his white frieze trousers.

"It's the fine gentleman she'd be wantin'," said Brigid mockingly, "and not a poor gobaun like you."

"How do you know what she'd be wantin'? You can't get anyone yerself, and yer as jealous as a hungry sea-gull."

Brigid pushed past him saying, "I've my work to be mindin' and not listenin' to an ignorant omadhaun like yerself."

Frank laughed, shook his head haughtily, and closed the

half-door behind him.

As Maura swung gaily along the road she never suspected for one moment that she would be the chief topic of the Kings' conversation. To-morrow was a holiday. It was the annual regatta day for Innisdall Island. Boats would come from the mainland and depart after the dance, which was always held in the school-house. Maura was absorbed in her own thoughts about the dance and the visitors. She thought of her arrival on the island three years ago, and how she had hated leaving her room to come here, as she believed, to a waste of unrelieved loneliness. Time, however, had changed her outlook on life. Now she loved the island, with its coat of black bogs sleeved with grey rocks and patched with blue lakes and green thread. All these afforded her material for her brush and pencil, and urged her creative instinct to manifest itself. The people and the children were also lovable. By singing for them, dancing with them, and talking to them, Maura had succeeded in breaking the veneer of timid reverence which all islanders display in the presence of strangers.

She sighed over her own thoughts, and was sorry to have arrived home so quickly. Her shawled landlady was leaning over the half-door when Maura reached the threshold.

After dinner she took a book and a canvas and walked to the west end of the island, where tall cliffs dipped their grey legs into the blue basin of the Atlantic. She sat down, tried to read, and found it impossible. She lay on her back in a crevice, placed the book under her head, and gazed at the blue sky with its cotton-wool clouds. Delicious images of the school-house, the dance, and the green field flickered before her mind.

That green field always brought thoughts of the home she would share with him she loved. Their home would be a long one-storeyed cottage nestling snuggly beneath its yellow thatch. None knew better than the islanders how to thatch. She would paint the woodwork green like the field. There would be a winding path from the road to the cottage door. The school-children would help her to make that path. They would carry the rough limestone boulders to her, and they would put the native rock plants growing between the crevices. Pateen Dan would bring wild maiden-hair fern from the wrinkled rocks in the boreens. Little Maura Dhu would bring tufts of sea-pinks, and Barbara Coneen would come with wild pansies so like her own wide wondering eyes. Her thoughts raced on. She would have a dresser like Sorha's with its row of blue-banded bowls. And "back in the room" she would have a little altar.

Her deft fingers itched for activity. She stood up and dusted the short grass from her black frock. Near-by a little stream chattered to the stones and sang for the sea. For Maura it was in tune with her present mood: here she was—restless, but enjoying life and its sounds whilst yearning for companionship and love.

The walk had soothed her, and her early impatience vanished as she entered the house. She went into her bedroom, pulled out a frock which she was making for the dance, and commenced working at it.

* * *

The school-house was packed with mainlanders and islanders for the Innisdall Regatta Dance. A melodeon and fiddle sent sprightly notes into the night air. A knot of men stood in a shaft of light at the doorway. Within, heavily-shod men and smiling girls danced with a joyousness that was infectious. Frank sat near the door, his white collar immaculate in the dull lamp-light. His face was aglow and his eyes restless as he looked reverently towards Maura, in her black dress and white lace collar. She was talking and laughing with one of the strangers, a tall, black-haired man dressed in a light-grey suit. Frank saw her light a cigarette, and his feet shuffled uneasily on the floor. He thought of Brigid's remarks and he bit his lip. But then, as he recalled the returned Americans he had seen smoking, he smiled gently. The man in the grey suit sang, and the audience clapped and shouted—"Arrish!" Frank nudged a man beside him and asked who was the singer. The man told him that he was a school-teacher from the mainland.

Frank clapped. He knew that Maura must know him since they were of the same profession. He watched the dancers and beat time to the music with his feet. He was wrapt in wonder and was awakened from his musings by the M.C. shouting above the babble of voices, "Take your partners for the six-hand reel—ladies' choice!" From the corner of his eye Frank furtively glanced at Maura. She was on her feet and approaching him. He assumed an air of indifference by talking to the man beside him. The next instant he was on the floor oblivious of everything but her presence and the thought that she had chosen him from amongst all the dancers. He never felt so happy, yet when he had resumed his seat he knew he had blundered. It was the last dance, and he hadn't offered to leave her home. A twinge came to his heart when he saw her leave the dance with the grey-suited teacher.

Frank was going home behind them. The night was one of intangible loveliness. The moonlight poured down on the grey rocks, filling them with cold gleams like patches of mountain lake. The limestone road was like a river of liquid lead. Frank could clearly discern the two figures—Maura and the stranger—silhouetted at times against the clear, cloudless sky. They were walking abreast, but far apart. Frank thought they couldn't be in love. They stopped at the corner of the green field nearest his house. He couldn't pass them; he stooped under pretence of tying his lace, and felt the blood rushing to his head. Maura's laugh, clear and silvered in the deathly stillness of the night, came to his ears. An inexpressible loneliness came over him as he entered the house and threw himself on the settle near the dresser. He took off his boots. He held one in his hand, looking at the sole and thinking of Maura, the dance, and his own discomfiture. The boot dropped with a clatter on the flags, and Frank went to bed with the consoling thought that on to-morrow the visitors would be gone from the island.

Next day the island subsided into its normal life. But in school Maura was abstracted. She heard Pateen Dan piping the addition tables in his childish treble as from a distance. Barbara Coneen's surreptitious pranks were not unnoticed, but were allowed to go uncorrected. After school Maura called on the Kings. Frank was out at the fishing. Maura told Brigid to tell him to call up in the evening.

That night Frank King found himself entering Maura's house. They were alone. They sat on opposite sides of a clean-swept hearth, gazing into a furnace of turfen fire. The girl broke the stillness.

"Frank, I have something important to tell you ... You're one of the best friends I have in Innisdall ... I want to remain here all my life, but this—depends on you."

Frank couldn't understand this riddling talk. "Is it proposing to me she is?" he thought.

Before he could speak Maura had continued, fixing her eyes on him and speaking tremulously:

"Do you know your green field?"

"Of course I do: the one the wee heifer grazes in," he replied, drawing his stool nearer the girl.

"Well, Frank, it would be the splendid place for building a house."

"Devil the sight's better in Innisdall, and it's close to the school, too. But what would ye be wantin' the house for?" continued Frank earnestly.

"Well, Frank, I want to get married and I want to know ..."

"But! but!" Frank spluttered as he twisted his grey cap.

"I want to know would you sell it?"

At the words "sell it" Frank was in a tranced state, something surged within him, his breathing quickened, and, glancing towards the door, he rose up quickly and went out.

Rain fell and a cold breeze blew in from the sea. The stone ditches made music with the wind—sharp and mournful like the keen. Frank shivered as he bent his head before the breeze. The sounds of the night, the wind, the rain, and the solemn andante of the sea invaded his brain in a fantastic resonance, increasing his feeling of hopelessness and misery ... Pebbles crunched under his feet, a square patch of yellow light caught his eye—he was home. He lifted the latch and entered. The wind shook a porringer on the wall. Brigid was in bed. He lowered the lamp and sat down heavily on a stool before the fire, which glowed with a quiet red. Steam arose from his wet trousers and melted around the blackness of his bent head. His

11

fingers combed his hair, and his sighs answered the chirping crickets. He thought long and deeply … Everything flamed into his mind … Maura would marry the teacher from the mainland, and he would take her place in the school …

Rising up, he crossed to the dresser, pulled out a drawer and rummaged for paper amongst the contents of fishing tackle. He found an envelope, and, tearing a piece of a white paper-bag, he wrote: "Dear Maura, the green field is yours and may you be happy always.— Frank." He folded it, placed it in the envelope, and went out softly by the back door. His feet made squelching sounds as he walked over the sodden grass of the green field. Jumping over its stone fence, he came to the school—grey as a ghost, deserted and abandoned, with the rain dripping heavily from a broken gutter. He stood very still, listening to the rain, and then, slipping the envelope under the porch door, he walked across the green field towards his home.

The Turf Stack

Irish Monthly, December 1932

It was a Saturday evening in late August. Kevin Black, a small, bare-foot, fair-haired boy of twelve years, sat on a limestone rock, that made a grey patch in the black-cloaked bogland of Illaunmore. His blue jersey showed holes at the elbows, and his grey homespun trousers with their frayed edges flapped gently in the cold breeze that blew up from the cliffs. The sun sent large, black, cooling shadows and golden shafts of mellow light across the hummocky bogland. The boy, sitting high above the sea, looked a glorious figure of freedom in the golden atmosphere of the setting sun. Beside him his shaggy brown donkey, her creels filled with turf, kept pushing her head with a melancholy persistence between a few tufts of heather; and lazily she nibbled at the sweet grasses she found there. The boy was alone and lonely. He had neither brothers nor sisters. His mother being dead and his father out at the fishing, he had no one to help him to draw the turf. Since early morning he had been working feverishly to build as big a stack as the Cloughmore boys. As he sat tapping the rock with a peeled stick, he recalled with a feeling of sadness the rhyme they shouted at him yesterday, and he coming from the school—

"Kevin, Kevin, Kevin Black!
Has only got a wee turf stack!"

Their laughs rang in his ears, and he found himself clutching the stick tightly. Then he thought of all the turf he had heaped at the gable-end of his thatched home, and a sweet unrest embraced him as he pictured the big stack he would build this evening. At that moment a hawk shivered in the air, and the boy's grey eyes steeled as they saw it drop like a stone, and then balance motionlessly above the cliff-heads. A gull appeared, and the hawk darted below the rim of the cliffs.

Kevin looked at a mark on his hand—a small red-blue gash where he ripped it in the desk at school. He licked it with his tongue, and then hearing the cry of a bird he jumped up and his tanned legs flashed like yellow paint as he ran to the edge of the cliff. Below him was the sea rolling sheets on the dark bed of rocks while gulls wheeled and dipped like scraps of white paper. He lay flat on his stomach and pressed the heather away from his nose. His eyes scanned the ledges of the grey cliff. Half-way down stood the hawk. Its beak was blood-red where it tore at a bird whose feathers fluttered like blown ashes. Kevin clenched his fist, rose up, and ran around until he found a stone. There was a crash. The gulls and guillemots peopled the air with terrified screeches, and the boy's blood ran cold. Fear overcame him and he raced to the donkey, caught the reins, and proceeded along a boulder-strewn bridle path.

Down! down! he hauled the donkey, and then getting tired he let her lead the way while he exhorted her with an occasional tap from his peeled stick. Kevin loved the animal, and to-day more than ever she was worthy of his love. She had been drawing turf since morning without even getting her usual rest at unloading time. The path stretched in front, falling and twisting down to the grey rocky plain of the island where a few fields of corn gleamed gold and green. As the donkey stopped to bray, Kevin halted.

His eyes, trying to sight his father's fishing curragh, scanned the sea. Not a boat could he see, and inadvertently his eyes wandered to the mainland with its innumerable whitewashed houses like the distant view of a cemetery. The mountains were bluish now, and Errigal had its little white bonnet, which his father told him was its night-cap that was spun by the fairies who lived in the clouds. It was only yesterday he had written this in his composition, and he smiled quietly as he felt again the teacher hanging over him, big and warm, and patting his head for what he had written. A curlew's cry startled him, and looking in front he saw his donkey ahead moving quickly as if

14

sensing home and rest and freedom. The boy shivered. He put the stick between his teeth, and as he ran he swung his arms backwards and forwards as he had seen his father do in the winter time.

The donkey drew up at one end of the house. Kevin unloaded her. Around him was the loose turf he had drawn all day. He immediately bent his back and commenced the stacking. The sun had now set and cool shadows like dark-blue wine filled the hollows of the island. The scattered houses were peaceful and dream-like. But for Kevin there was no peace; he must build the turf. He head ached, his heart thumped, and the evening air made him apply a sleeve frequently to his nose. A woman stopped on the road and shouted, as the boy straightened himself up: "Musha, Kevin, you are a great gasur to be building a stack like that; and did you do it all yourself?"

"I did it surely," replied the boy, stooping down to lift a sod of turf, "and it's the big stack I'll have for my father coming home from the fishing." She passed with a quiet smile on her face, and her words incited Kevin to harder work. The stack mounted higher and higher. Up on the top of it he got, and his back ached as he looked towards Cloughmore, where turf-stacks against white gable-ends pooped at him like black-faced sheep. He descended and sat down upon an upturned creel. Perspiration made his hair lie in streaks over his forehead as if he had been bathing. He pulled his shirt below his jersey and wiped the sweat off his face. His eyes wandered to the sea, and in the distance was his father's curragh with her nose high out of the water.

No smoke was to be seen as he looked up at the chimney of the house. He rushed in. The fire was out and there was no kettle boiling. He rummaged in his school-bag, tore leaves out of an old scribbler, lay down on the hearth, and piled turf round the crumpled paper. He got up, folded a rod of paper, and lit it cautiously at a little lamp that burned before a picture of the Sacred Heart. Soon blue-smoke curled up the chimney, and as he blew at the turf with his mouth, his eyes smarted and stinging pains jigged in his ears.

To the well he ran with a can, the dew-gathering grass

brushing coldly upon his legs. The boat was drawing nearer, but he would have the kettle boiled in time. Passing by the turf stack he paused for a moment to look at it. He felt hammering in his head and to his unnerved senses the stack seemed higher and broader. He went into the house, filled the kettle, and swung it on the crook. Down on his knees he got, and he blew at the fire until he felt weak, exhausted. Mechanically he arose, and, crossing to the poster-bed that was in the kitchen, he fell in a faint upon it.

When his father entered he threw his string of wet fish in the earthen floor and went over to lift the boiling kettle off the crook. His eyes wandered to the bed, and, seeing his son, he called out: "Kevin, allana, what's on you?" Kevin didn't hear him. His mind was a riot of revolving wheels—glittering wheels that grew and grew and then burst into myriads of epileptic sparks. White clouds took their place: clouds that jostled each other and flew about like fat, gigantic gulls ... The hit the mountains and exploded in spots of smoke ... The sea was rising up. The curragh was growing larger and larger until it covered the sky with blackness—a blackness that was slashed with golden bars of shivering light ...

Kevin opened his eyes and felt a queer lightness. People were talking, and a yellow light was on the wall. It grew larger and larger, and as it approached him he shut his eyes and it scattered like a bursting shell of liquid light ... His mind grew dark, and out of the darkness arose the turf stack. It grew up bigger and bigger; it was tall now, as tall as a mountain. Kevin saw it waver, and his raving mind burst into speech: "It's going to fall on me; it will fall on me! Hold it back!" ... it was weighing him down ... He clutched and felt a cold hand upon his forehead.

"It's me Kevin, *a vic*. Don't be afeard!" The boy's eyes opened wide, and in the light of the oil lamp his face looked like yellow-painted wood.

Raising up the boy's head from the pillow, his father offered him a bowl of warm sweetened milk, saying: "Take this and you'll be all right, with the help of God. Sure it's weak with the hunger you are!"

The boy sipped the milk slowly, and when he had finished he lay back on the pillow and fell into a deep sleep.

When morning came Kevin lay in bed looking dreamily round the kitchen. His father came in dressed in his Sunday clothes, and seeing the boy awake he went over and sat on the bed. "And how's my little maneen this morning?"

"I'm all right now, Daddy ... Did you see my turf-stack?"

"Musha, indeed then, I did; and wasn't it the talk of the people this morning and them coming from the Mass ... And I'm the proud father to be having a son like you."

The Boots

Irish Monthly, May 1933

Two new boots, with battalions of silver-grey nails in their soles, lay on their sides winking at a turf fire. Their young owner was in bed, but his granny, a short-sighted supple old woman, pottered about the earthen kitchen-floor in her bare feet. Crossing to the door, she drew the bolt, lifted the latch, and looked out. It was a damp May morning. Transparent festooned veils of mist drifted slowly over the island like the blown breath from some invisible giant. Through the mist the blurred forms of the mainland mountains showed as if viewed through frosted glass. Here and there on the island blue smoke rolled from white-washed chimneys and snaked away before the light breeze. The old woman heard a bucket rattling and someone calling excitedly to hens. She came inside, sniffed audibly, and went over to the bedroom door. "Padraig! Padraig! Get up me son. It's time ye were stirrin'," she said, her voice sounding flat and toneless.

For the past hour or so a well built boy of fourteen was waiting for this call. He couldn't sleep, for he was too excited. He had just left school, and to-day he was going to the hiring-fair on the mainland, where he would see trains, motor cars, and great big houses. The anticipation of all these new delights fired his boyish imagination. And then his granny had a surprise for him. What would it be? Eager with happy expectations, he hopped out of bed in his shirt, knelt down, said short prayers, and breathlessly appeared in the kitchen, tying on his woollen braces to his grey homespun trousers.

"God and Mary between ye and all harm," said his granny,

18

fixing a black porringer on the fire. "And ye, too!" he replied.

There on the hearth was his surprise—two new boots and grey stockings to go with them.

He lifted the boots, and his sea-blue eyes lustred as he rubbed his hands along the nails and stamped them on the flag at the hearth. He hugged them to his breast. Never had he worn boots, and never had he been so happy. "They're the good boots and the dear wans. I bought them off a pedlar six months ago, knowing ye'd be going to be hired," she exclaimed with pride, as she watched the boy pulling on his stockings and tying them above his chubby knees. He opened the laces wide and commenced putting on his treasures. The boy's feet had grown considerably since the boots were purchased. He stood up; his feet were tightly encased, but he thought all boots fitted and felt that way. His heels did not go fully into their new sockets, and the boy felt very tall and manly, as he stood stamping on the hearth and making his boots produce delicious, clicking sounds. As the old woman prepared his breakfast, he washed himself in a tin basin of water that sat on an upturned crock at the side of the dresser. He sat down at the table, made the Sign of the Cross, lifted his mug of tea, and at every sip his feet jigged an accompaniment.

"Take yer time and eat yer fill," said his granny, as she wrapped a grey shirt, stockings, and a phial of Holy Water in a brown parcel. "God knows it's the long journey that's afore ye this day; divil a bit ye'll be hired if it's sick with the hunger ye are."

He stood in the doorway, his curly head as black as a raven's wing and his cheeks aglow with a manly elation. The old woman held his hands, giving her final admonitions: "Bless yerself with the Holy Water night and morn—when at yer prayers; write every two weeks; take five pounds if ye can get it." He kissed her on the forehead, and as he stepped into the misty morning a flood of Gaelic blessings followed him. He walked awkwardly, and as he stumbled now and them on the rough road his face became wry with discomfiture. He bowed his head as a moist-laden mist passed over him leaving pin-point pearls on his grey coat and tatters of dewy gossamer on

19

the fuchsia hedges that bordered the limestone road. At a crest on the road he saw the stone pier, and along-side it the black boat that was to take him to the mainland. He could only see two men on the pier, so he had plenty of time. He stopped and pressed the toe of his right boot towards the ground, but his efforts at relief were futile. Leaving the road he went along the strand, where he watched with glee the dimpled pattern his boots made on the yellow sand. Their tightness was momentarily forgotten as he entered with untiring zeal into his new artistic game. A man whistled; on looking up he saw that the boat was ready. He lifted his brown parcel and cautiously began to run. At the pier some boys were in their bare feet and they eyed him with childish envy. They all got into the boat, and Padraig sat near the stern, his legs crossed like a tailor so as to show off the rows of nails. The sails, as brown as rust, bellied before the light breeze, and the boat moved away, filling the face of the bay with ripples of smiles and light laughter.

A drizzle of soft rain came down, and as it made sibilant sounds on the sea like the whisperings of countless fairies, a strange, ineffable loneliness stole over Padraig. All the boys in the boat were silent, and the mast creaked a soft, mournful monotone. The rain ceased; a spear of sunlight pierced the clouds; the mists melted into nothingness, and the grey and green of the receding island smiled in drenched loveliness. Drooped heads were straightened as a boy hummed. "O'Donnell Abu," and Padraig placed his feet on the bottom of the boat and jubilantly beat time to the tune.

"Is it sink the boat ye want to do, Padraig Sweeney, with yer ploughman's clogs?" interrupted the man at the tiller. The remark made the boy stop, but a wave of happiness enveloped him and washed his face with quiet smiles. The boat meandered into Burtonport between little islets.

Up the stone steps of the pier a group of boys hurried, clambering and talking, and elbowing and jostling. Padraig followed, and in a few minutes they were at the station. And there was the train! A big, black monster hissing and grunting with impatience. At each issue of steam Padraig retreated, for he feared that at any moment it would blow up or leap upon him. He surveyed open-mouthed the wheels, the funnel, the man with the glossy peaked cap—never had he seen such a black-looking man. Still watching fixedly the engine, and trembling with each hiss and snort, he sidled over to join the three Boyles from his own side of the island. They mildly repulsed his friendliness because he was well built and would sure to be hired in preference to any of them. Remembering the rehearsals of his granny concerning the tickets, he queued up, clutching his money with unnecessary energy.

Into a compartment he got; older and more experienced boys had already camped in the corners. He sat down clutching his brown parcel with one hand and the seat with the other. A whistle blew, and Padraig jumped. The train grunted, moved off, and the boy fell forward, righted himself, and grabbed hold of the seat much as a disturbed limpet would cling to a rock. Seeing how composed were most of his friends, he relinquished his hold, leaned back and commenced nibbling furtively from Indian-meal bread in one of his pockets. At Dungloe, more boys got in, and none got out. Some had to stand, and Padraig drew his breath hissingly through his teeth as some one trod on one of his new boots. Gradually he became warm, his eyes tired, the big mountains around Dunlewey no longer jigged at the windows, his head leaned on his neighbour's shoulder, and he fell asleep.

At Letterkenny—the place of the hiring-fair—the train stopped, and the noise awakened him. He blinked his eyes dreamily, and seeing boys jostling past the open door of the carriage, he jumped up, still holding his brown parcel. He tried to hurry, but his feet ached painfully, and he walked with his knees slightly bent. Out in the streets the big fat horses, drawing red carts with blue wheels, caught his eye. He stood on the kerb-stone, his eyes wide with wonder, while his mind evoked vividly the "An Capall Mór" chart which hung on the school wall. Motors whizzed by, filling him with awe and a slight apprehension. Looking up, he saw that all the boys were in front. He hurried, and his boots, as he trailed them along the hard footpaths, seemed as heavy as lead. And now he was in the market-place. Never did he see such crowds except at Regatta Day on the island.

He left down his parcel on the kerb and stood straight, as his granny had advised. Two men were approaching him, and his heart beat so fast that he feared he would faint. One of the men felt his arms, his back, looked at his legs, and, standing back, he told the boy to walk a wheen of paces: "It's a kind of stiff he is about the feet," the man remarked, with a shake of the head; "the cows 'ud be in the corn before he'd cop them." When they walked away with mocking laughter, Padriag felt the world go black and the people in the fair become intangible—a picture without a breath of life. He wished at that moment to be home; he would never earn money to send his granny. A group of barefooted boys awaiting to be hired focussed his attention. He sat down, saying "A-a-a-h!" as he removed each boot. Unrolling his stockings and tying his boots together, his placed than around his neck, as he had seen island visitors do when crossing swolen streams. Rejoicing with his newly-won freedom, he stood erect with his feet, feeling deliciously cool as the sun streamed down on him. A little bronze-faced farmer, driving a cart and horse, was watching. Padraig smiled and stood with his chest puffed out as the man halted and spoke. "Walk till a see ye … How much would ye be wanting for the six months?"

"Five pounds," answered the boy gallantly.

"Jump into the cart; it's four pounds ten ye'll get, and plenty of work."

Sweeney threw his parcel into the cart, jumped over the tail-board, and sat down on straw while his new owner urged the horse forward.

"And what may ye be doin' wi' the boots? They wouldn't fit a fairy. It's five shillings I'll give ye for them. They'll fit a wee handful of a boy o' mine." Padraig thought for a long time, unslung the boots, and asked for his five shillings.

The cart drew up outside the Post Office, and the boy alighted and went in.

"I sold me wee boots, and I want to send the money to me granny," he shouted, his red face pressed against the wire meshes that covered the counter. When he had answered every question of the kind postmistress, and being assured for the sixth time that his granny would get the money, he ran outside. The man gave him the reins and as he felt the pulsating tug of the horse, tears of delight welled into his eyes, and he forgot about his new boots with their silver-grey nails.

The Grey Goat

Irish Monthly, August 1933

Brendan Sullivan, a fourteen-year-old boy, sat on the creepy near a turf fire, idly making spiral designs with his toes in the grey ashes. His mother, standing in the earthen kitchen floor and wiping a delph bowl in her hand, paused, as she gazed through the paper-patched western window. "Brendan, it's time you were bringin' in the goat; the daylight's leavin' the house," she said, turning her head towards her son.

"All right, mother," the boy answered, rising immediately, "it gets cold for Bess above the cliffs when the sun goes down." Brendan lifted his tattered grey cap from a peg in the limewashed wall and went out.

He yawned and blinked his eyes as he looked at the land of the island sloping down in irregular patches of greens and browns, to a coast which clawed a calm sea with rough fingers. His bare legs were mottled and the stone flag at the door seemed to burn the soles of his feet with cold. He moved on to the grass-rutted road in front of his thatched home and from there he saw the darkening cliffs of the mainland and a grey rope of mist on Fair Head. Small steamers plying near the far-off Scottish coast sent up black smoke which remained suspended in a motionless horizontal cloud. "It's too clear; and it's little fish me father will have to-night again," he ruminated as he buttoned his grey jacket around his blue-knitted jersey. A little boreen flanked a patch of corn, and up this he went, the dew-wet grass under his bare feet feeling beautifully silky and soft. The summer evening was as still as death and yet the slender stalks of unripened corn gently bowed their heads, and whisperings came, like the sound of rain on dry leaves, from the little field. Brendan wondered at this; but nothing reached the inner consciousness of his mind except the thump, thump of his heart in the answering stillness. Midges gathered around his head and a daddy-longlegs rudely kissed his cheek and winged away buzzingly. It startled him slightly, and he began whistling as he skipped along over stone gaps and across heather-covered hillocks. Bess heard him, and before he saw her, bleatings of welcome reached his ears. Immediately he came in sight, the goat strained on her tether, rearing her head and dispelling the loneliness with impatient meh-eh-eh-he-ehings. In the light of the evening she looked white. The boy, on reaching her, stood scratching her moiled head, a ritual which made her tail wag with delight. Far below them was the sea, while around, stacks of stones with mountain-sods drying on their flanks, pimpled the hillocks, and in the little valleys, reedy lakes, slate-blue like the sky, smiled up with calm faces. The wing-rush of a flock of wild-duck made Brendan look up, but as Bess pushed her wet nose into his hand, he went and lifted the staple.

Instantly the goat pricked her ears, rose on her hind legs at an imaginary enemy and then, realising she was loosed, gave a few sideways jumps and rushed down the hill, with Brendan laughing behind as he strained on the tautened rope. "Wo-o-o, Bess, woe girl!—ye spulpin! It's out all night I'll keep you," he shouted, rolling up the rope as he was pulled along. When they reached the byre door, Prince, the sheep-dog, came forward, but as Bess bent her head in a fighting attitude, the dog scurried nervously to the side. Brendan milked the goat, gave her a handful of hay, scratched her head, and with a "Good-night, Bess," he went out, shutting the byre door with a wooden peg.

The paraffin-lamp was lit when he entered the kitchen and his mother sat near it, her needles flashing with points of light as they darted in and out of an unfinished grey sock. Hanging on the crook was a three-legged pot of stirabout, bubbling and spluttering on the fire. Brendan nodded to his mother, drew a stool up to the fire, and began carving into shape a little wooden boat.

Outside Prince barked in the night, gravel crunched under

heavy feet, and the latch lifted to admit the boy's father with fishing gear, but no fish. "Not a tail did we see; it was too clear," he said, tonelessly, as he hung the lines on the rafters ... "There's nothin' for us now to pay the rates except sell the few sheep and the goat ... I'll bring them over at first tide in the mornin'." Brendan stirred uneasily; he had no fish to gut and after taking his porridge quietly, he went disconsolately up to his room. His younger brother, Bob, and wee Ethna were already in bed. He needn't waken them; he'd wait until the morning with the tragic news. As he undressed, pictures of Bess as a little kid flickered before his mind: his feeding her on an improvised "bottle"; the laughter and the fun of Ethna and Bob, and now Bess—our Bess—was going away!

And morning came clear and bright and Brendan was up early to help his father to round up the sheep. On returning, the sun was strong and Bob and Ethna were out at the gable-end playing "school." Brendan ran across to them and when he told the news, little Ethna sucked her thumb and began to cry into her white pinafore. "Wisht, arra, that wid you," said the manly Brendan, "and don't let mammie see you."

He left them to their play, got the scissors and entered the byre. Bess arose from where she was lying and the boy edged her into the light of the open door. Her dark eyes, shiny as sloes, looked up at him full of a deep obedience and a captivating shyness. "Poor Bess, you'll never see Rathlin again!" he said as he cut off from her long grey coat three pieces of hair. The goat never flinched, for many a time she had provided Brendan's father with fishing flies of a silky greyness. But Bess's hair somewhat mollified Ethna, who immediately ran into the house and placed it in her prayer book. Young Bob disappeared for a time, and on a little hill behind the house he dug a grave with a spoon. Into the grave he reverently placed the hair, covered it with clay, and at the head he placed a flat stone with crude nail-carved letterings: "Our Bess—R.I.P."

When he returned Brendan was setting off with the goat, while his father was to follow with the sheep in the cart. Bob and Ethna went a piece of the road and, kissing Bess for the last time, they returned homewards broken-hearted.

The day was gloriously fine. The sun trickled down shimmering waves of heat on the land, while Bess's hooves beat the hard road with breath-like sounds. When they were passing the chapel, Brendan halted and hung the goat's rope on the iron gate-post. The gate creaked as he pushed it open. He went into the chapel. It was peacefully lonely. He dipped a finger into a delph bowl of holy water, and knelt down before a statue of St Anthony. "Please, St Anthony," he said earnestly, "don't let anyone buy Bess and I'll put a halfpenny in your box." Rising up, he thought he saw a smile on the face of the Saint and he emerged into the bright sunlight, feeling a little happier. The goat was chewing a piece of paper and looked up at the boy with mischievous irreverence in her eyes. The Church brae led to the quay and down this he hauled a now very "contrairy" goat. She jumped sideways, stopped rigidly, rose up in an attitude of defiance and then descended lightly, butting her head into the boy's hand.

In the small sailing boat the sheep lay with their feet tied, and Brendan sat near the stern with the goat's head lovingly embraced in the folds of his little jacket. The tall white cliffs of Rathlin seemed small when the boat reached Ballycastle. Bess was pushed on to the cement pier, her legs stiff and her eyes looking vacantly in front. After rubbing her legs, Brendan caught the rope near her neck and set off for the market-square. The motor cars frightened her and she became crotchety, sometimes standing stiffly until Brendan would give her a push from behind.

At last they reached the fair. Pigs squealed, cows mooed, hens cackled, shawled women at stalls shouted "yellow man— 2d. a pound!" while an old gipsy turned the handle of a barrel organ and out came "Danny Boy," protesting with many a screech and growl. But to all this medley of strange sights and sounds the goat, wedged between two carts, kept her island complacency; so contentedly did she chew her cud that Brendan got vexed and said: "It's maybe you want to leave us ... " His talk was interrupted as he saw his father and a red-faced man shaking hands after the customary spit of good fellowship. The boy's heart beat fast as he saw them enter a nearby "pub."

Maybe Bess was sold. In a few minutes they emerged, his father's face wreathed in smiles as he bade the other man "Good-Luck!" Approaching the boy he said gleefully: "Well, Brendan, me son, I got a grand price for the sheep, thank God." For a short time they stood together and then a fat red-faced woman, with a black shawl around her shoulders, came over to them. She eyed the goat critically, looked at its teeth, blew into its ears, felt its ribs and then, standing back, she bawled: "It's four shillings I'm offering you, and that's a shillin' too much, for I'm sure she'd die on me—the poor, thin, island crayture!" At these remarks Brendan's father straightened up and laughed loudly and good-humouredly. The woman tightened her shawl around her shoulders and went off with a shake of her head.

"It's likin' the goat for nothin' these people want, and them knowin' we don't like the trouble of boatin' her back … But, as sure as me name's Sullivan, back Bess will go this very day, and that's that! … Come on, me son!" said the father, his voice deep-toned with conviction.

The Letter

Irish Monthly, December 1933

Winter had come to Roecarra. A December wind blew over the naked-grey land, whistling sharply through the unmortared stone hedges and making the donkeys shiver in their beds of sapless bracken. The morning sky was ice-blue streaked with white skeletons of clouds. Whitewashed houses, which seemed like emanations of the earth itself, were cold and forlorn in their scattered nakedness. It was early morning and no life yet stirred.

Gradually a winter sun arose—a dull apricot above the mountains to the east. Its spent rays stole silently over the bare land, picking a white gleam from the houses and making the nearby sea blink with a sparkling coldness. But there was no heat from the light of this sun as the vicious wind lifted a curve of dust from the road and raced along shivering the scanty grasses and tugging at the leathern hinges on the crude donkey-byres. The crow of a cock pierced the wind, while a donkey roared hoarsely. A small boy stirred in his bed, twisted and turned, trying to draw heat from a wash-worn blanket that covered him. His head felt cold and he awoke blinking at a cardboard-patched window in the room.

The room was bare and the cobwebbed beams that held the thatch were brown with years and turf-smoke. The boy sniffed and drew in a wheezing breath of cold air. He was about to coil himself up again when his mother called from the kitchen: "Are ye asleep, Tameen? It's time ye were movin' for the school." The woman who spoke was small and thin and her eyes were red-rimmed and watery and she tried to stir into life a fire of sticks and turf mould. Her teeth chattered as she pinned a green-black shawl more tightly around her throat, and her bare feet on the stone flags were numb with cold. She paused at the dresser looking sadly at a jug of buttermilk and a spoonful of flour that lay in a tin basin. She muttered something inaudible and her eyes turned towards the Cunard Line calendar which had hung on the wall since Teresa, her only girl, had gone to America. "Mo leun géar that Teresa hasn't written. It's workin' hard she is surely and it is so near the Christmas—four full weeks now and no work!" Her thoughts were interrupted as Tameen appeared in the kitchen, dressed in a blood-red petticoat and grey jacket, while his feet were bare and brown. For a moment he stood, looking at his mother standing by the dresser stirring the flour. "Tameen," she said tonelessly, "run over to Mrs Quirke's for a quarter stone of flour. Maybe, with God's help, Teresa's letter will come to-day and we can pay her in the evenin'." The boy's lip dropped when he heard this, and dolefully he opened the door and went out into the coldness of the winter morning. It seemed to him that he was continually going to the shop asking for little things. He didn't mind going when Teresa's letters arrived, for the had always a fistful of money with him and Mrs Quirke always gave him an acid-drop. With the long delay that was now on the letter the shop-keeper had got angry and sceptical and each day Tameen was scolded and told not to come back.

Now he drew near the shop and he went more slowly, keeping close into the stone-hedge of the road as if he were bent on something evil. He could see it clearly, it was the only slated house in Roecarra, and the frost whitening the cold-blue slates repulsed the boy with unfriendliness and filled him with a sickening feeling of solitariness. He would rather go to school hungry than face the shopkeeper again. But his mother had told him to go and he trudged on reluctantly till he came in front of the house, which was situated in off the road. A big fat collie dog lay at the closed door and got up, barking furiously as he ran towards the barelegged boy. For a moment Tameen halted, wishing that the dog would bite him or knock him down. A fat woman, very tall with large jowls, and sleeves rolled above her mottled arms, called the dog in a deep, commanding tone—a tone that sent great fear into Tameen's heart and made the dog's tail drop limply between his legs. Shyly and nervously the boy entered the shop and the same smell of soap and paraffin oil and aniseed balls reached him. "Well, I suppose the letter has come and it's in to pay me you are?" said Mrs Quirke sarcastically as she leaned over the counter with her brows furrowed and a scowl upon her coarse features. The boy, his hands toying at his red petticoat, didn't reply, but looked at his bare toes making patterns on meal that had fallen on the cement floor. "What is it you want now?" she continued sharply as she began opening a fat black notebook. "It's a quarter of flour me mother wants and it's surely to-day that Teresa's letter will come." "Hm! if it doesn't ye needn't come back; for if it's not flour, it's tea or sugar ye do be wantin'," she retorted giving her copying-ink pencil a lick and writing something in her black book. As she weighed the flour into a black paper bag, dropping it in with economic exactitude, the boy yearningly watched sweets that winked yellow eyes at him from a glass bottle at the side of the counter.

It wasn't long until he was home again, and it wasn't long until he set off for school, warm within from the warm cake made from Mrs Quirke's flour and cold without from the biting wind. He started to run, his little cotton bag, tied around his shoulders with cord, bobbing up and down in his back. It was good to get into the one-roomed school and it was better to get near the great fire of turves which roared up the chimney. Through the large low windows of the school Arran could be seen lying ever so far out. Often when the master turned his back Tameen's head turned towards the window, trying to sight a big steamer moving up to Galway. Nothing could he see except darkening patches of water as the wind scurried across it. There'd be no letter to-day, and to-morrow it would be himself would be going to Mrs Quirke's again. The thought chilled him, but as the teacher rapped the blackboard with his knuckles Tameen jumped. The master began a lesson on Australia, and as he talked about the goldfields Tameen's mind wandered again. He saw himself digging in the rocks behind his

31

house and coming on gold—not raw gold, but gold coins he pictured. And he bought his mother shawls, and bags of flour, and flithches of bacon to hang from the rafters just like Mrs Quirke's.

When school was over he rushed on, not waiting for the other boys, until he came to the post office. The post-car had just arrived and a string of people waited anxiously for letters, while old men hobbling on sticks came for the pension. Every day for a long time Tameen had waited for the letter and each day he returned home tired and sad. But to-day was different. His mother's name was called out and he went and received the letter; he looked at it; there was the same red stamp with the queer man's head and the wavy black lines across it. But the handwriting was different. It wasn't Teresa's and there might be no money in it. He placed the letter in a book in his bag and started to run.

His mother was looking out for him, and when she saw the wild hurry that was on her son she came to meet him. Breathlessly he told her of the strange letter as he drew it from his bag. She opened it carefully with a hairpin and pulled out a folded sheet with a number of dollar bills within it. Delight came on them at the sight of the money. They sat down at the glowing fistful of turf on the hearth and the mother handed the letter to her son to read the English that was in it. Tameen, his eyes bright with understanding, took it in his hands. But as he haltingly read, the mother clutched at her shawl—Teresa was dead and her friend had sent the letter with all Teresa's savings ... Realisation came slowly, drained out of the bare silence, and flowed around them, chilling their bodies. A cry broke from the woman, a sound like a stiffled whine; Tameen's eyes went round with wonder, his young lips quivered slightly, and he burst into tears. The mother drew him towards her, held him tightly as if he, too, were about to be taken from her, while the crumpled money lay on the earthen floor and the blue wind keened outside.

The Wild Duck's Nest

Irish Monthly, April 1934

It was evening in late March. The sun was nearing its setting, its soft rays gilding the western limestone headland of Rathlin Island and washing its green hills with wet gold light. A small boy walked jauntily along a hoof-printed path that wriggled between the folds of these hills and opened out into a crater-like valley on the cliff-top. Presently he stopped as if remembering something, then suddenly he left the path, and began running up one of the hills. When he reached the top he was out of breath and stood watching fan-shaped streaks of light radiating from golden-edged clouds, the scene reminding him of a picture he had seen of the Transfiguration. A short distance below him was the cow munching at the edge of a reedy lake. Colm ran down to meet her, waving his stick in the air, and the wind rumbling in his ears made him give an exultant whoop which splashed upon the hills in a shower of echoed sound. A flock of gulls lying on the short green grass near the lake rose up languidly, drifting lazily like blown snowflakes over the rim of the cliff.

The lake faced west and was fed by a stream, the drainings of the semicircling hills. One side was open to the winds from the sea, and in winter a little outlet trickled over the cliffs, making a black vein in their grey sides. The boy lifted stones and began throwing them into the lake, weaving web after web on its calm surface. Then he skimmed the water with flat stones, some of them jumping the surface and coming to rest on the other side. He was delighted with himself, and after listening to his echoing shouts of delight he ran to fetch his cow. Gently he tapped her on the side and reluctantly she went towards the brown-mudded path that led out of the valley. The boy was about to throw a final stone into the lake when a bird flew low over his head, its neck astrain, and its orange-coloured legs clear in the saffron light. It was a wild duck. It circled the lake twice, thrice, coming lower each time and then with a nervous flapping of wings it skidded along the surface, its legs breaking the water. The boy with dilated eyes watched it eagerly as he turned back and moved slowly along the edge of the lake. The duck was going to the farther end where bulrushes, wild irises and sedge grew around sods of islands and bearded tussocks. Colm stood to watch the bird meandering between tall bulrushes, its body, black and solid as stone against the greying water. Then, as if it had sunk, it was gone. The boy ran stealthily along the bank, looking away from the lake, pretending indifference to the wild duck's movements. When he came opposite to where he had last seen the bird he stopped and peered closely through the gently-sighing reed whose shadows streaked the water in a maze of black strokes. In front of him was a soddy islet guarded by the spears of sedge and separated from the bank by a narrow channel of water. The water wasn't too deep—he could wade across with care.

Rolling up his short trousers he began to wade, his arms outstretched, and his legs brown and stunted in the mountain water. As he drew near the islet, his feet sank in the mud and bubbles winked up at him. He went more carefully and nervously, peeping through the avenues of reeds and watching each tussock closely. Then one trouser fell, and dipped into the water; the boy dropped his hands to roll it up, he unbalanced, made a splashing sound, and the bird arose with a squawk and whirred away over the cliffs. Colm clambered on to the wet-soaked sod of land, which was spattered with seagulls' feathers and bits of wind-blown rushes. Into each hummock he looked, pulling back the long grass, running hither and thither as if engaged in some queer game. At last he came on the nest facing seawards. Two flat rocks dimpled the face of the water and between them was a neck of land matted with coarse grass containing the nest. It was untidily built of dried rushes, straw and feathers, and in it lay one solitary egg. Colm was delighted.

He looked around and saw no one. The nest was his. He lifted the egg, smooth and green as the sky, with a faint tinge of yellow like the reflected light from a buttercup; and then he felt he had done wrong. He left it back quickly. He knew he shouldn't have touched it and he wondered would the bird forsake it. A vague sadness stole over him and he felt in his heart that he had sinned. Carefully smoothing out his footprints he hurriedly left the islet and ran after his cow. The sun had now set and the cold shiver of evening enveloped him, chilling his body and saddening his mind.

In the morning he was up and away to school. He took the grass rut that edged the road, for it was softer on the bare feet. His house was the last on the western headland, and after a mile or so he was joined by Peadar Ruadh; both boys, dressed in similar hand-knitted blue jerseys and grey trousers, carried home-made schoolbags. Colm was full of the nest and as soon as he joined his companion he said eagerly: "Peadar, I've a nest—a wild duck's with one egg."

"And how do you know it's a wild duck's?" asked Peadar, slightly jealous.

"Sure I saw her with my own two eyes, her brown speckled back with a crow's patch on it, and her little yellow legs and—"

"Where is it?" interrupted Peadar in a challenging tone.

"I'm not going to tell you, for you'd rob it," retorted Colm sensing unfriendliness.

"Aach! I suppose it's a tame duck's you have or maybe an old gull's," replied Peadar with sarcasm.

Colm made a puss at his companion. "A lot you know!" he said, "for a gull's egg has spots and this one is greenish-white, for I had it in my hand."

And then the words he didn't want to hear rushed from Peadar in a mocking chant: "You had it in your hand! She'll forsake it! She'll forsake! She'll forsake!

Colm felt as if he would choke or cry with vexation. His mind told him that Peadar was right, but somehow he couldn't give into it and he replied: "She'll not forsake! She'll not! I know she'll not!"

But in school his faith wavered. Through the windows he

could see moving sheets of rain—rain that dribbled down the panes filling his mind with thoughts of the lake creased and chilled by the wind; the nest sodden and black with wetness; and the egg cold as a cave stone. He shivered from the thoughts and fidgeted with the ink-well cover, sliding it backwards and forwards mechanically. The mischievous look had gone from his eyes and the school-day dragged on interminably. But at last they were out in the rain, Colm rushing home as fast as he could.

He spent little time at his dinner of potatoes and salted fish and played none with his baby brothers and sisters, but hurried out to the valley, now smoky with drifts of slanting rain, its soaked grass yielding to the bare feet. Before long he was at the lake-side where the rain lisped ceaselessly in the water and wavelets licked the seeping sides leaving an irregular line of froth like frost on a grey slate. Opposite the islet the boy entered the water. The wind was blowing into his face, rustling noisily the rushes, heavy with the dust of rain. A moss-cheeper, swaying on a reed like a mouse, filled the air with light cries of loneliness. The boy reached the islet, his heart thumping with excitement, wondering did the bird forsake. He went slowly, quietly, on to the strip of land that led to the nest. He rose on his toes, looking over the sedge to see if he could see her. And then every muscle tautened. She was on, her shoulders hunched up, and her bill lying on her breast as if she were asleep. Colm's heart thumped wildly in his ears. She hadn't forsaken. He was about to turn stealthily away. Something happened. The bird moved, her neck straightened, twitching nervously from side to side. The boy's head swam with lightness. He stood transfixed. The wild duck, with a panicky flapping, rose heavily, squawking as she did so, a piece of straw and a white object momentarily entwined in her legs. The egg fell on the flat wet rock beside the nest, besmearing it with yellow slime. A sense of tremendous guilt seized Colm, a throbbing silence enveloped him as if everything had gone from the earth leaving him alone. Stupefied, numbed to every physical sense, he floundered across the black water, running wildly from the scene of the disaster.

The Trout

Irish Monthly, January 1935

For a long while Coilin lay in bed listening to the rain, the thatch dripping, and the barrel at the gable-end spluttering to the fast-falling drops.

"If it keeps on raining like this," he said to himself, "there'll be no school for me to-day." He got up, wiped a peep-hole in the little window with his shirt sleeve and looked out. The slanting rain fell like thin segments of fine wire, and across the darkened bogland cheerless hills rose up with shawls of mist on their shoulders. Gleefully the boy returned to bed. By the time the rain had stopped he would be too late for school and then he could go fishing. Outside it pelted with great vigour, rattling in the buckets like hailstones. The sound sent a happy shiver through him and his toes waggled with delight.

His eager mind began planning an expedition to the lake and the trout going mad after the rain. Then something happened in the room. A strange stillness pervaded it and Coilin raised his head from the pillow, listening. The rain had ceased, and the room was slowly brightening as the wet sunlight filtered through the dusty window and splashed on the cement floor in a golden patch of light. It washed the darkness from the walls and pushed into relief a large loom that straddled in a corner like some ancient musical instrument. Coilin fixed his attention on the loom, on the sunlight running up and down its barred threads. Thinking that it was soon his father would be coming in to start work, he arose from his bed.

When he entered the kitchen it was empty. The fire on the hearth was lit and a black kettle hissed steam up the wide chimney. He opened the back door and had another look at the morning. The wind had torn the shawls of mist and scattered the rags upon the laps of the hills. The sky was a deep blue, bolstered with billowy clouds, and the land below shimmered coldly with jewelled drops of wet sunlight. Small lakes gleamed blue like the sky, while brown rivers filled the air with great noise.

"'Tis wild the trout will be this day," muttered Coilin as his eye focussed yearningly on a crack in the hills that led to Loch Cam.

He turned into the house as his mother entered by the other door, cans of milk in each hand and pieces of grass sticking to her wet boots. She swung a black shawl from around her head and hooked it to a nail in the wall. The boy dropped his eyes when his mother looked at him, and as she prepared his breakfast he went outside to the byre. A long bamboo fishing-rod lay along the wall on three nails. He carefully took the line off it, rolled it into a nest-like bundle, and hid it under three sods of turf at the corner of the stack. In the kitchen a mug of steaming tea, an egg, and a large farl of buttered bread awaited him.

"It must be well on, Coilin. I saw a few scholars going the road and I milking. Hurry, *a vic*, and don't be getting the rod for being late."

Coilin's face lengthened. Guilt was written all over it as he sat at the table in his shirt and trousers, his back to his mother. When he had finished he pulled on a white home-spun jersey, which made his hair look redder and the freckles on his face brighter. His mother handed him his coarse-linen schoolbag and as he was going out the door she stopped him to shape his hair. As the coarse comb ran through his head Coilin's eyes puckered, he made faces, and his bare feet shuffled impatiently.

"'Tis late I am now," he added petulantly, hoping his mother would agree and keep him at home.

She raised her eyes to the sun and replied: "Plenty of time you have still if you don't dally on the road."

He passed the byre door, ran to the stack, lifted his line and stuffed it into his bag. Then with great haste he scampered off, stopping once to wave to his mother, who stood at the door looking after him. Not a soul did he see on the rough road stretching in front and he slowed down, convinced that he was late. Some part of him wanted to go to school, but his feet lagged behind as a persistent voice said: "It's no use going now, for you're dead late." A thrush perched on a stone fence bubbled out in song, and Coilin was sure it sang "You're late! You're late! Don't go! Don't go!"

Conflicting thoughts warred in his mind and momentarily ceased when the boy reached a crest on the road. Stretching gently below him was a land of rock and little homes, and far to the right the one-roomed school looked like a sheet of white paper. Two little black figures were running towards it and Coilin pictured the master raising the cane and the two laggards going to their seats with stinging palms. An emptiness came over the land and the boy felt as if every living thing, except himself and the lakes and the mountains, had been sucked into the black mouth of the white-faced school. Without a thought he suddenly left the road scampering behind rocks, hiding and dodging as if the world were now full of spying eyes. His feet led him across rocky bogland to the crack in the hills. A stitch in his side made him stop.

Far off he heard the rumble of a 'bus and his eyes spied it moving along the main road like a great red beetle. His mind raced to it and he wished that he was the conductor punching tickets all day long from here to Galway. The 'bus stopped outside the Gárdaí barracks.

"It must be ten o'clock," he said to himself, and he saw the master adjusting his specs, saying: "Now, Sixth, you learn your spellings and woe betide any of you that miss." The master was a holy terror on spellings. Coilin smiled, rejoicing in his forbidden freedom. Near him a dog barked and he crouched as a man passed over a hill after sheep. Then the boy arose, hid his schoolbag in a drain, leaving a stone beside it to mark the place. He was now carefree like the wind, for if he met anyone he could say he was looking for a stray sheep.

Presently the hills around parted and Coilin found Lock Cam in front, its corrugated surface running before the wind like a flowing river. Rock-scarred hills sloped down to it and boulders, like giants' heads, littered the shore. Beside him a stream, covered by a mass of rushes and arching bracken, rattled over hidden stones, and where it entered the lake there was a mad tossing and jabbling of water. Near the mouth of the river, but separated from it by a causeway of stones, was a dark bite of water with high shelving jaws of rock. Here Coilin stopped to tear up seeping sods in his search for worms. There was a damp smell of sodden bracken and bog water.

He baited the hook, clambered up a rock overlooking the pool and into it he threw his line, which fell with a gentle plop into the muddy water. He lay flat on the rock, line in hand, watching dreamily a fringe of froth gathering around the cork, and the wavelets polishing its brown surface. A shadow passed over the water and a gull hovered, its little legs dangling in the air, and the snowy whiteness underneath its wings glowing in the sun. He fell to wondering what it would be like to be a gull flying far over the lake and out to sea … The line chugged and the cork sank. Coilin scrambled excitedly to his feet, his eyes staring at the white gleam from the fish turning in the water. A thin blade of dripping gold wriggled in the sunlight and soon the trout lay on the grass, its mouth gaping, its fins shivering, its eye a glistening bead encircled by a wet-gold ring.

Tightly holding the ice-cold trout, Coilin extracted the hook and rebaited. For a while the released fish flailed the grass with its tail and then suddenly stopped. Cold tremorings convulsed the tiny body as its wet colouring drained away in the hot sun. The boy covered it with grass. He climbed exultantly back on the rock, all thought of school banished from his mind.

Overhead the sun streamed down and honeycomb reflections quivered near the feet of the water-lapped rocks. Its rays fell on the pool and filled it with brown dust. But the boy paid no heed to the sun as fish after fish was lifted up the rock and onto the bank. Soon six little trout were lying in a row like knives. After that they stopped biting. The water cleared.

Coilin could see the leaf-brown bottom of the pool, and the dark fish approaching his bait, sniffing it and turning away with a whisk of their tails. He knew the day's fishing was at an end and lying on his stomach he dropped pieces of worms into the water, looking at the trout sucking them greedily into their mouths. It thrilled him to observe the delicate movement of their leaf-lined fins and the perpetual motion of their gills. He often wondered how they could drink so much but his own reflection now engaged his attention. He began making faces, pulling ears and spitting at the grotesque head that grinned back at him from the water. A cloud of midges danced into his line of vision and Coilin got up irritated. He pelted them with stones, but the midges danced on oblivious, and the boy lay down on the bank defeated, exhausted.

When he went to his fish they were all stiff, their wet loveliness dried into a pale rainbow of colour. He put them on a piece of string and made off by the little river to where he had hidden his bag. He wondered what time it could be and as he wondered, fear and remorse now took possession of him. What could he tell his mother? The more he thought, the more doleful he became.

Along bypaths through he bog he came out on the road that led to his home. He sat down. Then his eyes rested on Granny O'Connor's cottage with its sack-coloured thatch and clean white walls. On warm days she was always seated outside, moving her chair with the sun. Now Coilin saw her hunched figure clear against the gable-end and he knew it must be after school time. He got up and ran down the road, little clouds of dust rising at his heels. He reached the house to see his mother standing with a tin basin in her hand calling the hens.

"You're late, Coilin. What kept you? Who gave you the little trouteen?"

Coilin didn't answer, but when she asked again he replied without looking up: "Jimmy, the Poacher."

"And where did you meet him?"

"He was going east, the road coming from Lock Cam, and he gave me the little ones from his bag."

"He always had great nature," said the mother, smiling to herself at the smallness of the fish. Coilin fidgeted on the stool, listening to the clacking of the loom and watching the flour-coated trout frying on the pan. Their smell was good.

The boy sat into the table, his troubled face brightening in front of the white plate. He put a fork-full of fish into his mouth just as a ragged man with a bag on his back crossed the threshold. It was Jimmy the Poacher coming with a bag of spun wool for his five-yearly suit. The boy looked up at him, the fish in his mouth suddenly turning as tasteless as the scribbling paper he often chewed in school.

"Musha, weren't we just talking about you ... Sit in and have a bit of the fish."

"Arrah now," said Jimmy smiling, "it's shame you should have, frying those bits of things."

"Well, let me tell you," retorted the woman good-humouredly, "it's fun you're making of your own fish, for they're the ones you gave Coilin this very day."

The poacher, perplexed, looked up at the woman. There was silence, broken only by the rattling loom within. Without speaking they turned to the boy seated at the table, his face ablaze, his head hanging in shame.

Aunt Suzanne

Ireland Today, March 1937

The McKinleys all went down to the station to meet their Aunt Suzanne who was coming to take care of them now that their mother was dead. Mary, the eldest, was fifteen, Annie was eleven, and wee Arthur, the baby, as they called him, was nine. They boarded a tram at the foot of the street and, after much pleading and hauling, Arthur got them to go up on top. He loved the top of the tram, to kneel on the ribbed seat, and to feel the wind dunting his face and combing his hair.

To-day he leaned over the iron railings looking down at the top of the driver's cap; the cap was shiny and greasy, and a large lump knuckled up in the centre. Arthur tried to light a spit on it when Mary wasn't looking, but at last she spied him, slapped his hands, promising that never again would she come on top with him. The kneeling on the seat had imprinted red furrows on his knees, and he fingered them till a passing sandwich-man caught his eye. He stood up, looking bewilderedly after the walking triangle of boards, watching the legs of the man and wondering how he could see out. When he asked Mary how the man could see, Annie chimed in: "You're a stupid wee fella; did you not see the peep-hole in the board?" Arthur made up his mind there and then that he would be a sandwich-man walking round and round the street, just like a motor-car.

At the station they had to wait, Mary telling and retelling Arthur not to be forgetting his manners, occasionally taking his hands out of his pockets, and pulling down the brown jersey. Overhead arched the glass roof, pigeons cooing along the girders and sparrows chirping in and out. Three taxi-drivers sat on the running-board of a car reading a newspaper, and near them a cab-horse fed wheezily out of a nose-bag. There was plenty of time, and Mary put a penny in a chocolate machine, letting Arthur pull out the drawer. The chocolate was neatly wrapped in silver paper, but when she went to divide it, it was so thin it crumpled in her hands

As Arthur ate his chocolate he was fascinated by a huge coloured advertisement—a smiling girl poised on a white-rigged bottle that splashed through the sea. He could read some of the words and Annie helped him to read others, but when he asked unanswerable questions about the bottle, Annie told him to look out for the train and play at who-would-see-it-first coming in along the shiny lines.

A bell began to ring somewhere, and the taxi-drivers got up, dusting their clothes. Mary moved along the platform where the red, steel bumpers and the porters with their noisy trucks filled Arthur's mind with nameless longings. Presently there came a vibrating tumble like thunder and the train came panting in, smoke hitting the glass roof with all its might.

Mary fidgeted, "Now you two hold on to me tight. Don't get lost; look out for Aunt Suzanne. She's small; she'll be in black; she has a— She has a— She has a—Oh! I see her! There she is!" People hurried past, brushing roughly against wee Arthur till he was ready to cry from fright, but Mary's gleeful shouts sent a breathless, weak excitement over him. And then, as if she had jumped out of the ground, he was looking up at Aunt Suzanne.

She was a wee woman, not as tall as Mary, with a black plush coat, a yellow crinkly face, and a black hat skewered with enormous hat-pins. But as he looked down below her coat, he saw something funny: he saw one boot, and where the other should be was a ring of iron. Mary nipped him. "Aunt Suzanne's speaking to you."

"And who's this?"

"That's Arthur."

"A lovely little boy, God bless him," she said, touching his cheek with a cold hand.

"And what book are you in?"

"Third," Mary replied for him.

"Third! Isn't that a great little man! ... and this is Annie. Well, well, she was only a wee baby when I saw her last, a lovely wee baby. Tut, tut, tut. How the time flies!"

Annie relieved her of a band-box; Mary took her black glossy bag and, linking her by the arm, they began to move off slowly along the cement platform. Occasionally Auntie Sue would stop and say: "Well, well, it's like old times again!" But the clink of the iron foot on the pavement made Arthur twist and turn so that he could see how it moved. When Mary saw him gaping she scowled at him, and for the moment he would look in front, fixing his gaze on a horse or a tram, but always there came the clink-clink of iron on stone, and always he'd turn his head and gape at the foot, then the iron, the boot again, and then the—

"Walk on a minute, Auntie, Arthur's boot's loosed." Mary pushed Arthur to the side and began to untie his laces and bow them tightly again, until Aunt Suzanne and Annie were out of hearing. "Now," she said. pointing a threatening finger at him. "If I—get—you—looking—at Auntie's leg there's no telling what I'll give you. Do you hear me! Come along and be a good boy. You'll never get out with us again! Never!" She tightened up his blue and white tie and pulled him along by the hand.

Into a tram they got, Annie and Arthur sitting opposite Mary and Aunt Suzanne.

"No, no, child dear, I'll get them," said Aunt Suzanne when the conductor came along. Mary handed the tickets to Arthur to look at, but he only turned them over in his hand, and then his eyes swivelled to the iron foot that didn't reach the floor. Once he looked up at her face staring at it fixedly. Below her hat were two wings of grey hair, and from the corners of her buttony nose were two deep lines making a letter A with her mouth. There were a few white hairs on her chin, and her eyes were brown and sunken. Suddenly the eyes narrowed, and wee Arthur returned his Auntie's smile. He decided that he was going to like her, but he hoped that he hadn't to sleep with her because of her iron-leg.

Passing up the street he felt that all the wee lads would be looking at his Auntie, with her clop-clink, clop-clink. If she'd only cover it with a stocking and put paste-board inside it. nobody'd hear it or know what it was. Suddenly he left them and ran over to three of his companions who were standing with their backs looking at a baker's horse. To show off before his Auntie he ran under the horse's legs and out by the other side. "Holy misfortunes what a child!" said Auntie Sue, frightened to a standstill.

"Arthur!" Mary yelled.

Arthur came running back and Mary gave him a stinging smack on the jaw. "You've been working for that this day." All the way to the house, and into the house, he sobbed and sniffed. "Wait'll me da comes home till yez see what yez'll get!"

"That's just it," said Mary, "Me da has him spoiled!"

"Sh-sh-sh, big little mans don't cry, Tut-tut," pleaded Auntie Sue. "Give me my bag till you see what I have for you, and none for the rest," she continued, casting a wink at Mary and Annie. When Arthur heard the happy rustle of paper his sobs became less frequent, and when he received a piece of sugar-stick coloured like a barber's pole, he sat on the fender sucking contentedly, and even suffered Mary to wipe his face with a damp cloth.

Aunt Suzanne rested on the frayed couch looking with admiration at the clean tiles on the floor, and the white-scrubbed table, then up at the mantelpiece where two delph dogs stood guarding a row of shining brass-ware horse-shoes, two candlesticks, a rigged ship, and a little three-legged pot containing a bunch of matches.

"Yiv the place shining," she said proudly. "Did you do it all by yourself, Mary?—You and Annie. Och-och, but it's nice to see two sisters agreeable."

Mary took the band-box and the glossy bag and put them in a room off the kitchen. Then she poked the fire to hurry on the kettle while Annie spread a clean newspaper on the table and laid down the cups and saucers. Aunt Suzanne stretched herself out on the sofa, and wee Arthur was sent out to play till the big people had finished their tea. From the table they could see, through the cotton-lace curtain on the window, out on to the street and the red-bricked houses opposite; and many's the question Mary had to answer about the neighbours; the gossipy ones, the friendly ones, and the borrowing ones.

Just when they had finished their tea Arthur came crying into the yard and battered impatiently at the scullery door.

"What's up now?" asked Mary, letting him in. He didn't answer, but ran to Auntie Sue. She took him in her arms and nursed him, but he scratched his cheek on a brooch in her breast and cried all the more.

"What's wrong my pigeon? What's wrong my darling? Tell your Auntie Sue."

"The wee-lads called you iron-hoof and cork leg!" he whimpered.

"There's a cheeky lot of gets about this place," said Mary. "Wait'll I get my hands on some of them."

"And what did you say to them?" asked Auntie Sue, shaking him to and fro.

"I said you hadn't a cork leg," he replied, bursting into more tears.

"There! there! there!! " consoled Auntie.

"Maybe God'll give some of them a bad leg before very long," put in Annie.

"God forbid, child dear; sure they're only childer, and mean no harm."

They were relieved when Arthur stopped whimpering, for they never knew at what time their father would step in on them and find Arthur in tears. It was late that night, however, when he came home from work in the flour-mill, and they had all gone to bed except Auntie Sue.

Whilst he shaved in a looking-glass hung to a nail in the mantelpiece, his face under the gas-light, he kept up a chat with her. Later he talked about old times and about Armagh where Suzie came from, and then he fell silent for a long time, looking at the flames nodding and leaping in the fire, and the flakes of soot shivering in the wide chimney. She, too, fell silent with her hands joined on her lap, looking at the wrinkles of flour in his boots, and thinking of his poor wife, her own sister. And then without preface he turned to her: "Tell me, Suzie, are you off the bottle?"

"Off the bottle!" she started. "Not a drop of strong drink has wet my lips this many a long year. I forget the taste of it; that's the God's truth, Daniel!"

"I'm glad to hear it. It's the divil's own poison. Poor Katy, God be good to her, would be here now only for it."

"Aye! Aye!" she nodded, taking a handkerchief and dabbing her eyes.

He looked at her awkwardly for a minute and said: "You'll be dead tired after journey ... Be good to the childer, Susie and keep a tight eye on wee Arthur ... Good-night now!"

After the first week or two, wee Arthur and Auntie Sue became great friends. He no longer stared at her iron-leg and no longer paid heed to its stamping up the stairs or its clinking across the tiles. Auntie Sue was good to him and paid him halfpennies for gathering cinders. With a battered bucket, a piece of card-board covering the hole in the bottom, he would go out to the waste-ground at the back of the long row of small houses. There the neighbours flung out their ashes, cabbage stalks, and potato skins. He would squat for hours on his hunkers, rummaging with a stick for the blue-black cinders, carrying the bucket in front with his two arms under the handle. Aunt Suzanne would open the yard-door at his knock. "That's the man; them'll make a grand fire; there's nothing like cinders," and out would come the black purse, and a penny or a halfpenny would be squeezed into an eager hand.

One warm day when Annie and Mary were down the town Arthur wanted to earn a penny for the pictures and he took out the bucket to gather cinders. The cinders were hot under the sun, and near him barefooted boys sat with broken mirror-glass sending leaves of sunlight into the cool corners of the houses. Men, waistcoats unbuttoned, sat with newspapers over their heads, and when the wee lads shone the mirrors on them they got up and chased them. On the yard-walls thrushes and goldfinches in their cages sang madly in the sun. Dogs stood about with hanging tongues and heaving sides. But Arthur worked on.

The sun scorched down on him and a creak came in his neck,

but only a few cinders lay in the bottom of the bucket. He sighed, wiped the sweat from his face with the sleeve of his jersey, and hoked on.

He felt very thirsty and came into the yard where the blue tiles burned under his feet. All the doors were open, but the air was still. Two fly-papers covered with flies hung from the clothes line in the kitchen. He looked around for Aunt Suzanne and pushed open her room door; there she was sitting on the bed with a flat bottle of gurgling yellow liquid to her mouth.

"Aw, give's a slug?"

"Merciful God, where did you come from? You put the heart out of me!" She put the cork in the bottle. "Pw-pt-th," she said in disgust, making wry faces. "Rotten medicine! Worse than castor, but poor Auntie has to take it!"

She went to the sink in the scullery to get him a drink, the splashing tap spilling coolness into the air. Arthur held the wet-cold cup in his two hands and drank noisily. He drank two cupfuls, finishing with a deep sigh. She gave him a half-penny. "Don't tell your da that poor Auntie has to take medicine, he'd be vexed to hear it. Now go and gather your cinders."

Later he returned with an almost empty bucket and found Aunt Suzanne snoring on the sofa. He started to sing loudly so as to waken her, and she got up and poked the fire vigorously.

"Give's a penny for the pictures?"

"If I'd a penny I'd frame it, and you with no cinders!"

"G'on," he whimpered, "or I'll tell me da about your medicine."

"Get out of me sight! Do you think I'm made of money!" she said crossly.

"G'on!"

She lifted the poker in anger, and Arthur raced into the yard. He barricaded himself in an old disused goat-shed and started to sing:

> Boiled beef and carrots,
> Boiled beef and carrots,
> And porter for Suzanne.

He was innocent of the cruel implication, but it riled Auntie

Sue and she hammered at the door with the poker and flung jugfuls of water in at him through the loose boards. "The divil has the hold of you, me boyo. Wait'll yer da hears this and you'll get it!"

He yelled louder; and, thinking of the neighbours, she went in and left him. He heard the bar shoot with finality in the scullery door and her last words: "You'll not get in the night! G'on now about you business."

All the evening he was in the dumps and sat far out on the waste ground at the back of the house. Annie came out with sweets in her hand and coaxed him in, assuring him that Auntie Sue was not going to touch him. And sure enough she had a Paris bun for his tea and jam for his bread. Then she kissed him and packed him off early to bed.

That night the father returned to the nightly ritual of family prayers which had been upset by the arrival of Suzanne in their midst. All knelt except Auntie Sue, who sat on a low chair with her rosary beads twined around one hand the other resting on her lap. She closed her eyes as she answered the responses, and when she opened them there was always something to distract her: a new seat was needed for Daniel's trousers; a stitch in Annie's dress. Then she fell to dreaming as she looked at Mary's two plaits tied at the ends with green ribbon; hair like her poor mother, God rest her. And then Annie's one plait with a broken ivory clasp; that's what she'd buy them at Christmas, two nice clasps, and maybe brooches with their names on them. A creak from Daniel's chair brought her mind back with a start, and she asked God to forgive her for such distraction as she turned to her beads again. But when he said solemnly "All now repeat the Heroic Offering after me," she felt weak, and her heart pounded so loudly she thought they'd all hear it.

"*For Thy greater glory and consolation, O Sacred Heart of Jesus* ... God forgive me for telling lies to that saintly man. *For Thy sake to give good example* ... and wee Arthur saw me swilling it. *To practise self-denial* ... and me with a bottle under a board in the room; but I didn't take much this day. *To make reparation to Thee for the sins of intemperance* ... God forgive me! God forgive me for being a hypocrite! I can't repeat the next of it. *I promise to abstain from all intoxicating drinks for life."*

She listened to the end of it with tightened lips, afraid to profane the sacred words, and thankful for the way the children almost shouted it. She was glad to get into the comfortable darkness of her room where she lay twisting and turning for a long time before sleep came to her.

After that Auntie Sue was cautious and always had a secret slug behind a locked door and kept the bottles under a loose floor-board. It was Arthur she feared. He was always appearing at surprising moments, stalking her, playing at Indians, pretending to himself that she was a squaw on horseback, her iron-ring reminding him of a stirrup. But Annie and Mary were the sensible children!

They looked forward to Arthur's bedtime, for with their father at some Sodality meeting, they had their Auntie to themselves. They would ply her with questions: about her school days; about Armagh, and the games she played when she was young. And Auntie sitting on the sofa between them, Annie hugging one arm and Mary the other, would turn to one and then the other looking down at their anxious eyes as she told them scraps of her life. Before Daniel would come in she'd sing for them verse after verse of "Lady Mouse."

> Lady Mouse are you within?
> Hm, Hm—m—m—m,
> Lady Mouse are you within?
> Yes, kind sir, as she sat and spun,
> Hm, Hm—m—m—m.

They had it by heart now and all three hummed the hm—hms that ended each verse. Sometimes the hm-hms would be so prolonged by Annie and Mary till one or other would burst out laughing, and Auntie Sue would hold her sides. "I'll be kilt laughing, I'll be kilt."

She sang for them songs of the countryside; courting songs and songs of Ireland's heroes and Ireland's traitors; and maybe she'd give them riddles and phrases to say quickly. "Three grey geese in a green full of grazing, grey were the geese and green was the grazing." She taught them how to knit and how to crochet. Then of a Sunday she'd read to them out of her prayer book, and though the print was as big as that in a child's primer she always followed the words with her finger.

In the long November nights when the pains would come into her legs she'd go off to her bed early, and then Annie and Mary would come slipping into the room with a mug of hot tea for her and two big slices of loaf bread. They'd light the candle and sit on the edge of the bed. While Auntie would be sipping her tea and dipping the bread in it her eyes would travel round the Holy Pictures that she had tacked to the wall. "I have a quare squad of them around me and there's none of them like that fella there," she'd say, pointing to a picture of St. Patrick banishing the snakes. "A decent fella, a real gentleman, many's a good turn he done me."

Up through the long winter months she drank little, and now and again at the family prayers she was on the verge of promising to abstain for life, but something told her she'd never keep it. Christmas came and she taught the children how to bake and she bought them brooches like her own with the words "Annie" and "Mary" in silver-white stones, and for Arthur a tram conductor's cap and a ticket-puncher.

Then one cold winter's day when the snow had fallen and Annie and Mary had gone for messages, Auntie Sue was in the house alone. The coalman hadn't come, and there was little coal for the fire. She felt cold. She closed all the doors, but still there seemed to slice through every crevice in the house a wicked, icy draught. Her teeth chattered and she lifted the wrinkled quilt off her bed and put it around her shoulders, looking miserably through the kitchen window at the white street and the light fading from the sky. Her thin blood craved for a drop of warmth; and not as much as a thimbleful of "medicine" in the house to wet her lips or make a nip of punch. Without waiting to talk it over in her mind, she left two-and-fivepence on the kitchen table for the coalman, put on her black plush coat and hat, took her umbrella, and out with her.

The hard snow lay deep in the street, yellowed by cart ruts and blackened by coal-dust. In the sky a few stars were coming out. She put up her umbrella though the snow wasn't falling. She passed neighbours cleaning their doorways with shovels, and now and again heard the wet sad sloosh of a brush. A few snowballs thubbed on the top of her umbrella and she hurried on, her iron-ring cutting circles in the snow. Then wee Arthur came running up and she gave him a penny to buy sweets for himself. She turned the corner on to the main road, saw rags of snow on the wheels of a cart, and the rich glow on a coal-man's face as he lit his swinging lamp. The snow slushed in her boot and she shivered.

She went into "The Bee Hive" and sat in a snug near the stove. There was dry sawdust on the floor, a smell of new varnish, and a great glow of heat. She'd have a nice drop of punch. She held out her hands to the heat and smiled sweetishly as she heard the tight scringe of a cork coming out of a bottle.

That night the children were long in bed and Auntie Sue had not returned. Daniel was seated on the sofa in the firelight, a pair of his trousers drying on the back of a chair and the children's wet boots in a row on the fender. A quilt of snow fell from the roof into the yard. A knock came to the front door. Daniel lit the gas, and when he opened the door, there was Aunt Suzanne paralytic drunk hanging between the arms of two men. They linked her into the kitchen and plopped her on the sofa, her skirt and coat dripping wet, her hair in rats' tails about her face, her hat feathered with snow. She sang to herself pieces of "Lady Mouse," and then burst out laughing. "Three gay grease," she said. "No, that's not it. Poor Auntie Sue can't say "Thee geese geen'——.""

Daniel stood in the middle of the floor looking at the wet miserable woman on the sofa. She looked up at him with half-shut eyes, "as dacent a man as ever walked in shoe leather."

He went into her room and bundled all the things he could find into her band-box. He opened the door and looked up and down the street. It was empty and all the kitchen windows lit. A gramophone was playing and a child crying. The snow was falling, falling with a sparkle against the lamp lights, and falling quietly on the window-sills and the shut doors. Over the white-silent roofs the cold sky was sprayed with stars. A man with bowed head passed and said: "That's a hardy night." Daniel heard him kicking the snow of his boots against a doorstep, and a door closing. He came inside. Auntie Sue had leaned back on the sofa, her hands listless, her eyes shut. He took his trousers from the back of the chair, put out the gas, and threw an overcoat over the huddled figure.

In the morning Auntie Sue was leaving and they all went down on the tram to see her off. Arthur knelt on the seat looking out, and no one chastised him when he pursed his lips against the window. They spoke little. They could find no words to say to each other.

At the station before getting into the carriage Aunt Suzanne gave Arthur a penny. Her eyes were wet as she held Annie's and Mary's hands and stroked them lovingly. They couldn't look up at her, but stood awkwardly swaying to and fro. The train slid out and they lifted their arms and waved them wearily, tears filling their eyes. Arthur stood watching the smoke and the back of the receding train. Then he plucked at Mary's coat. "Come on quick," he said, but they didn't seem to hear him, and he ran on in front to to the chocolate machine with the penny Auntie Sue had given him.

Leavetaking

Ireland Today, July 1937

"Run down to your Uncle Robert's with the paper. You mightn't get a chance of seeing him before you go away."

Colm loved to go to his Uncle Robert's. Robert always told him yarns and sometimes Aunt Maggie gave him a farl of warm potato bread with butter oozing across it. He brought Rover with him and went in his bare feet. He had a half-penny for sweets, so he cut down to the right-angular row of houses that was the island village, called in the shop, and took the loose stony road along by the sea. Around him walls of limestone hedged the shingly fields, and yellow, wizened rocks stretched long arms into the sea. This part of the island, he often told himself, was white; his own place was grey, because of the rocky hills; and his Uncle Robert's black, because of the lake and the stones that came out of it.

Rover sniffed at a black beetle that was tumbling over the sharp stones on the road; and bending down, Colm barred its way with a twig, amused to see it climb with its thready legs and then curl itself up, pretending to be dead. He smiled at its cunning, and gently turned it on its back, where its thin legs wriggled wildly. "You're not dead now!" he said aloud as he prodded it with the twig. Its back was covered with grit and it lay perfectly still. He scooped out a small channel in the loose pebbles and left it to escape.

The road climbed gradually out for the village, up into the hills where the air was clear and cool. Here he could see Fair Head and dark Knocklayde bulging strangely near. Away beyond that lovely mountain he would soon be going to Belfast and as he looked at its cold, sodden folds, he wondered if he would be able to see it from the town.

Standing on a hill facing the road which he had ascended, his eye took in the long, crooked arm of the island; white houses with their backs stuck into the hills; the East Lighthouse like a brooding gull on the cliff-top; and far away over a grey sea a fleet of clouds moored to the cheerless hills of Scotland. He turned away like one looking on it for the last time, and slowly his head disappeared behind the hill that held in its lap his Uncle's cottage.

As he drew near he saw the hens about the open door, a bucket lying on its side, and a brush against the window. But no smell of baking bread came to him. Maggie was turning a heel in a sock, and got up when he came in.

"That's a brave day, Colm," she said. "Just go on down to the room; Robbie didn't stir a fut the day; the rain in the mornin' scared him."

Propped up in the bed was Uncle Robert, his forehead seamed with dirt, a woollen shirt on him, and his scapulars round his neck. He was rubbing a hand over his bald head when Colm entered with the paper.

"Och, och, is it you?" he said. "A'm glad to see you. My pains were that bad I didn't budge the day ... A'm watchin' them thieves of swans that's after comin' to the lake. They'll not leave a pick of feedin' for the ducks."

Colm looked through the four-paned window at the three swans sailing near the house. One of the swans ducked its neck under the water, its tail in the air waggling, and its black feet almost above the surface. It came up with a long, green weed dripping from its bill.

"Aw, but that's the thief for you," said Robert, shaking his fist at it. "A hould you them buggers are from Scotland."

Near the swans Robert's ducks paddled amongst the black stones, and above them on the short grass sprawled a grey shirt with its sleeves pegged down with stones. The swans moved towards a little bay which was yellowed with chaff from an emptied bed-tick. The chaff gathered on their wet feathers as they made tracks in the yellow scum. Colm watched them for a while and then sat on the bed without saying anything.

Robert's woollen shirt was open at the neck and as he bent over the paper there could be seen blue mast-tips of a full-rigged ship tatooed across his chest.

"Is there anything in the paper the day?" he asked, as his cordy arms opened it out. "D'ye know I can't see a stime without my glasses. Maggie! Where's my glasses?"

Maggie brought him a pair, their legs mended with white twine. As Robert scanned the paper Colm sat gazing around the familiar room, crammed with old trucks and boxes. Patched trousers hung by their braces from a dinged knob on the bed, and under a chair lay Robert's clayey boots with corn-holes cut out in the toes. On the mantelpiece he saw for the hundredth time an old dusty piece of palm leaning like a feather out of a white vase, and, beside it, lying on its side a green bottle containing a ship in full sail. It was always a puzzle to Colm to know how the ship was got through the neck of the bottle and everytime he asked his uncle, the only replies he got were a fit of laughing and: "Think it out, boy; it's simple if you think it out." He was wondering now if his uncle would tell him and he ready to go away from the island in a week's time.

"God-a-god, would you look at that poor craythure," interrupted Robert, tilting the paper towards him so that he could see the photo of an old Tyrone woman, aged 104.

"If she doesn't die soon she'll turn into a crow," he added giving the paper a smack.

Just then Maggie came down to the room with a mug of tea and three pieces of bread balanced on the mouth of it. As Colm chewed the bread she leaned over Robert's shoulder, glancing at the paper, and arranging the pillows at his back.

"Hm, there's quare wickedness in the world," she says, addressing a photograph of Bangor girls in bathing suits. "Look at them bold heelers, and not as much clothes on them as'd dust a flute!"

"Woman, dear," Robert turned to her sharply. "Don't meddle with me when I'm readin'; leave me in peace, and I'll send it up to ye in a wheen o'minutes."

"Aw, but that's the cross man for you, Colm. He's as cantankerous as a clockin' hen when he doesn't get the air."

Colm smiled. They always seemed to be fighting; yet he felt there was a great oneness between them. He recalled an evening, not long ago, that Robert took the queer wild notion to fish from the rocks by himself. And how Maggie had come up to the house crying and lamenting: "He'll be killed and drowned this very night. An old man like that with no eyes in his head and no foot under him; he'll slip on them rocks. Go down, Colm, and keep an eye on him." And later how Robert roared at her when he found her coming to look for him, to help him home, as if he were a drunk man. The recollection brought a smile to Colm's eyes as he sat with the empty tea-mug in his hand and Rover begging up at him for more bread.

"It bates all, the number of words in that paper and nothing in it," said Robert, closing his glasses. "A body'd be better keepin' his penny; but, all the same, ye like to get it, afeard ye'd be missing' something. Och, och, but it's queer the notions we have whiles … And you'll be going away soon. It's sad to see so many young people leavin' the island and none comin' back. There'll soon be nothin' on the island only rabbits—with nobody marryin', the ould dying', and the young goin' away."

From that he drifted into telling about the time he himself left the island, the towns he was in and the boats he stokered to India. And now and again he sat straight up in the bed and bent his arms like a boy showing off his muscles, and shot them out and in again with great force.

"I was a tight one in me day, a tight fella. And look at me now, Colm, a done man with my blood dryin' up and the dregs of it clogged with grit and dirt—a body can't get a night's rest with it. God forgive me, but a man'd be better dead when his blood's astray and no comfort in his body. Whiles I think the roof's leakin' when I feel the swirls of air about my head. But it's the blood, Colm, all dried up from stokerin' them bloody boats to Indya. Only for the the ould pipe," lowering his voice now, "and Maggie, the craythure, I'd be a lonely ould man."

Colm's hand rested on the bed-clothes and old Robert gripped it tightly.

"Whisper, Colm, yer goin' away soon. Listen to me, son;

pay heed to an ould battered man. Say yer prayers when yer young; it's then ye love life and if ye give a bit of yer time to God 'tis better than givin' a big bit when yer old. D'ye hear me? It's hard to restore an ould limpy ship."

A scorching sensation came into the boy's throat as he listened to the quavering voice of the old man, and he turned his head to the window. A wet light seeped out of the sodden sky, shining weakly on the black lake water and whitening the sailing swans.

The hand gripped more tightly his own and he blinked his eyes and gave a nervous little laugh.

"And whisper, Colm, put yer heart in the work; if the heart's not there the work's no good … Deed troth, we'll miss you."

They fell silent. A wet sun shone into the room, splintered in a thousand pieces upon the lake, and withdrawing its light, lost itself in a bundle of clouds. Colm lowered his head and stretched out a hand to the dog who licked it and jumped joyously on to the bed.

"Get down out o' that or ye'll have the place full of fleas," shouted Robert. "Maybe now he'd hunt the swans for us. Give him a race at them for we'll have a flood of rain before long."

Colm and Rover went out. Along the edges of the lake the water was greyed and wrinkled by a little breeze, but the middle reflected the yellow glow of the sky. A wet-gold light dripped from the clouds and a clammy air breathed against his bare legs. The queer light frightened him as he screwed up his eyes to watch scattered gulls flying high and silent. The dog barked and the swans slid out from the edge, breaking the ripples and leaving a smooth trail behind them. He threw a stick into the water and the dog splashed noisily after it.

One of the swans rose heavily, and with loud flaps from their wings and white splashes from the water the others followed. Necks a-strain they circled the lake and as they flew low over the cottage old Robert heard with delight the bing-bing of their powerful wings. Sadly Colm watched them flying northward, while the dog jumped around him barking with joy.

"He done that well; he's a good dog," said the Uncle, when they came in again. "But keep him outside or he'll dreep the place."

Colm stood in the middle of the floor, his legs apart and his eyes on the green bottle on the mantelpiece. He lifted it and looked at the schooner inside, turning the bottle with a perplexed look.

"Uncle Robert, are you not going to tell me how you got the ship in the bottle?"

The bed creaked with the laughing. "Ask yer clever town boyos when you meet them; they'll tell you how."

"Ach go on and tell us!"

Robert laughed the more, and Colm questioned Maggie.

"Deed, child, sure if I knew I'd tell you. I'm thinkin' the ould codger doesn't know himself."

Robert closed one eye cunningly and stuck out his crinkled tongue at them.

"It's little you have to do but to be tormentin' childer," said Maggie. "None of yer nonsense and tell the poor child how to get a ship in a bottle."

"Are you tryin' to get it out of me, too? It's a secret, woman, a secret! And Robert McCurdy, Rathlin, the County of Antrim, would be known the world over if he let it out. The black niggers of Indya and the yella Chinamen of China would give me a fortune for it. I've sailed and stokered boats the world over. And did I tell my secret?" He points his finger at them. "No!" and finished with a loud laugh.

"Good God, would you listen to him, and not as much in his pocket as'd buy an ounce of tobacco."

Maggie went up to the kitchen, and Uncle Robert and Colm sat looking through the window at the sky swirling with ragged clouds and the lake growing mysterious and cold.

"That's a wicked, festerin' sky," put in Robert. "You'd better sit and take your ease for there'll be a quare blatter of thunder and a shockin' shower."

A cold draught flowed into the room. It grew dark and the room cowered. A cheap watch ticked loudly from a nail in the wall and a few scales of rain glistened on the window. Lightning jigged in the house and Maggie rushed into the room and sat on the edge of the bed. She blessed herself as thunder crackled over the scraw of a roof and rain fell battering on the bucket.

Robert turned his back on them and coiled himself in the bed-clothes, drawing great comfort from the rods of sound.

"Whistle to me when it's over. Hm, afraid of a spoonful of rain and a chopstick of thunder. Aw the storms I seen in the Indya Ocean and the rain—monsoons, they called them; ye'd think the ocean was turned upside down."

Maggie clicked her teeth and shook her head with disdain. She was thinking of the shirt at the edge of the lake and the eggs under the hen in the box; they'd be ruined now; not a bird would be left in one of them.

Colm's eyes were steady with fear as he listened to the brattling thunder. His mind followed a line of swans flying through the rain and beating cold sprays from their wings; then in a flash he saw the white stony road passing lonesomely by the grey-drenched cottages; the grit being washed from the beetle's back, and water plaiting itself in the pebbly channel he had made in the road.

The thunder grumbled and barged as it sped over the sea towards Scotland. Sheep bleated from the hills and the lake clopped on the stones.

Colm got up to go and Maggie sent him out for a cabbage leaf, as she had some fresh butter for his mother. The garden was dark with rain and the black soil squelched up between his toes. Shining puddles lay in the furrows and rain freckled the cabbage leaves; when he broke off a leaf it creaked like new leather and the drops rattled off it like pebbles. He stood up and looked towards the north and thought of the swans flying through the wet mists of the mountains and their black feet alighting in the cold water of a Scottish lough.

It was dusk when he left the cottage, a pair of hand-knit socks for himself in his pocket and the butter snail-cold in the cabbage leaf under his arm. He hurried and took the road. The dog panted by his side, and the night cool air, soft as the touch of a child's balloon, fluttered against his cheek. He splashed in the rain puddles here and there on the road, and all the time his mind kept thinking of the ship in the bottle and his Uncle with

61

he gritty blood; but as the thickening darkness hardened the hills and brightened the speckled stars, he became afraid. Rocks and bushes took queer shape, while in front lights glimmered in the scattered homes and the light-house revolved spokes of light in the darkness.

Passing by an empty house he whistled loudly; frightened rabbits thudded out of danger and the dog raced after them. As he drew near home he began to run. He halted when he reached the door. The square of light in the window and the noise of his mother talking brought his courage back. And looking around now at the ships' lights far out at sea, he thought again of the dusty green bottle on the mantelpiece and the swans pushing into the shelter of rushes in the night-grey waters of a lonely lough.

Journals 1934-1936

1934

Burns stands out from English poetry. There is no place in English literature for him. He had homeliness in his poetry which had gone out of English poetry since the Renaissance.

Burns, a very human poet, cared very little for what people thought, was influenced more by human beings. Matthew Arnold the very reverse. Cloistered life, brought up in Colleges.

* * * * *

The Irish, not being of a philosophic temperament ... must not be intolerant by condemning literature, poetry etc.—that treats of philosophy. Everything was objective and given objective treatment by the old Gaels.

* * * * *

1935

O'Faoláin's analysis of Corkery's stories is apt and incisive. Corkery's stories are, in the main, consciously written; they romanticize the Irish Peasant attributing to him a deep culture that exists in the mind of Corkery and not in the mind of the peasant. They curb his spontaneity and are therefore inferior as art. Literature, however, should not only reflect but *affect* the mind of a people. To maintain a connexion with the best of the past is to ensure a solid connexion with any future worth arriving at. If a vestige of a past culture remains in a people it is an artist's function to deepen it, to heighten it, as in Corkery's case (The Ploughing of Leaca-na-naomh) so as to affect—or arouse an awareness in a people to the culture that is deep-rooted but not dormant in their minds. To keep us Irish and Gaelic is Corkery's intention. Anyway, it's the last paragraph of "The Dead" that raises the story in English eyes above the ordinary run—their materialism taking cognizance of the immortality of the soul.

*　*　*　*　*

1935
The more Joyce strives to escape from the bonds of Catholicism the tighter they become—blasphemy upon blasphemy he vomits on the Catholic Faith and its ritual, yet in spite of all Catholicism remains with him. From *Ulysses* their arises in us a disgust, a hatred of sin—a good effect; but we get also a hatred of all humanity—a bad effect.

*　*　*　*　*

1935
Joyce
The corruption of mankind due to the Fall is portrayed vividly—the rottenness of original sin, the vile-eaten minds of those without God. (Morally sound) But we make these deductions unconsciously. In the *Portrait,* he shows sin and goodness (a contrasting picture). It is the better book for this reason—takes congnizance of the whole man. Furthermore in *Ulysses,* except in two instances, there is a lack of genuine feeling. What is man without emotion? Lives deprived of God's grace put no censor on their daily thoughts, hence a valuable experience from the book.

Even when Joyce is farthest from God, as in the brothel scene when our senses are stenched in sin we feel in the words of St. Augustine—"For thy omnipotency is not far from us, even when we be far from thee." Stephen's mother rising up and praying for him, praying for a repentance that we feel will come some day when pride shall no more roam in that sad-torn heart of his. In *Ulysses* he is preoccupied with one side only of man and that is evil and sordidness.

The monologue at the end does not seem to be an outgrowth of any situation in the book. It is stuck on like an artificial gargoyle. Obscenity is the only name for it.

*   *   *   *   *

18 September 1935
Contrast the moral struggles, reactions, that Shakespeare's characters undergo when sin has been committed with the indifference, the equanimity of the so-called "characters", (men and women) that parade in modern literature. If literature is an art that treats of life, then moral principles must always be applied to the conduct of the characters. Contrast Macbeth and Lady Macbeth with present-day murderers in fiction and dramatic literature.

*   *   *   *   *

1936
A Short Note on Séan O'Faoláin's *Bird Alone*.
It is a novel, like all good novels, difficult to outline. It is written in the first person by one Corney Crone, a builder. He traces his boyhood, his family, the city of Cork, his love for a girl, Elsie. Both himself and Elsie are Catholics, and it is their mutual love-making and the ensuing spiritual struggle that form the main structure of the book.

Corney loses his religion in his "free" love; he erects moral standards of his own and in doing so brings misery to himself and the girl he loves. He tells her that their free love-making is no sin; she confesses to the priest and Corney is outraged. In secrecy and unknown to her righteous and loving parents she is going to have a baby. It ends in her death.

It is beautifully written—too good for one with the trade of builder. The style is spoiled by interpolations and parentheses. There are scenes—the tragedy in the sea—and the hero's Act of Contrition into Elsie's ear, which is wrung with deep pity.

In the final church scene he reveals his own inner corruption and his pride; and he utters—"I denied life by defying life, and life has denied me."

He should have added: "I tried to find happiness by ignoring God's law and now I have found that all is misery."

Irish Fiction

Part of Text of Unpublished Talk to Young Ulster Society

27 February 1940

... We have taken writers now from Belfast, Dublin, Donegal and the West. Munster remains to be explored, and to the reading public Munster means Cork. Probably that county has more writers to the acre than all the rest of Ireland.

I suppose Daniel Corkery, Seán O'Faoláin and Frank O'Connor represent it at its best. Corkery is the eldest of the three and I think that at one time, as a schoolteacher, he taught O'Faoláin and O'Connor.

He has given us one novel: *The Threshold of Quiet*, and four volumes of short stories. The novel was published in 1917, and it is still being read; it is a beautiful novel and many writers, like O'Faoláin himself, regard it as a perfect novel. (Mr N. Brown* introduced it to me some eight years ago when I had the pleasure of attending a course of his lectures on Anglo-Irish literature— I read it then, but it made little or no impression on me, for I was at the stage when I wanted action or when a thundering writer like Liam O'Flaherty appealed to me).

Corkery's book is quiet, mellow, thoughtful and inactive—it bears all the evidence of maturity, a mind turned inwards and catching for us fragments of a life which youth passes by. There is nothing in it of the rebellious stir of youth; there is a love theme threading through it, but it, too, has all the unobtrusiveness of age. The book is prefaced with a phrase of Thoreau: "The mass of men lead lives of quiet desperation."

It has atmosphere, the atmosphere of autumn: firelight

* J. Nelson Browne, sometime Head of English at Belfast College of Technology.

leaping at the windows; water hens creasing a lake; amber skies; and man himself, with his own thought—quiet, perhaps, but with a growing note of desperation. Its construction is perfect and it is steeped with that love of place which is characteristic of many Irish writers.

Here is a girl sitting sewing outside a cottage in the mellow evening sunlight.

> She put the thread between her teeth and broke it. With a little clatter the scissors fell to the dappled ground. There it remained. A robin, quite suddenly, winged across her and was lost in the sun-flecked foliage. Stitch, stitch, without hurry. The garment was held up and examined. She stopped and her fingers, but not her eyes, searched for the fallen scissors. Far away in the crowded valley a convent bell was ringing for evening Benediction. Then again, suddenly, the robin flung out a little phrase of melody. It ceased, but the far-off bell continued, very sweet, very faint. The scissors once again fell to the ground. There it remained.

It's a subtle book, one that makes demands on a reader's intelligence.

One of the characters, Stevie Galvin, seemed to me a little artificial; queer, perhaps, but then I have been told that there are many queer people about Cork. And certainly if their literature is a reflection of their life we need not doubt it.

Frank O'Connor has one or two queer people in his novel, *The Saint And Mary Kate*. The novel begins well: for eight chapters it has abundance and extravagance of life, and then something happens; it sags (all the juice, as it were, seems to go out of it).

It has some lovely scenes; the death of the hero's mother is brilliantly done, but it is spoiled here and there with the author's irritating obtrusiveness:

> The truth is, as the more acute of my readers may already have recognised …
> It is right for an author to dwell for a moment on this conversation …
> But her chronicler, as a disciple of the realist school …

These spoil the illusion of reality and make you feel that the author is looking over your shoulder as you read.

But there is no doubt of O'Connor's ability and I wish I had time to talk to you of his short stories.

This novel was written eight years ago and we wonder what has been in process of gestation since. I must say I like his short stories; some better than the novel.

The last of the trio is Seán O'Faoláin, and his long novel, *A Nest of Simple Folk,* is his best book, one that, for some reason, did not catch the eye of the reading public. It is an impressive novel and I am inclined to think it is a great novel. It has as many characters in it—all brilliantly alive—as would serve a dozen novels: policemen, schoolteachers, farmers, boys, sailors, old men and old women, young girls and young men, and genteel ladies fondling kittens, gazing into the fire and thinking of old glories. The book is soaked in atmosphere: he writes of Cork city, of Limerick, Rathkeale, the Golden Vale and the slow-moving sedgy rivers that trail across it—a plain where the clouds hang low and are forever shaking out rain. All I can say to you is read it; it is a book that will live and O'Faoláin will never write anything half as good.

Most of the writers I have mentioned are somewhat melancholic and tragic; their stories are plunged in sorrow and some, alas, are a little bitter (born as they were out of a country that has borne and suffered much). But here is an Irish writer—a writer of literature—who can shake the tears of laughter from our eyes. James Stephens (Read *Charwoman's Daughter* p.126).[1]

And now I have finished. I'm sure what I have said will provoke a discussion. We can learn, I think, from the writers I have mentioned; their best work has grown out of their own environment—they have not as writers mistrusted their own experiences, believing also that what is happening to people in their own country has that common element of universal humanity.

In a recent book of literary criticism a writer paraphrasing Lessing has given this advice—"Unless a writer sink himself in the heart of his own people, he will never (let his own gifts be what they may) accomplish work of such a nature as permanently satisfies the human spirit."[2]

[1] Author's note for quotation.
[2] Daniel Corkery in *Synge and Anglo Irish Literature,* Cork & London, 1931.

Letters 1940-1941

Knock,
4th Nov. 40

To Julie Kernan[1]

At last I am able to send you the remaining chapter of my book. My delight last night in typing out the words, 'The End,' was inexpressible. And yet the relief in finishing the book was tinged with a little sadness, and for this reason—the characters so preoccupied my mind the I now feel lonely at despatching them into the world.

I am pleased with the book though I agree with you that it may not make a great appeal.[2] I feel however that within the short compass of time in which the action takes place that I have successfully depicted three generations of people and their different attitude to life: The old woman with her thoughts on death and her spiritual struggle against selfishness; Johnny and Kate preoccupied with the struggles of their family; Hugh and Eileen—Youth—with their doubts, hopes, and ambitions; Hugh's selfishness (not having reached the stage when he'll be a family man like his father and can forget the "self" in the rearing of children) and then the incipient stages of Eileen's pregnancy manifesting itself in her anxiety for the children. For Eileen and Hugh the wheel will go full circle and they'll pass in time through the whole gamut of existence as that of the two previous generations.

I have tried to make the book taut with suppressed emotion—suggesting rather than describing. I have pared the

[1] Julie Kernan, editor at Longmans Green & Co., New York.
[2] *Lost Fields.*

prose to the very bone for I believe that intensity in literature is only achieved when prose is a bleak and sinewy as a wintry oak.

I hope that the completed book shall please you all

P.S. I am enclosing with these last chapters a revised version of Chapter 1 and page 134 of Chapter IX. On second thoughts I have retained the Hopkins quotation.

I hope Chapters XII-XVII arrived O.K. I sent them by Air Mail on 14th October.

* * * * *

Knock,
5th April, 41

*To Phyllis Neale,**

Enclosed is the requested paragraph on my book *Lost Fields*.

God forgive me if I have made claims for it which it does not possess.

Lost Fields

In this novel the Irish author of *Call My Brother Back* reveals— within a short compass of time and with consummate technical skill—the attitude to life of three generations of people.

The story concerns the Griffin family, their neighbours, and their continual makeshift employment. An old woman is wheedled from her home and fields in the Antrim countryside to live with her son's family in the noise-swarming streets of Belfast. Against her uprooted life in the city she is in revolt; and it is only her spiritualized struggles against selfishness that persuade her to remain with a family for whom her old age pension brings comparative wealth. Her cantankerous moods, her recurring threats to leave for the country and her daughter-in-law's counter-manoeuvres to get her to remain, and the death of the old woman provide scenes of tenderness, humour,

---

* Editorial Assistant at Jonathan Cape Ltd.

and deep tragedy. Then there are her son-in-law Hugh and his girl Eileen against whose marriage the old woman bars the way.

Amongst the neighbours there are many unforgettable characters—Stick McCormick forever whistling and chopping sticks in his back-yard; the cup-reading Liza McCloskey and her good-natured husband with the foolish habits; brilliant studies of children, a boy's reformatory, and a girl's vocation for the convent.

It is all told in a prose pared to the bone and taut with emotional intensity; and throughout the book the lyrical urgency of the style evokes for us the rainy streets of Belfast and the quiet fields around the lonely reaches of the river Bann.

* * * * *

Knock,
9th April, 41

To Julie Kernan

Thank you very much for the cheque received to-day via the Bank of Ireland.

The book at this side will be published in the summer by Jonathan Cape. Longmans, I think, intended to publish it all right but they suffered severely in one of the air raids and their whole stock of books was destroyed. I can well understand their position with regard to the publication of new books when so many old ones have to be replaced. I see by the papers they are still doing their best to carry on.

I have almost completed a chapter of a new book about which I shall let you know shortly.

P.S. I suppose you have heard the sad news of the death of Edward J. O'Brien.* I never had the pleasure of meeting him but the little correspondence that I had with him convinced me

* Edward J. O'Brien (1890-1941), editor of *New Stories,* 1933-35, and *The Best Short Stories* (ann) 1915-1940.

of his genuine sincerity and his endeavour to help young writers. It was he who introduced me to you and it was he who encouraged me when I was scratching out my first short stories.

*   *   *   *   *

Strangford,
2nd June, 41

Thank you very much indeed for your very kind letter of April 24th. I have survived the air-raids, thank God, and I am now teaching evacuees in Portaferry, a little seaside town near the entrance of Strangford Lough. I am living at the above address and every morning I cross the Lough in a small boat. I am delighted with the change, and later on when I get settled down I shall be able to do some work at my next novel.

I shall be pleased to see the dust jacket when it comes along. I am more than grateful to you for undertaking the proofs. You'll not overlook the dedication—*To Joseph Fitzsimons*—I can well understand now your publishing in the autumn, for I hear that during the intense heat of your summer people do not read books. I am sure you'll find everything in order when you write to Cape including the Canadian rights etc.

As soon as I find time I'll type out the opening chapter of my new novel and send it out to you.

*   *   *   *   *

Strangford,
23rd Nov. 41

Pardon the long delay in acknowledging the clippings and reviews which you kindly sent to me. I was delighted to get them and to see that the critics appraised it.

About my next novel: I shall send you out a chapter or two as soon as I get time and energy to type them. I really haven't a minute to myself these days; the evacuated children have all gone back to the city again and of course I, too, was sent after my group. I am now bus-travelling from here to the city—it's tiring, but it's a problem to know what is best to do.

I'm sorry Cape haven't written to you about publication at this side. It was announced in their Summer and Early Autumn list but I think the publishers here are all experiencing great difficulty with the paper shortage and binding. They hope to have it out early in January. I shall send you some reviews of it from this side.

Journals and Criticism 1941

1941
The Novel
For me a novel:
- (i) must be in serious relation to actual living.
- (ii) The characters must be normal, credible.
- (iii) Each sentence should have significance.
- (iv) Technical ability and poetic sensibility.
- (v) The style depending on the compulsive quality of the matter in hand.
- (vi) The events to be inevitable (no forcing).

A novelist should recreate reality and illumine it.

A novelist who shows in his work that he had been dead to the central problem of his time is hardly worth taking seriously.

Barrie was dead where the life of his times are concerned.

A good novel should be to future readers as much a history of the country as well as a permanent human document.

The descriptive matter should be integral.

The writing should have tenderness and delicacy—a respect for human feeling.

*   *   *   *   *

1941
My attitude to reality must never be false even if it reveals weakness in the clergy, the convents, or our educational system. I have no time for the contorted masterful monkish stories or the pietistic novel that smells of incense and crushed flowers.

The truth! The truth! is what I want and sincerity. Nothing

written that would shock, abhor, or lead others into sin—it all needs delicate handling.

* * * * *

1941

To write well one must become *absorbed* in his creations—the characters and their environment. To communicate with precision—the scenes and the emotions. To make the reader feel physically present—that is *art*.

* * * * *

1941

The incidents in a novel should be related to a central theme—a spiritual unity—producing an affirmative judgement on life.

The left-wing writers are, to my mind, too crude, too photographic. They seem to be insentient—insensible to the fair things of life. Their sensuousness is completely dulled; and without deep, keen sensuous impressions a novel fails as a work or art. Their crudity: wall-paper the colour of dog's vomit, the moon like a pool of horse's urine—and so on ad nauseam.

* * * * *

1941

A Nest of Simple Folk had all the qualities that make for permanence—the Land—incipient growth of our struggle for Independence—the delineation of two backgrounds—urban and rural. The characterisation is deep; the prose evocative—there are scenes of childhood, of excursions to the sea, that are enshrouded in a delicate, poetic atmosphere.

* * * * *

1941

Jacob's Room—Virginia Woolf.

I read it in Killard during Easter holidays, 1941, and I found a great sincerity in the thoughts of her characters and in their reaction to natural phenomena or physical sensations.

Virginia Woolf's strength lies in her observation—her ability to describe a hot day at the seaside, her feeling for a captive crab, or her poetical enumeration of the details that evoke for us the size, shape and smell of a town ...

But she seems to me to be interested only in externals—the shape, colour and sights of landscape ... We look on from the outside—they don't move us to pity or joy or sorrow ... it is the circumference and not the centre (the heart of life) which she aims for.

*   *   *   *   *

1941
The Novel
Introduction (Fragment of unpublished essay)
When one speaks of literature at the present time we find that the vast majority of the names mentioned are names of novelists. Literature today is dominated pre-eminently by the novel. The novel has undergone many changes within the past hundred years and has become by time the vehicle of sociological criticism, propaganda, thinly disguised autobiography, or sometimes travel book material used as background to a mediocre romance. Since the end of the last war the novel, due to the break-up and disintegration of society, has become more "inward" or more individualistic. We have only to think of Joyce, Virginia Woolf, Dorothy Richardson and their numerous offspring to realise that something had gone wrong with our age: that our society was not stable, that there were no common beliefs. When this happens writers look inward, technical innovations follow to compensate for common belief. They try to produce something solid from their own consciousness. The results are often unintelligible except to the author himself or to the coterie in which he moves—we find this more amongst the poets. To try to stabilise society or to commonise certain beliefs many authors adhere to some system, and the majority of the present day ones adhere to the objectives of Marxism, believing that his age of disintegration

or transition must gradually coalesce into a stable society informed by Marxism because regenerated by it. There is no doubt that this commonised belief has spread, is spreading, and may spread when the war is over, but whether or not it will regenerate civilization is a matter for conjectural sociology than for literature's immediate concern. The poets have gone Left and many, to my mind, have gone wrong—are eaten with dry rot, because they are writing and practising strange inhibitions by writing for the comrades [... phrase illegible] that first freedom that comes from an individual. Auden would have been a better poet for remaining as *Auden* and not as one of the folk.

As Daiches says (p.15): "More and more writers are accepting a common formulation for a rejuvenation of civilization and are writing in accordance with that formulation."

An artist should be able not only to record and re-create life, he should be able to interpret it and this interpretation should be ... If you write with truth and sincerity you'll always be new and fresh in a world that is constantly changing. We have no call—as many moderns do—to advocate restraint and economy and yet when they come to a description of sex relationship they seem that restraint, economy, or the soft pedal is out of place. A man stripped of his flesh (as the Jansenists would have us do) is only half-alive—Man is good and evil—and it is in the integration of these that ...

* * * * *

1941

On Modern Poetry

There is a self-conscious attitudizing in many of the moderns—lack of that spontaneous utterance which we expect of all good poetry. None of them can sing of "summer in full-throated ease." They are deficient in all that fresh simplicity that is one of the primary elements in poetry—some of them may have thoughts but the thoughts, one feels, are superimposed and do not grow from the organic nature of the work in hand. One is aware of this in the poverty of their compulsion—in the movement of their verse. They are too premeditated; a grim proposition before they write—a sort of gathering of the materials and then writing out a knowledge of poetry—achieved from too much theorising. The same fault prevails, I think, in many of the short stories being written at the moment—one yearns for a bit of freshness, a bit of freedom and less of that restrictive attitude imposed by the theorist in their search for perfection of form. Invariably the greatest innovators are those who do this work instinctively—the theorists arrive afterwards to underline and deduce the rules by which such exquisite art was achieved. The imitators rush forward and try to do likewise thereby destroying at one sweep their own individual approach.

(Write article on Hopkins from notes already made: his verbal power; his Journal: his weakness, viz., lack of a socialized attitude, too much "ego." Put other poems alongside etc.)

Poetry should enlarge our understanding, our experience of life. If its meaning is sacrificed to sound (music) then it's debilitated.

* * * * *

1941
To The Lighthouse
The book is too static. In her attempts to grasp the whole of life by way of people's thoughts she misses much in life that makes life interesting. She misses laughter; she misses the pang of sorrow that we get in Tolstoy. She draws a small circle round her people and she holds them confined within it. It is cramped, and the people, with the exception of Mrs Ramsay, and Cam's thoughts about her father and the boat, have dry irony but little sympathy. They are selfish and egotistical.

* * * * *

1941

In literature (poetic drama apart) I have a deep and lasting affection for the writers who portray the ordinary in life. It is easier to write falsely, of romantic incidents that falsify life, but it takes a great artist to take the ordinary and make it interesting. Tolstoy did it, Joyce, Chekhov, K.A. Porter and Katherine Mansfield in her New Zealand stories. Mauriac, with a rare exception (*Vipers' Tangle*), can't portray the ordinary. Joyce told his brother that would continue to write of "the dog bites man." Proust could also deal with the ordinary (cf. Aunt Leonie, Swann, Odette, the Vaudins).

* * * * *

1941

In the Murtaghs' story don't forget about the crib in Joe's story: the curtain rasping and jerking over. The angels singing; the dark eyes of one of them—then Fell!

"Ould cry-in-the-stable."

The nun in tears: "Oh, you bold boy! You've spoiled the concert!" The audience laughed. I hopped out of the cot and St. Joseph tried to stop me, but I kicked at him and got away.

"I want my mammie!"

* * * * *

1941

Read Oliver Gogarty's Poems.

They are disappointing in bulk, few are perfect and few will live.

He has some lovely lines e.g.

> O the stillness of well water
> Waiting for the blessings of the
> Crozier-holding fern.

But then one meets the lines and words that are mildewed and long worn out e.g. "ineffable and perfect word," "immemorial," "antidote" etc.

* * * * *

1941

A really fine short story or novel will have its own style and idea and will not remind you of anyone else.

● ● ● ● ●

Real art can't be successfully analysed; it can only be experienced. There is a mystery in it, a magic, which we sense but can't measure. To try to measure it is to reduce art to a science—a thing it is not.

● ● ● ● ●

Pride is love of self.

● ● ● ● ●

In a novel or a play it is a wise plan not to reveal the characters completely in the earlier stages. They should be revealed bit by bit: there should be an air of mystery, or wonder, about them. James's characters in *Portrait of a Lady* are revealed slowly. Madame Merle is brilliant in this respect.

Mary, the mother in Eugene O'Neill's *Long Day's Journey Into Night* holds our attention. She holds the interest because of the author's witholdingness. The characters in it are warped. They mean well but their weak nature makes them say the evil, hurtful thing and not the good.

● ● ● ● ●

Anger is a horrible sin. Man loses his reason and descends to brute level; there enters into the unguarded mind all the vices that flesh and spirit are heir to.

* * * * *

1941
Downpatrick—the roads—people—Nature—books—feeling *Language*—edge of dark—cutting away—heel of evening—moon in full bloom—blossom on the sun today.

moon in full bloom—blossom on the sun today.

Avoid stale phrases—read poetry.

Unless a writer sink himself ...

Yeats and cobwebs—Parochial and World—Not Plot—Mood and Atmosphere

K. Mansfield's Journal.

Elizabeth Taylor—K.A. Porter.

Your own stories.

The Senses: MacNeice.

Proust.

D'Patrick: love to live there; any road that comes.

People—Nature—language—Books.

Corkery: Unless a writer sink himself into the heart of his own people.

Cather: Whatever is felt upon the page without being specifically named there.*

Dog bites man. The normal.

Significant detail—

Vision: Chekhov: Tolstoy: Turgenev.

* * * * *

17 July 1941

I was speaking to an old man today and he was complaining about the scarcity of the crops.

> I seen me sowing the corn and the ground like powder and lifting the pickles three months afterwards and no growth on them.
>
> The grass is only a shadow this year. There's no crop in it and I remark that the flies and clegs is very scarce the year. In the fields I've seen the noise of the machine makin' them rise from the grass and them flyin' round you in clouds. There's the swallows: they used to build in these houses; they'd fly in and out above our heads, but whatever's the reason they've gone too.

• • • • •

* Willa Carther, (1873-1947), American novelist, in *Not Under Forty*, 1936.

I hear that the sea's thick with fish.

• • • • •

The sea-air kills the frost.

• • • • •

Thatch is a bothersome roof

• • • • •

"He's as light as a kite".

• • • • •

The days were very warm. The tops of the stones in the stream were dry; tomorrow if it would rain during the night the tops would be wet and slippery.

He lay on the sand, it was warm, and he lifted handfuls of it and let it filter through his fingers.

• • • • •

An old man told me that the North-West is a listening wind. "You'll hear it dulling away as if it was listening! Then it'll come rushing at the house like a thousand cannons!"

* * * * *

1941

In Toome there travelled around the district an old tramp who gathered empty bottles—Paddy Bottle they dubbed him. He used to call regularly with the P.P.—a man who was fond of a drop. He was good-natured and kind and fond of banter. One day when Paddy called it was the priest who answered the door.

"Have you any bottles, Father?"

"I have. But they'd be no use to you, Paddy. They're all dead ones!"

"They'll do all right, Father. I'm sure none of them died without the priest."

* * * * *

1941

D'Patrick.

I went into D'Patrick and called in Alms House. It was founded by the Southwells in 1733 as a Blue Coat scheme and has been enslaved ever since by the rentals from Land. There is a finely wrought iron gate at the main entrance adorned with the Southwell coat of arms. One section of the house is for old men and another for old women. The outside of the building is tidily kept but the living quarters (in the men's section which I visited) are flimsy and ill-kept. Each man is given a small plot of ground to labour—his kitchen and his room are free. At Christmas they are supplied with coal. I spoke to one old man. He was 87 and had been in the House for ten years.

• • • • •

Coming home in the bus the men were talking about the price of cattle, the condition of their crops, their fowl etc.

"There's nothing like oul' slushy rotten wrack from the shore to give to hens. Let them hoke through it and damn the pip or ache they'll take. It's great health for young birds!"

"That corn's light," one said looking out the window at the fields.

"How the hell can it be otherwise! Corn can't grow well in the sand and gravel of the shore."

* * * * *

1941

Belfast 1941—After The Blitz

All morning the train had gone past the suburban station of Knock, but when a delayed action bomb was discovered on the line near the Belfast station, Knock became the terminus for in-coming and out-going trains. The little station was crammed with people old and young, their baskets, suit-cases, birds in cages and bed-sheets with portable furniture wrapped in them lay at their feet. The station-master was exhausted as he made out tickets to all parts of the line: some of the tickets, to less-frequented parts, had remained untouched for such a length of time that they were covered with dust. Time and again he had to call the porter to get him change.

"Is there no small change amongst you people at all? You made sure Hitler didn't get your big notes."

The sun came out strong, and people, tired of waiting for a train, tired from the sleepless nights and the sound of guns and bombs, lay on the grassy embankments. Some were sleeping, others talking about the terrible night they had put in. "Hope I'll never live to see the like again."

Suddenly the siren went and a nervous hush spread cross the people, and those who were lying got up and stood about. The silver barrage balloons were put up; an old man looked at them contemplatively: "You might as well put me up!"

The crowd laughed. Presently there was a noise like machine-gun fire and the crowd raise their eyes to the blue sky. But the sound faded; it was only an old motor car running over broken slates on the road. Silence again. Then there came a faint drone like an aeroplane, and once again all raised their eyes. Then from a wooden box spread out at the feet of two women an alarm-clock suddenly went off and the people jumped away from it in fright. Then they laughed at their folly and the old man again said with contempt: "We can take it!"

*　*　*　*　*

In the train a young man sat beside me. Everyone was talkative. The young man's face and hands were dirty. He told me how he had remained in the shelter all night. When he went back to his house in the morning the windows were broken by the blast and the [...] were streaming into the house. The floor was littered with glass and plaster. He missed the bird-cage that always hung at the window and he found it flattened out in the scullery as if a steam-roller had run over it. "I didn't search for the finch, for I thought it was killed but when I was poking at the fire I looked down and saw the finch perched on the [...]. It was all bone on one wing where the blast had blown off its feathers. You'd wonder how it emerged. I opened out the cage again and rigged it up and put the bird back in it. He flittered from perch to perch as if nothing had happened to him."

* * * * *

October 1941
The potato gatherers in the field: the wind cold—the sea very blue—water lying in the upturned limpet shells on the shore—the sun shining on them. Evening—a silver light combed out between the clouds.

* * * * *

1941
On my way to Mass this morning it was dark and I hadn't time to shave, but knew that in the dark no-one would notice me. I thought of the poor old woman and her two sons who used to live near us and how, because their clothes were shabby, they went out to six o'clock Mass in the Monastery—Clonard Monastery.

The Young Poets

Published in *The P.E.N. in Ulster* (Belfast 1942),
with articles contributed by well known writers of
Belfast Centre.

1942

That there are so many young Ulster poets at present writing good verse is evidence of a literary resurgence in our midst. A transition period is not the time to speculate on where they are tending, but their highly individualised approach and freshness of perceptions, the human factor in their work, their vital contact with their own times, exhibit a vigorous faith in themselves and in their work. It was lack of faith that crippled us for so long and has, compared with other parts of Ireland, arrested our literary development. That period seems to be at an end.

They are exploring the resources of the language, incorporating in their poetry many of our own full-bodied words which have not as yet been defaced by too much literary usage. They are highly articulate, displaying a nervous tension and feeling for words; and one notices a quickening of tension, and intense impulsion that makes the rapid changes of their imagery convey the temper of the times in which we are living.

The poetry of W.R. Rodgers is typical and individual. His verse is crammed tight with urgency: "the winds of words pouring like Atlantic gales over his ears"; and then the spontaneous delight he takes in his material compels one to read him aloud in order to get the full, fresh flavour of his words.

Out of the emotional and intellectual interpretation of life these poets are conveying feeling and thought in concentration, and as their poetry in general manifests that man has more than natural needs to satisfy they will probably escape from the materialistic conception of life that impoverished much of the poetry of the 1930s. So far they have evaded the schools of poetry that are already cropping up with ready-made tabulated ingredients and prepared plans. A poet should write as he himself feels; it is his task to elucidate and integrate his experiences and if he possesses a Christian philosophy of life his work will, I think, be more universal and greater as literature.

Journals 1942

1942
Portaferry

As I was passing by the sea wall I saw an old tramp accosting two soldiers and asking them for a penny.

"I couldn't give you a penny until pay-day," one of them said.

"When's that?" asked the tramp.

"Friday!"

The soldiers laughed and walked past him. The tramp looked after them coldly:

"Umph! The army's gone to hell. My God, when I was in it we were paid every bloody hour!"

* * * * *

1942

When I was on my way across the ferry this morning the boatman was in bad humour.

"Did you pass that big horse on the road?" he asked me.

"I did!"

"He's an ignorant big brute!" he went on. "When we were taking him across this morning he walked up and down the boat and left his load in all parts of it. An ignorant fellow! We were only drivelling thro' the water—if you went hard he'd kick the boat asunder."

* * * * *

1 July 1942

I watched them shaking out the dulse this morning and spreading it to dry on the beaches and on the stone quay, and on the footpaths.

"There' good money at it! 4/6 a stone," one of the men told me.

"It didn't take long to dry on the footpaths—it's the cleanest too. There may be some spittle here and there but I believe the tar on the paths poisons them."

On my way back from school I saw them rolling up the dry dulse the way you'd roll a carpet—each strip having dried and stuck to the one beside it. I thought of the "poisoned spittle" and the droppings of the geese that paddled across the dulse on the way to the shore.

*   *   *   *   *

1942

I was reading a few stories by Gorki and some snatches from his diary. I am surprised at the eminent name he has achieved amongst literary people. I can see no reason for it! He seems to me to be a "made" writer—one who knows the tricks of the trade but lacking in that fibre which gives muscle, bone, and life to prose. He is like a student who had no brains, but just by hard work and plodding manages to arrive.

*   *   *   *   *

1942
D'Patrick—Strangford Bus

The women with baskets crushed their way on to the bus. A little workman was pushed to the side and he could hear the women shouting out to the bus-driver where they wanted off—some of them only a short distance away. Finally the bus was packed and the little man who intended to go the full distance was left standing on the road.

Letters 1942-43

To Julie Kernan

I am sorry to say that I haven't the novel completed yet. I have been living a lazy sort of a life recently: listening to the radio, reading worthless war books, and giving an occasional lecture. But I am now getting into the swing of work again and once I get the mood for writing and the feeling for it I'll be able to push ahead rapidly.

I am enclosing the first chapter of the new novel and from it, I think, you'll be able to extract the flavour of the entire book.* The whole scene of the book is centred around the entrance to Strangford Lough and the small town of Downpatrick.

The four copies of *Call My Brother Back* arrived O.K.— thank you very much or sending them. I am glad to see that it is still selling.

Good-bye now and good wishes for the New Year.

*   *   *   *   *

Knock,
3rd June 1943

Here are a few more chapters of my book which I hope will please you. I'll let you have some more at the end of the summer vacation.

I have no idea when I'll be able to have the entire work

---

*In This Thy Day, published by Cape and Macmillan in 1945.

complete but now that I have my teeth in it I'll forge ahead. I find it difficult to write, to contemplate, in times like these when the whole blood-boltered world is growing more dehumanised. I trust in God it will all end soon and a blessed peace follow after it.

Good-bye now and good luck to you.

Journal 1944

Gerard Manley Hopkins

(Notes for a talk delivered to the Belfast group of P.E.N., The Society of Authors, May 1944)

He displays throughout a keen sensuous delight in the objective beauty of the world. But it suffers from a decided lack of homeliness, and when he does make a simple home statement: "I'll put on my shoon and let thee out" we wish and yearn for more like it. He chats occasionally with the lay Brother—nearly all Irish—and notes their phrases: "I wouldn't put it past you ... Sorrow mend you ... It puts me to the pin of my collar ... as weak as a bee's knee." When, however, he uses all the conventional paraphernalia of the dull travel-book—endless description—he does so with this difference. He conveys to us the intense excitement aroused in him when he gazed at the objective beauty of the world. He didn't obscure anything. Rather we could say that he felt his way into anything he looked at; for instance: "The thunder rolling in great floors of sound ..." (Synge & Rilke).

> The bright woolpacks that pelt before a gale in a clear sky are in the tuft and you can see the wind unravelling them and rending them till they are unravelled to nothing and consumed.

He saw a lad burning big bundles of dry honeysuckle, the flame was

> brown and gold, brighter and glassier then glass or silk or water and ran reeling up to the right in one long handkerchief and curling like a cartwhip ...

paved with wind—saw the waves break into bushes of foam and ships of scum blow off and gadded about without weight in the air ...

On a hot day—one could feel the air as it rippled and fluttered like linen, one could feel the folds and braids of it.

The young lambs toss and toss, it is as if it were the earth that flung them not themselves.

I looked at the pigeons down in the kitchen yard strutting and jod-jodding with their heads. The two young ones are all white and the pins of the folded wings (quill pleated over quill) are like crisp and shapely cuttleshells found on the shore. Then others are dull thunder-colour or black-grape colour except in the white pieings, the quills and the tail, and in the shot of the neck. One moved its head and a crush of satin grew, came and went, a wet or soft flaming of light.

Crush Silk Poppies

Now these few descriptions—the book* is full of them— have the virtue of being distinctive. They aren't really descriptions at all. They are essences—he feels his way into the thing described (it's a quality that distinguishes literature from journalism) and this distinctiveness, he designated by the name of "inscape." For him it could be said no common nouns existed. (The *thread* convolution for instance ...). The use of the word "crush" (or the "floor of sound") convey the physical distinctiveness. They are three-dimensional and they, so to speak, bulge out from the page. The words have body— carrying simultaneously sight, sound and touch. It is this close, sharp, perceptive quality which has, I think, had the most influence for good on the moderns and not his elaborate theory of metrics. But for Hopkins this inordinate pleasure in the natural beauty of the world caused him many tormenting hours for he was troubled in trying to reconcile this with his spiritual vocation—how to be a priest and poet at the same time. The

* *Notebooks and Papers of Hopkins*, ed. H. House, London, 1937.

sharp pleasure he got form his perceptive gift can be evaluated from this entry in his Journal of a self-inposed penance:

> I would have looked again at the reaped fields on returning home but during dinner I talked too freely and unkindly and had to do penance going home!

However, he came on the work of Duns Scotus, the Franciscan philosopher, and as he remarks in the Journal:

> It may come to nothing or it may be a mercy from God. But just then when I took in any inscape of the sky or sea I thought of Scotus.

Scotus, it seems, justified him in his approach to nature and enforced him to understand "that the utmost concentration on the details of visible objects, so far from distracting from thought of God, was the most urgent of all reminders of Him." This reconciliation, I feel, gives all his rural poems a unity— they give them height—pointing upwards to God, the Father of all created Life. In one of his poems he refers to Scotus "who of all men most sways my spirits to Peace."

It would be appropriate to read at this stage one of his poems which may help to give significance and sequence to what I have already said: "Pied Beauty."

This rapturous delight in the beauty of Nature and feeling at the same time its loveliness as the breath of God dominated and unifies, it seems to me, most of his rural poems:

> The world is charged with the grandeur of God.
> It will flame our, like shining from shook foil.
> (The simile here is odd but one feels it is inevitable).

Again from his Journal we read:

> As we drove home the stars came out thick; I leant back to look at them and my heart opening more than usual praised our Lord to and in whom all beauty comes home.

This quotation refers us to his poem "The Starlight Night"—it is well-known and I need not quote it here.

To us removed in time from him by over sixty years and hardened, I suppose, by the "dull blows and buffets" of the world it will be difficult to comprehend the real sense of pain that comes to him when a tree is felled or when a city besmudges on the countryside with its trade and smells. An utterance like the following may come to us with a sort of shock:

> The ashtree growing in the corner of the garden was felled. It was lopped first; I heard the sound and looking out and seeing it maimed there came at that moment a great pang and I wished to die and not see the inscapes of the world destroyed any more.

This was written in 1873. Such sensitivity, I feel, is foreign to a world like ours. Six years later (1879) this intense sensibility towards nature had not hardened, or coarsened, for seeing a row of poplars being felled at Oxford, he wrote a poem ("Binsey Poplars"). I like it very much and I would like to see it included in anthologies. Although he himself was a classical student very few words of classical derivation obtrude upon his work–Anglo-Saxon—intense sharp—harsh—penetrate to the bone. In a letter to Robert Bridges he wrote once:

> I cut myself off for the use of *ere, o'er*, well nigh, what time, say not, because, though dignified, they neither belong to nor ever could arise from, or be the elevation of *ordinary modern speech*. For it seems to me that the poetical language of an age should be the current language heightened, to any degree heightened and unlike itself, but not (I mean normally: passing freaks and graces are another thing) an obsolete one. This is Shakespeare's and Milton's practice and the want of it will be fatal to Tennyson's Idylls and plays, to Swinbourne, and perhaps to Moore's.

Like many another poet he realises that the sharp, bleak words—which are all Anglo-Saxon—penetrates to the bone.

In another letter to Bridges he said: "I do not think you have reached finality in point of execution, words might be chosen with more point and propriety, images might be more brilliant."

Here are a few of his own images:

(the hawk turning on the wind)
… the fuddling and gnarls of the water
… the back draught shrugged the stones together and stacked them one against another.
… as a skate's heel sweeps smooth on a bow-bend
… bright-plucked water swaying in a pail…

The thrush singing:-

does so rinse and ring the ear, it strikes like lightning to hear him sing
—a tree whose boughs break in the sky—
—with hills of rime the brambles show …
—the clogged brook runs with choking sound—
… like water soon to be sucked in
will crisp itself or settle and spin—
… live and lancing like the blowpipe flame—
the cobbled foam-flare.

His poetry is full of these sharp and exquisite sensuous impression but Hopkins, from his remarks about Keats ("a life of impression instead of thought") was not content with poetry which rested on the senses alone. Like many another major poet he realised that the lyric is the primary element of poetry, but for a poet to continue to grow he needs to have some attitude to the world about him. He must reveal that he is alive in his own age to the condition of the world or to his particular part of the world. With Hopkins embracing and absorbing the philosophy of the Church of which he was a member, his work gained as he grew older a fine positive and intellectual control. It is true that one who shares his beliefs may get more spiritual value from his work then one who doesn't, but one does not fail to notice that there is behind them a unification of experience—not to grow is to live in a world "that's all in pieces, all coherence gone" or as Mr Yeats remarks: "Things fall apart; the centre cannot hold; /Mere anarchy is loosed upon the world."

"Leaden Echo and Golden Echo"—there may in this poem be too much verbal decoration, too much baroque or brocade for our minds to return to it continually but since it states something positive I'll read sections. It is original in thought and execution. The long lines are not rhythm run to seed: everything is watched and timed in them. Wait till they have taken hold of your soul and you will find it so.

Bridges quarrelled with him about his originality which he maintained was odd:

> The effect of studying masterpieces is to make me admire and do otherwise. So it must be on every original artist to some degree, on me to a marked degree. Perhaps then more reading would only refine my singularity, which is not what you want ...

Some months later on the same topic:

> You are peculiarly liable to echoes. Echoes are a disease of education, literature is full of them; but they remain a disease or evil ... a kind of touchstone of the highest or most living out is seriousness; not gravity but being in earnest with your subject—reality.

Hopkins is always serious, never cheap and never flashy. His longest and greatest poem is "The Wreck of the Deutschland": Our Lord's Passion: Death—Sin and Suffering in this World—the Redemption and eternal glory. The Dense and Driven Passion and frightful sweat.

But since literature is full of echoes: Pick:— "theological and not literary."

As I said: The Catholic outlook on the world gives his poems unification. At the same time—Journal—lack of interest in ordinary common humanity though restricting his range does not weaken the effects of what he had accomplished.

Destined to remain on the missions—Liverpool or Sheffield—"Felix Randal" " ... turned utterly sullen in the

Sheffield smoke-ridden air." He came to Ireland and now his poems are plunged for the most part in a bleak and self-torturing analysis. They are for me his best poems. They have been the cause of much controversy. Read: 41:45:50.*

As regards the doubt I'll quote a letter he wrote to Canon Dixon—*Frustration*—coupled with ill-health—neuroses—a country where he felt completely uprooted.

But whatever the cause they are great poetry and Ireland in a negative way is responsible. His frustration, his inhibitions are written in "sweat and blood." To get anything like them we would need to go back to Shakespeare. This conscious theorising and application of sprung rhythm are swept aside by the intensity of his vision, the words somehow come with a rush, a burst of energy that burns up all idea of poetic theory.

* Author's note for quotation.

Letters 1944-1947

30 Deramore Drive
Belfast
4th May 1944

To Julie Kernan

Here are two long chapters XIII-XIV which contain, I think, some of my best writing. I have about three more chapters to send you and then the book is complete. These will follow within the next six weeks but I don't suppose that will give you sufficient time for your autumn list. However do whatever is convenient. I am terribly sorry indeed to have disappointed you so often but many things upset me. I trust the book will do better for you than my last.

About a title: what would you think of any of the following:
Bread of Sorrow (it's taken from a psalm)
A Fire in Spring
Stony Limits.
You may of course have some interesting suggestions.

I am now living in a new house well out from the smoke and smudge of the city.

Good-bye now and good luck to the book.

* * * * *

Belfast
27th Nov. 44

To Jonathan Cape

Thank you for your letters. I am enclosing the paragraph and hope some of it may be of use to you. The only alternative title, which I feel suits the spirit of the book, is the biblical one which I already suggested: *In This Thy Day*. For the life of me I can't think of anything else. I told the editor of *Modern Reading* that this was the title, and as I have a story appearing in his Xmas number I am sure he will mention that title in his *Notes on Contributors*. On this account maybe we should let the book sail ahead under title: *In This Thy Day*.

The position with regard to America is this: Before I had finally completed the novel at the end of July Longmans had already seen three-quarters of it which they liked very much and urged me to hurry up so as to be in time for their fall list. But since sending them the remaining chapters at the beginning of August I am still waiting for a reply. I have cabled them to-day asking for their decision and I shall let you know the result of this. But to tell you the truth I would like a change of publisher in America. Longmans certainly produce a book nicely but somehow, from their lists they sent me from time to time, I feel they are interested more in Philosophical and Educational books than in Fiction. It was the late Edward J. O'Brien who introduced me to them and I must say they are the only American publisher to whom my work was every submitted.

Enc.: Publicity
For the background of his new novel Michael McLaverty takes a small parish on the Irish coast of County Down.

On the day Ned Mason's father dies the Devlin cottage goes on fire and Ned, disregarding what would be thought of his behaviour, rushes to help the neighbours to quench the flames; but his mother, distraught with worry and anger, appears amongst them. She insults the Devlins and reproaches her son for disgracing his father's name. The ensuing conflict between the two families provides a psychological penetration of many characters. Mrs Mason, in full possession of the farm willed to her by her husband strives to dominate her son and so bring peace to her family. She finds, however, that peace of mind, which she passionately seeks, seems to evade her. In contrast to her outlook on life the Devlin's grandfather, always in intimate relation with the natural beauty of the world, finds life's fulfillment in the work of his hands and in rejoicing with the young. Throughout the story an earnest priest, working for co-operation amongst his people, is beset with worries of his own: an old housekeeper wishes to die in harness to escape the loneliness of the workhouse and a good-natured chimney sweep flees from the parish because of gossip.

It is all blended with a fine coherence and written with that quietness of tone and fresh lyricism of phrase that characterised his previous novel, *Lost Fields*.

* * * * *

Belfast
28th Nov. 44

Since I last wrote to you the other day the final decision from Longmans has arrived and I am now enclosing their letter. Their suggestion about the ending of my novel seems to me to be preposterous and as I don't intend to alter the inevitable sequence of the story I am now free to make a friendly departure from Longmans and seek a publisher who would like the story in its present form. Whom do you suggest and how do I get in touch? I haven't got a copy of the script myself and I am wondering would it be O.K. to send them out a corrected copy of your proofs when they come to hand. I am very grateful indeed for your help in this matter.

* * * * *

To Julie Kernan

Your letters arrived two weeks ago and I thank you for them
and for the cable. I have given your suggestion much thought
but for the life of me I cannot accede to it as I feel it would
destroy the entire spiritual fabric of the novel. The whole spirit
of the book rests, I feel, on the ruination of lives caused by a
woman whose soul is poisoned by a spite shrouded in self-
righteousness. It is true that in the last chapter the presence of
death resurrects for her the futility of her sham religious life,
and on her way home from the priest's house a genuine
neighbourly feeling does possess her for the once, but to effect
a complete transformation at that stage and to end hopefully
would, I think, disintegrate the realistic unity of the story. The
hint given in that final chapter fits in with the title: In this thy
day if thou hadst known the things that are to thy peace.
Neighbourliness, love—old Dan has it and Luke—that is the
positive life-giving force of the book and not Mrs Mason's
which concerns itself with negations, a soul-destroying
attitude. However, the book may have failed to reveal these
implications and the fault therein lies with me. Though the
reading public may despise the book my faith in it will not
alter.

It was kind of you to suggest passing it on to another
publisher and as I have been told that Devin-Adair Company
(23 & 25 East 26th Street) are interested in Irish books you
may send it to them for me and I will write to them to-day to
expect it. I am conscious that I owe you a small debt (money)
for this trouble, for cabling, and for copies of books received
sometime ago. If you will kindly render an account of all this I
will settle it not on the Day of Judgment but now.

I thank you for all the kindness, courtesy, and consideration
that I received while I was with you.

*   *   *   *   *

To John O' Connor

A letter like yours, unexpected and unsolicited, brought me keen satisfaction and made me feel that the writing of novels is worth while. The fact that you quoted a few passages increased my satisfaction and scattered, somewhat, an idea that I was forming about novel-readers, namely that they do not read but skim, following the physical aspects of the story, that only and no more, My idea may be true of the mass of readers but, on them, literature does not rest for sustenance, nor to them does a creative writer primarily address himself. More and more I realize that reading is becoming a lost art; the tempo of our age is against it, the masses rush and race thro' the pages of a book, reading with a hurried and harassed eye, and into that tide an artist must launch a book, and, knowing its strength, he will expect little or no notice from it. We are, I feel, losing the power to sit still, and, as I wrote elsewhere, we are losing the power to contemplate and without contemplation there can be no real art and no response to art or just appraisal of it.

I am glad to hear that you are a writer yourself and I hope you will continue to be so and not be discouraged by a shoal of rejection slips. I have had many in my time and the cry is still they come. What matter (if you have faith in what you do and what you set out to do). And if reviewers praise you for the wrong reasons do not blame them; they are hard-pressed, have too many books to review, and no one expects them to be able to respond to the spirit in any of them. You will always write to please yourself, not to follow the prevailing fashion and please the multitude. Write with truth, for if an idea is true, generally true (not commonplacely true), it will remain so for future generations.

Author's note
*O'Connor=John O'Connor who later published a novel called *Come Day, Go Day* (M. McL. Nov. 1964).
This lad, I believe, has since died in Australia (M. McL. 4.4.70).

I haven't come across any of your work yet, so I give you my advice for what it's worth. Avoid romantic ideas and treating them realistically—the abyss of many of our Irish writers; stories, like these, may and do please for a while, may, catch the ear of foreign audiences, but Time and the author's own people will eventually bury them. Before you write spend days upon days upon what you are going to say—live with it, feel your way into it, and then the day will come when the idea will write itself. If you identify yourself with what you are writing, then you will write with intimacy, closeness, and an intelligent reader will feel himself physically and spiritually present in what you are doing.

Rilke's surge of perception, or any artist's, seems to be achieved by contemplation—slow and unhurried. How penetrating he is comes out even in translation (Leishman's):

> ... and let
> the shepherd's daily task seem possible to me,
> as he moves about and tans, and with measuring stone-throw
> mends the hem of his flock where it grows ragged.
> His slow but laborious walk, his pensive body,
> his glorious standing-still! Even to-day a god might secretly
> enter that form and not be diminished.
> Alternately lingering and moving like day itself,
> While shadows of clouds
> pass through him, as space were slowly
> thinking thoughts for him.
> Let him be for you what he may. As the blowing night-light
> is placed in the lamp's chimney, I place myself within him.
> A light grows peaceful. Death
> may cleanlier find his way.

Now all that is close, and originally perceptive. Lawrence had moments of it in *Sons and Lovers*; and we Irish, at one time, were endowed with the same gift of intimate vision—have the years of exploitation, and of our struggle for freedom, maimed or destroyed it, I wonder.

I must end now as I want to hear over the radio what L.A.G. Strong has to say of Yeats's "Fisherman."

Did you ever try any of your stories on American mags. You should send one or two that you have already published at this side to FATHER RALPH GORMAN, C.P., (Editor)—The Sign, Monastery Place, Union City, N.J. A story of mine that I published in *Modern Reading* and another in *The Bell* I republished in *The Sign*. The editor is on the look-out for Irish writers and I am sure he'd be interested in your work. He will pay you handsomely for them. If you wish you may tell him that I gave you his address.

Good-bye now and good luck to you. Should you ever be in this part of the world call to see me.

* * * * *

Spring 1946

To Padraic Fiacc*

I read your essay amidst the noise and distraction of a school-room, and now, in peace and quiet, having read it again I write to tell you how fine and sane and balanced it all is. Have no fear about your future—a young man who can write so calmly, so detached, about his friend need have no misgivings, and your poetry, too, will be appreciated. And since you express a love for the sharp and bony-structure of Anglo-Saxonism then I would advise you to cut out ruthlessly words like (I quote from memory of the 3 poems I read) "diaphonous clouds," of kindred brogue or decorative language; which only draw attention to themselves and dissipate one's immediate and spontaneous wooing of a poem. I'm not a poet—wish to God I was! But I love poems that have in them the rhythms of common speech (Yeats drew towards that in his later days and how fine and striking O Lord his poetry then is)—"live and loving like the blowpipe flame" in Hopkins' words. Your time

---

*Padraic Fiacc, poet, (1924-   ), born Patrick Joseph O'Connor. Fiacc lived in America until 1946, when he returned to Belfast. His correspondence with McLaverty dates from that time.

will come but you must have patience and faith in your own work and since that is sincerely wrought and the expression of sincere emotion—then wait, wait.

What the reading public think is of little importance—the masses doesn't read; they skim and literature will never reveal its secrets to the skimmer.

When I get back from my holidays I'll introduce you to Roy McFadden—a chap of poetic temperament is always revitalising.

My good wishes to you always,

*　*　*　*　*

Belfast
20th August 47

To Jonathan Cape

I am sending you for your own personal library a volume of some of my stories which has just been published with much success in America.* I enclose a few reviews of it which you may return at your convenience. I would be glad if your firm would publish them sometime after my next novel which I'll be sending to you within the next few weeks or so. If there is any story you dislike I could substitute another for it—but we can arrange all this at a later date.

In This Thy Day may be published in Spain, and when the contract and advance royalty comes to hand I shall send you it to make a copy and also 10 percent of all royalties in accordance with our agreement on that book. Macmillan, by the way, did well with it in the States and to date it has sold some fifteen thousand copies since last March—all this after three American publishers had rejected it. I have an idea that it was you who put Cecil Scott of Macmillan on to it.

With good wishes to yourself,

*　*　*　*　*

* *The Game Cock and Other Stories*

I was glad to get your letter to-day and to know you will publish the novel in 1948[1] and the short stories in 1949. Within a week or two I will let you know what new title comes to my mind and what title Macmillan may suggest. I was in two minds about the quotation on the title page: wondering if I should dispense with it altogether or substitute one from Eliot's *Family Reunion:*

> I believe the moment of birth
> Is when we have knowledge of death.
> I believe the season of birth
> Is the season of sacrifice.

A quotation that would be congruent with the characterisation of John and Nelly and in a negative manner with the tattered rag of a life that was the old country draper's.

You will be glad to hear that the volume of stories was selected as one of the outstanding books of the year by the Yale Review, their criticism ending with: "There are few elements of popular appeal in Mr. McLaverty's stories; but those who are interested in Irish literature, or, indeed, those who are interested in the art of the short story, should not neglect them. Michael McLaverty is a creative artist of a high order."

You ask me about Joseph Tomelty.[2] I know him well, and about two years ago when he gave me the first half of a novel to read I thought it truly magnificent and I advised him to submit it to you when he had it finished. I am wondering if that is the same novel you are now considering. I can still remember sharply his re-creation of the fisher folk of Portaferry (his native place) and the loneliness of a lone young man whose mother had died, and in his loneliness forgetting to milk the goat out on the hillside and her cries of pain attracting the passing postman who drained her udders into the ground.

[1] *The Three Brothers,* (New York & London) 1948.
[2] Joseph Tomelty, (1911-   ), playwright, novelist and actor.

I don't think the novel would fail you; Tomelty is known throughout Ireland: he is manager and chief playwright of the Group Theatre in Belfast; one of his plays ran for six weeks in the Abbey Theatre, and he, himself, was adviser to the film *Odd Man Out* and also played the part of the old cabby.

Good-bye now and my good wishes to you,

* * * * *

Belfast
2nd November 47

To Dr Cathal B. Daly*

Though the laneways of my life seem to be crazy-paved with promises, broken or made whole, I venture to succumb to the blandishments of your letter by promising to write an article for you. When and on what subject? Early in the new Year and on, say, *Literature and Propaganda* in which I may be able to satisfy your suggestion by taking a glance or two at the raked-up ashes of the 1930s Communist inspired literature.

At present I am trying to make whole a promise to *Irish Writing* and *Transition* by writing a story for each. When these are complete, and should I not happen to be beguiled into the writing of another novel, I will settle down to the article for your magazine—though whether or not it will receive your Imprimatur remains to be seen. However, there'll be no harm done should you send it back to me. But to tell you the truth I would rather "talk" it than write it, and, indeed, I am sure to do this ten times over with myself before I put it down in the black and white of the typewriter.

For a while back I have been turning over in my mind problems confronting Irish Catholic novelists and wondering if our novelists have not—where they treat it at all—an unbalanced and narrow conception of sin: sex as the totality of

* Most Reverend Dr Cathal B. Daly, now Bishop of Down and Connor, then lecturing in Department of Scholastic Philosophy at Queen's University, Belfast.

life. And I have often wondered why, say, the truth of their ways—to pervert this truth for the sake of a political party as the Communists do or to pervert it for the purposes of edification as some Catholics do is to become a propagandist: either way defeats its purpose.

In poetry, too, the same remorseless pursuit of truth is necessary for in the long run pietistic or propagandist verse does more harm than good. A poet must believe in suffering, in the Cross, and not bedevil himself with regressive tendencies like settling down in Inisfree with nothing for company but a few noisy bees and nine rows of miserable beans. "I am gall, I am heartburn. God's most deep decree bitter would have me taste ..." The verse of Hopkins with its cries of spiritual anguish would hardly be the book that a young girl would take on her holidays and mark with a rose-leaf or a crushed forget-me-not!

The whole problem is between truth or sham, and for the Irish scene, at least, something concrete may be thrashed out among literary laymen and a few priests who feel endowed with a sense of literature as well as philosophy. Unfortunately once the Catholic lay writer enters into this kind of criticism he runs the risk of having his work fine-combed for subtle nuances of Catholic propaganda. It would be worth it all.

*   *   *   *   *

Belfast
17th November 47

To D. A. Garrity[1]

This is to thank you for the fine reviews you sent recently and to ask you to send me six copies of the book before Christmas.[2] I have signed up with Cape for its publication at his side but it will not be ready for some time and, due to scarcity of good paper and binding, will not be able to compare with yours in

---

[1] Devin Adair Garrity (1905-1981) , President of Devin-Adair, New York.
[2] *The Game Cock and Other Stories,* Devin-Adair, New York, 1948, Cape in 1949.

general format. They have also taken my new novel and this is now with Macmillan—its publication will, perhaps, give the stories a fresh spurt of life in the New Year. It is, I feel a good novel—not in the "plot" sense but in its search for a meaning in life—congruent with Eliot's

> I believe the moment of birth
> Is when we have knowledge of death.
> I believe the season of birth
> Is the season of sacrifice.

Thank you for all your kindness.

The Novel and the Short Story

1947

In reading O'Faoláin's defence of O'Connor's *Common Chord*, and in reading his criticism of the short story in *The Bell*, it seems to me that he is formulating a critical analysis to justify his own "romantic" products.

Joyce's *Dubliners* is read now and will, I venture, be read and reread in the future because what Joyce has to say and the people he presents are true and will remain true for the majority of readers. One is never in doubt about the reality of his short stories: we feel that they deal with real people and real experience. We never have the same sense of truth when reading *The Common Chord* or many of O'Faoláin's stories, e.g. "The Man Who Invented Sin." We feel that the authors are out on the cod; if we could feel that they are fantasising as, say, Stephens' delightful *Charwoman's Daughter,* we would enter into the spirit of the fun and have our fling. But this does not happen; the authors wish us to read them as realists, as portrayers of truth. They are only deceiving themselves, and trying to deceive the reading public. When they are caught out as "realists," they say that we are being unkind to them: "We were only having a bit of delightful and imaginative fantasy."

Behind a flimsy facade of fantasy they seek a justification for their naked realism, their falsification of life. O'Faoláin instances the fact that O'Connor is read by Saroyan and printed in *The New Yorker*. The French always think it an ominous sign when their authors are read by foreigners:

> Three of the replies specified that Proust is read specially by foreigners. This is always an ominous note where a French writer is concerned, for is this not just what happened to Guy

de Maupassant and Anatole France. (Justin O'Brien in the N.Y.T. Bk. Review—28 December, 1947).

O'Faoláin and O'Connor should remember Dr. Johnson's words:

Nothing can please many and please long but just representations of human nature ... the mind can repose only on the stability of truth.

Letter to a Young Novelist

Published in *The Key* (London, 1948)

Dear Frank,

I wasn't surprised to read in your last letter that you intend to be a novelist. You were always a great reader, fastidious and implacable, and I am sure you will now transfer to the study of human nature some of this intense assiduity. But why must you feel the urge to leave your own provincial town for London? You say that your town is arid, intellectually backward, uncultured, and unstimulating. These remarks are nothing new: every young writer from a provincial town, here or in the U.S.A., possesses them and airs them occasionally. Giving verbal expression to your dissatisfactions is a definite way of disabusing your mind of them and finally settling down to the job of writing novels. Should you go to London you will probably align yourself with a literary coterie, read Kafka, Sartre, and Gide and write novels in the what-is-the-fashion. To turn your back on your own experience and your own environment would in time lead you, if you happen to produce at all, into a stultifying artificiality. Those who write for the world write for the moment, those who grow and write within a tradition, nourishing it and being nourished by it, write for posterity. Remain rooted in your own town would be my advice to you; there you will have leisure to contemplate your material and this contemplation would affect your style with the intimacy and particularity which are disappearing from the prose of many contemporary novels. Freshness and intimacy, it seems to me, are the products of writers who are humanly close to their material: D.H. Lawrence in his earlier novels has it in abundance, and with him I would mention the Brontës, George Eliot, and the dialogue of Jane Austen.

We feel close to all this and we feel, too, that the passages were written by one who was completely immersed in his material; it is not hurried writing, not cipher writing—it is writing that comes directly from life, from genuine human experience.

You say you are reading the "Europeans," and among them, I notice with some pleasure, you mention François Mauriac. From these writers you can learn much; you can learn technique but you should be careful not to be affected by the spiritual climate of writers who have no affinity with your own mood or with the characters who are to populate your novels. No living writer can surpass Mauriac in his compelling power to lay bare the ramification of evil (pride, greed, lust, hate, money-worship) in the individual soul and the soul of society. But having said that, I feel he has defects. He does not achieve the bitter-sweet in life—the duality of experience:

> I will complain—yet praise;
> I will bewail,—approve;
> And all my sour-sweet days,
> I will lament,—and love.
>
> (G. Herbert)

Hopkins, too, was aware of it: "with swift, slow; sweet, sour; adazzle, dim;" or "Enough! the Resurrection. A heart's clarion! Away grief's gasping, joyless days, dejection ..."

It seems to me that Mauriac's novels are for the most part cast in a puritanical gloom: there is no *Servite Domino in Laetitia*, no *Laetare Sunday*; there is a stifling depression, a preoccupation with the forces of evil that fail to make their complete impact because they have not been offset with analogous effects of joy, charity, kindness and humour. He usually attaches an epigraph to each of his novels and I often wish he had come round to writing one with, say, this extract from *The Shepherd of Hermas*:

Clothe yourself with cheerfulness which always finds favour with God and is acceptable to him. Rejoice in it. For every cheerful man does good, has good thoughts, and despises melancholy. Cleanse yourself of this wicked melancholy and you will live to God.

Lest you would take this hint and founder in the other extreme I hasten to add this remark of Cardinal Newman:

> Christianity, considered as a moral system, is made up of two elements, beauty and severity: whenever either is indulged to the loss and disparagement of the other evil ensues.

It may all be, however, that the fault of Mauriac's one-sided view of human nature may rest in the society which he recreates. If it does then he seems to me to have been born in unfortunate suroundings: his society is without laughter, and when people cease to laugh death has set in.

A novelist needs more than his share of commonsense. He must look upon life as it is in all its baseness and beauty, and not force any thesis on it. Everything needs a right ordering, and that ordering is first of all in man's total nature and his relation to his eternal destiny. From the shuffled material of experience the novelist must integrate and clarify the night and day of life, its sorrow and joy. He must be true to his people and to their ways and thought; he must represent life as it is but over and above that—and it is here that an integral Christian philosophy will help—there must be a summoning forward to a life that "ought to be" (Aristotle). Where human nature in all its weakness falls short of this a novelist produces that clash of opposites that reinforce his work with a genuine criticism of life. No matter how objectively he may strive to be, his own attitude to life will impose itself on the characters of his imagination, and if he is a Catholic novelist and writing of a Christian people he will reveal a world other than that perceived by the senses. A Christian philosophy comprehends the whole of life and gives meaning to all human experience.

Journals 1948

1948
Thoughts
... When all seems lost; seems as if God had forsaken us, that is the time to hold firm in faith, even when everything done to us seems absurd, against reason, against justice. For good Christians there's a meaning in it all if we but have patience to wait and not rebel. God gives his grace to the courageous. He delights when man, whom he has made in his own image, confronts difficulties and endures suffering with patience and with acceptance. "That which I have made I am proud of ... You have shown me that there is great stuff in you ... You, the great of heart, I will help. You of little faith put me to shame ... Have I not told you: Consider the lilies of the field etc."

*   *   *   *   *

23 February 1948
When you feel at peace with the world and at rest, if you feel no more within you a struggle against this world and your soul's salvation, then is the time to re-examine your conscience ruthlessly. To be lukewarm and indifferent is to be in danger. A soul is alive when there is an unceasing daily struggle.

*   *   *   *   *

25 February 1948
One cannot pray properly without fervour. Where fervour is absent our prayers are thin—like breath in the wind. God sends

117

suffering and sorrow in order that we will turn to him with fervour and cease relying on ourselves. Fervour is like a blaze in dry twigs—burns itself out in white ash and does not smoulder.

When we are lukewarm and merely mechanical there is no lifting of the heart of God. Do not allow dry habits to root themselves in your soul.

*   *   *   *   *

26 February 1948

To accept pain and sorrow is to live, to flee from them is to die. Think of all the maimed people lying in hospitals, think of the people paralysed for life since birth, think of the hungry children and the destitute and you'll cease lamenting over the trifle that has crushed in upon your comfortable life. Suffering, in some form or other, will come to us all. To seek always after comfort is to seek for the death of your heart, because indifference will grow and come with it, and to be indifferent is to be lukewarm—"I will vomit thee out of my mouth."

*   *   *   *   *

25 January 1948

I have just read Mauriac's *Thérèse*, and found it a book of unrelieved gloom, a dark pool full of weeds that seldom stretch towards the light of day. There is something fundamentally lacking in Mauriac—a morose and warped type of Christianity—a man, it would seem, who believes in fatalism, in predestination. There is no joy and no humour—serious defects in a writer whose quest is for completeness, for wholeness. Where this duality of life's experience—its joys and its sorrows—is not achieved, one couldn't attribute the word "great" to Mauriac. There is too, in this book a static atmosphere of carnal love—an emphasis throughout on, it seems to me, an abnormal eroticism that is almost animal and subhuman in its delineation e.g. the young girl (Anne) moving around the garden "like a bitch in heat."

The relationship between Thérèse and George is drawn to the point of absurdity.

One wonders was the book worth writing; its philosophical content is obvious to us all; i.e. we can't completely live in the world and mix with people without spreading, however unwittingly, some suffering, some vice that escapes legal justice, and yet is as bad as a murder. The point is: Thérèse was conscious of her crime and suffered for it—the rest of us commit crime and vice—and do not suffer for them.

Letters 1948

Belfast
8th May 48

To Dr Cathal B. Daly

I am sorry for the delay in sending this out to you. I have been in and out of bed fighting off 'flu since I last spoke to you and I couldn't settle myself at anything. I am afraid, too, that the article is rather bony and scrappy and needs fattening in places.* However you may submit to the editors and see if it is along the lines they expect; I can then lengthen it if they wish by references to the work of Yeats, Lewis, Barker, and the early work of Spender.

This is only part 1 of the article and I will follow it if you wish with *Night and Day: a note on the Modern Novel;* in it I will show that Mauriac's greatest novel is *Viper's Tangle* but that in *Thérèse* the life depicted is all Night—no joy, no humour, no Laetare Sunday: a perpetual Lent without hope or joy of a Resurrection. But he is strong where Irish writers are weak—his sense of evil is not confined completely to concupiscence; at the same time I feel that there is something maimed and morose in his attitude to life—one wishes to the good God that he knew how to laugh!

You can let me know at your convenience what you think of this. Should the editors say that it is no damned good don't be timid in relating their message to me.

* * * * *

* No copy of the article exists, but the title *Night and Day* is used in a later lecture. See pages 142-148.

To Jonathan Cape

You must have forgotten that you had already seen a copy of *The White Mare* when it was published about six years ago.* Mr. Richard Rowley sent you a copy as he thought that you might have imported sheets for the English market. At the time of its publication paper was scarce and of an inferior quality and as far as I can remember you stated in a letter to Richard Rowley that it was not the policy of your firm to import sheets and that each book issued by the firm bore a distinctive format in typography, binding, and paper; I think you mentioned the possibility of reissuing it in your *Travellers' Library*. I am writing from memory and I may have things a bit mixed.

The Mourne Press is no longer in existence, its owner and editor Richard Rowley having died about two years ago. But the copyright of the stories always belonged to me, and when Rowley asked me for a few stories for his Mourne Press booklets I gave them to him to help Irish Letters in this corner of Ireland. I received no payment or royalties for them, and I asked him to confine its sales mainly to Northern Ireland and not to send review copies to England. He was an old man and forgetful and he slightly overlooked the later clause, at least two copies for review being sent across.

If, however, you would like a written statement from his wife that The Mourne Press had no right in the stories I could get that for you. But I can assure you that everything is in order. I am separated at present from my files and it's possible that I may have a letter from Rowley that would show you that all is O.K.

I will be away in Brittany for the next two or three weeks and when I return I will answer any letter you may happen to send during that time.

---

* *The White Mare and Other Stories*, published by Mourne Press, Newcastle, Co. Down, 1943.

Michael McLaverty Explains His Methods

as he sketches background of The Three Brothers

August 1948

I write each novel as carefully as I write a short story, endeavouring to make each sentence and each passage of dialogue carry their full complement of meaning, and trying also to sketch the background which forms and had formed the lives of the characters in my books. The background I regard as fundamental and I can never treat it in a casual manner because I feel that character and background should coalesce in such a way that one is unthinkable without the other. So when I am writing my novels I have a real place in my mind's eye: house, village, river or country road, and I am continually seeing these places, in all their seasonal or physical changes, from the angle of my characters.

The village, which forms an essential element in *The Three Brothers*, is a real place though I have altered its name, and to this day there are to be seen the pump, the level crossing and the unalterable river with its falls. As I write of these things, surrendering myself to them, there comes over me a flow of perception: the very sounds and feel of the place, the smell of dust on the road, the inflection of the people's voices and their gestures when they are angry, laughing or at rest.

By identifying myself with everything I describe, I experience something that has a physical quality. I feel for my people and with them; they are not, for me, creatures in a book but people as real as the fingers in my own hand. Though in the main I imagine them, yet who is to say where imagination ceases and memory begins:

"the woven figure cannot undo its thread."

Contemplation is what we are all in need of—writers and readers alike. Without contemplation there can be no real art, and without a slow contemplative response on the part of the reader or observer there can be no adequate appraisal of art.

I am not interested in the abnormal or violent—violent men are usually weak men and those writers who follow that incline usually lose themselves in a maze of melodrama by an insistent emphasis. It is the half-said thing that produces intensity of expression. "To be told nothing and yet to hear and feel everything," Coleridge said of Shakespeare.

Not what an author says about his characters but what the characters say and do is what gives life to a novel. A novelist is a creator, not a commentator; his chief function is to present his people truthfully—in *their* ways and not *his* ways.

I usually visualize my novels in terms of conflict: a conflict arising out of characters with environment, characters with their inmost selves or a clash of character with character; and in seeking to resolve these conflicts in an inevitable and natural manner, incident flowing to and out of one another, I strive to produce a coherent pattern that not only records experience but evalues and illiminates it, thereby affecting the reader's sensibility and not pandering to his curiosity.

In that pattern there is the conflict of life as it is, with what it ought to be. In the final chapter of *In This Thy Day* where Mrs. Mason is neighbourly and friendly with her enemies she feels a lightness of heart for which she can give no name—it is the fruit of charity but it has come to her too late: it is life as it is, with what it ought to be—the pain that we bring upon ourselves but blame others for causing. A novelist can only signpost the way; he cannot drag his recalcitrant characters along with him—to do so would be to fail as a creator and become a propagandist.

In this new novel there is a conflict among three elderly brothers—John Caffrey, Uncle Bob and Uncle D. J.—and this conflict, by involving the subsidiary characters, affects and changes, for better or worse, their sense of life's responsibilities.

Uncle Bob, the village draper, heaps unhappiness upon

himself because he erects a barricade of selfish comfort to guard his peace. His selfishness and love of money have so stultified his life that he fails to realise that a grudge is the worker of death, that you cannot liquidate people who are a bane to your self-comfort—you have to bear with them, not desire their death but their repentance. "And here the faithful waver the faithless fable and miss." In contrast to Uncle Bob is his half-sister, Aunt Nelly, who by sacrificing her ambitions discovers a rich and satisfying fulfillment.

Eileen and her sister who teaches school, their mother and father, and the two boys, Brendan and Frank, are all affected by the joy and sorrow that form out of this family conflict. For them, life is neither tragic nor joyous—it is a mixture of both; to strive to escape for the sorrows in life is to make the cross meaningless, to strive to shut out the joys in life is to make the resurrection meaningless.

Life's experience is the author's raw material but his function is to clarify its night and day, its joy and sorrow, and sin and grace, and give them a coherent form. That form is in life's inevitable wintering and summering.

(Published in *Forecast,* the journal of the Catholic Literary Foundation, Milwaukee, Wisconsin).

Letters 1948-1949

Belfast
24th August 1948

To D. A. Garrity

I am glad you have decided to publish a selection of Corkery's short stories—no one deserves it more. Since you asked me what stories of his that I like best I must confess that most of them are in his latest volume "Earth out of Earth." The Cork school of writers (although they would deny it) have a tendency to seize upon romantic ideas and treat them realistically—so in reading them I have always a doubt as to what is "real" and what is "imaginative," "fake," or "story." I have never that doubt when reading, say, Joyce's *Dubliners*—the realism in those stories (i.e. their truth to life as it is lived and not life as "imagined") is as clear as daylight. Now in *Earth out of Earth* Corkery is more real than in his previous volumes of stories; mind you I am not despising a writer's imaginative flights for one must agree with Aristotle that "a likely seeming fiction is better than an unlikely seeming fact"—and there's no other corner of Ireland that has the natural gift of story-telling, and that tradition has coloured all their work—it is in Corkery—in O'Faoláin, in O'Connor; it has given them facility and colour and grotesque humour but, in many cases, it has also pulled them away from complete reality. But to ask them all to be Joyces would be tantamount to asking a tree not to spread its branches.

Of Corkery's stories here is a list of the stories that I often find myself re-reading: the first, "Vision," is a little masterpiece.

From *Earth out of Earth"*
1. Vision
2. Children
*3. "God Forgive us all"
4. The Lilac Tree
*5. Old Men have a Day Out
*6. A Terror of a Man
7. Richard Clery's Sunday
8. Strange Honeydew

From *Stormy Hills*
9. The Awakening (a very beautiful piece of work)
10. The Emptied Sack
11. Carrig-an-Afrinn
12. A Looter of the Hills

From *Munster Twilight*
13. The Cobbler's Den
14. The Spanceled

From *Hounds of Banba*
15. Cowards
*16. The Child Saint

The stories marked with * are very popular at this side of the Atlantic. The above would be my choice but if I started to re-read the four volumes again it's possible I'd include others. But the above made a deep impression on me on my first reading of them. There's lovely humour in "The Old Men Have a Day Out" and in "God Forgive us All" where the old drunk puts his coat and hat round the new statue and takes off the old bags and rags that the people had used. Corkery has taught us all!
Note: I did not send this letter—I wrote a shorter one containing a list of the stories only—Michael McLaverty

*   *   *   *   *

To Daniel Corkery *

I am sending you this volume of some of my stories in the hope that you will send me a selection of past stories from your own four volumes by the same publishers; I'm sure they'd be pleased to get that. Recently I listened to a broadcast of your story "Vision" and it still enthralled me—all the bleak wonderment of that boy writing at the table—and listening and feeling the darkness outside is nothing short of wonderful, and the use you make of "sharply" to give us immediately the character of the mother. That story and P. Colum's "The Journey" (unknown to many people) are for me two of the loveliest of all Irish short stories. In "talks" I have given I have never tired of quoting from both of them; and also of analysing the changes of mood and circumstances in your story "Richard Clery's Sunday"—stories like yours do not depend on "lower cravings of curiosity" but on mood and character. When the meaning is grasped they explode and illuminate; and one can re-read them always with the joy of fresh discovery.

I read recently that you have retired from University life. I hope that you will have many a long and happy year. Maybe you'll give us another *Threshold of Quiet*.

I didn't get to Cork for the summer that I intended. I went north to Rathlin instead. But I may go this summer. I got the idea for "The Road to the Shore" when cycling south from Cork out by Inishannon. I happened to see a car load of nuns who had unfortunately knocked a cyclist into the ditch.

My good wishes to you always. You may not be aware of it but it is to your work that I owe my beginnings.

Michael McLaverty

* * * * *

* Daniel Corkery (1878-1964), novelist, short-story writer and literary critic.

To Jonathan Cape.

Thank you very much for sending me copies of the two broadcast reviews of my last novel; I was glad to get them as I only heard the one from Radio Eireann.

I am wondering if you have decided to include "Six weeks on and Two Ashore" in the *Game Cock* volume—I do hope that you'll include it. I could, if you wish, send you another copy of it. When the proofs are ready I hope you'll send me a set for I am dying to make a few corrections in the American edition which was sent to you and from which edition you are working.

With good wishes for the New Year to all of you.

*   *   *   *   *

Belfast
16th Jan. 49

To Horace Reynolds *

A short while ago Macmillan sent me a sheaf of reviews of my last novel and I wish to tell you that yours and the one in the Sat. Review and one in a Scranton University review pleased me greatly. How I loved your emphasis on Bob! When I was writing that novel it was his character above all others that intrigued me, and each time he appeared I entered into his creation with a joy that I have seldom experienced before, and in spite of myself his stinginess and his blindfolded and unconscious moral weaknesses wrung some compassion from them. The book is doing well for Macmillan, and at this side it has produced some fine reviews from Irish critics.

Have you ever come across Mary Lavin's work? I didn't think much of her novel except in spots but some of her short

---

* Horace Reynolds, American critic and reviewer.

stories afford me intense and constant satisfaction. Time and time again I return to them as I do to Joyce's *Dubliners*; they are true and will remain true for at no time do we feel that there is falsification or romanticising of the material. Not that Mary Lavin hasn't written a dud story—she has: the four stories in *The Becker Wives* I found so unbalanced that I feel they are only prentice work. But stories like "The Will", "Brother Boniface", "Miss Holland", "The Cemetery in the Demesne", "At Sally Gap" are unforgettable. She goes her own way unhampered by any short story formulae; it seems to me she can do anything she likes with the short story, entering into it with a freshness and freedom that are instantly compelling. But what delights me above all in her work is the way she can capture mood by the rhythm of her language. Some modern stories give the impression they they were written by an pneumatic drill but hers have ease, urbanity, growth, and inevitability. Rhythm in language is disappearing from English prose style and the defect is due to the want of total immersion in the theme so that the resultant mood engendered can gather round itself the rhythm necessary for its total expression. Synge had it and so has Mary Lavin. "Brother Boniface" had it in abundance but for an obvious example take the opening of her "Dead Soldier"; when I read it aloud it excited the same rhythm and mood as I got from Synge's description of the Aran funeral. It was Dunsany who introduced her to the public; he has also introduced a novel *Bridie Steen* which I did not like at all.* I found its entire landscape covered with cart-loads of clichés and such a marked disparity between its narrative passages and dialogue that has left me wondering how he arrived at his extravagant estimation of it. At no time was there an artistic fusion between her language and the people she was writing about. Place it alongside O'Faoláin's *A Nest of Simple Folk* and it disintegrates into facile journalism.

Under separate cover I have sent you on a few books which may interest you. Farren's book has a good hard grain and I think he is aware that a change is coming in the course of Irish

---

* *Bridie Steen*, (New York, 1948) by Anne Crone, (1915-   ), novelist.

verse. AE said somewhere that the centuries have not brought us the philosophic mind—one does not stop to wonder at that when we consider our political history; one wonders at how much it has contributed to the world's literature. And when our poets ascend and grow from their indigenous lyricism into a world of co-ordinated thought how much more will they able to contribute! I believe a time will come when one will not be able to cast at them Yeats's valedictory poem:

> ... All that I have said and done,
> Now that I am old and ill,
> Turns into a question till
> I lie awake night after night
> And never get the answer right.
> And all seems evil, until I
> Sleepless would lie down die.

P.S. After reading this I must add that I have never met Mary Lavin; I only know her through her work and that is enough for anyone.

Journals 1949

30 January 1949

Many critics quarrel with writers who are too contemplative—it is a niggling sort of criticism to condemn man for the nature which God has endowed him with. If all through his life he has met "chaste, quiet and virginal women," why should a critic condemn him for writing about the life he knows. To write otherwise would be to write what is untrue to himself—to what he knows and feels and thinks.

*　*　*　*　*

1949

… a novel like Mauriac's *A Woman of the Pharisees* which treats of spiritual pride would not suggest itself to Irish writers, or his *Vipers' Tangle* which reveals with devastating power the hate engendered in a man's soul by the lack of love and sympathy from the good and pious Christians who fill out the horror of his days. Is our spiritual health so numbed and weak that it cannot deal with these subtle refinements of evil or is it that the centuries of struggle for political independence have diverted our energy from spiritual growth, bequeathing us a blurred conscience that sees only one deadly sin? Where are we to look for this rot, for this unfruitful attitude? Catholic continental writers—though some of them like Mauriac can be too doctrinaire at times—have a conception of sin which includes the seven deadly fellows but I doubt if these exist for the Irish writer outside the Penny Catechism. And more fundamentally, have the Irish people this lofty conception? If it does exist in the conscience of our people then our Irish writers who write of "conscience" and take cognizance only of "Sixth thou shalt not commit adultery" are certainly falsifying the lives of our people. If, however, there is present in our people only one way of committing evil then it would be an equal falsification if our writers wrote of them as beings torn with spiritual remorse (in fact I have heard Irish people rend one another's character with the same concentrated vigour as they shred a nutmeg and with the same happy abandonment).

* * * * *

Saturday 5 March 1949
Annoyed to see in the *Irish News* an inaccurate and stupid account of "D. O'Donnell's" lecture.* I am reported to have said that I regarded Mauriac, Green and Bernanos as "unimportant." I felt like writing a letter to deny this puerile allegation—thought it better to suffer the foolish reporter in silence. 'Tis a pity I didn't say in the discussion that Mauriac's *Viper's Tangle* is for me the greatest Catholic novel ever written.

* * * * *

6 March 1949
On reflecting on Donat O'Donnell's lecture on "The Devil in Catholic Literature," I am convinced of a certain intimate familiarity in all the characters of Mauriac, Gide, Thebault, Daniel-Rops, etc.—all their characters and brilliant psychological reactions have a family resemblance to one another and to their parent, Stendhal. In totality they convey the impression of literature and not on life. One feels it is their living so closely together in Paris that accounts for their resemblances; it's a pity, like Cézanne, they don't go back to their villages and provincial towns. The change would infuse life and vitality and variety into their work.

* * * * *

* Donat O'Donnell, pseudonym of Conor Cruise O'Brien, (1917-   ), historian and critic.

1949
Mauriac

Because I suggested that the total impression of Mauriac's work is one of despair and gloom does not mean that his conclusions of *Thérèse* and *Vipers' Tangle* and *The Woman of the Pharisees* are not hopeful—they are, but one feels that everything was prearranged to point to *that*; one, however, is aware that the "hope" and "sorrow" do not alternate throughout the chapters of each book: it is 99% gloom and then the glimmer at the end. Does not truly reflect human experience—the disruptive forces in man's nature are paramount in his books.

*   *   *   *   *

1949
François Mauriac

"Wring thy rebel, dogged in den,
Man's malice with wrecking and storm."

That quotation from Hopkins could serve as a motif to the best novels Mauriac has written: *Vipers' Tangle, Thérèse, Woman of the Pharisees.*

In each of these, the chief protagonist has to undergo a crucifixion of experience in order, at the end of the demolition to be brought face to face with the real spiritual foundation, the image of God. It is only the realisation of that factor that can teach us that life (our real life, our spiritual life) can only grow and be fulfilled by one way, the way of the Cross.

In his lecture delivered before Cardinal Suchard on the closing day of the Semaine des Intellectuels Catholiques, 1949, he says,

> Yes, necessity and circumstances are our mentors. Seen from this perspective the catastrophe of man's history are like agents in the job of turning the Christian from what on his own he has not the strength to renounce.

In God's love for man He often uses wrecking and storm to

bring him face to face with what is fundamentally the root of all life.

In Mauriac's *Thérèse,* Thérèse goes down into the depths to be shown the way. But this philosophical approach to a novel, and because of its high seriousness, often scoffs at much of that life that reveals life in all its wholeness. Mauriac's lack of humour etc. It tends to become a clinical study of evil.

* * * * *

7 November 1949

"Why do you not write a book every year?" Trees do not grow in a year. Flowers grow quickly and so quickly fade but a tree remains even when it loses its leaves. I want my books to be tree-like—slow to mature but solid.

* * * * *

8 November 1949

I have read B. Kiely's *In a Harbour Green,* and think that it is a good as O'Flaherty or O'Connor.* It prompts comparison with O'Faoláin's *Bird Alone,* but one, in all honesty, must declare that O'F.'s Elsie Sherlock is a truer picture of Irish girlhood than Kiely's May Campbell. With May Campbell there is no moral struggle when she enters and succumbs to the urgings of the flesh. Like the majority of the characters in the book (Pat Rafferty the exception) life among the young and, with Fiddis, the middle-aged, is lived on a naturalistic plane—it failed to reach a mature Catholic novel because the supernatural was only a slight addition.

Many Irish writers mistake promiscuity as life. Sex is an essential element in human experience but is not its totality as most of them think, and when a writer touches on pharisaical pride the critics are so dull-witted they don't notice it.

Kiely goes out of his way to interlace his book with sexuality—e.g. the passages given to May to recite ("Troilus

* Benedict Kiely, (1919-), novelist, short story writer and critic.

134

and Criseyde"—why?)

He has an addiction for knees and thighs and silk—rather adolescent habiliments.

But he will write a fine novel when he gets over the growing pains of love.

*   *   *   *   *

1949
On Writing a Novel
I think over it daily; at first ideas and incidents are confused and have no coherence except that of place—then gradually and inevitably they merge together and I am ready then to put them on paper. *Everything comes easy* after long and loving contemplation. *There must by a raison d'etre* for writing it—to uncover truths.

*   *   *   *   *

3 December 1949
Lectured on G.M. Hopkins last night to the English Society at Queen's. My throat was rather tired and husky. I wished it had had a clearer ring, as one needs full voice and vigour to read Hopkins's poems.

Letters 1948-1949

Belfast
21st Nov. 48

To David Marcus [1]

It is very decent of you to review my book seeing that it reached you by an unprescribed route. You need have no fear that Cape has any particular objection to sending books to you. The truth is that they seem to me to be under the opinion that *The Irish Times* covers the entire reading public of Ireland. My novel *In This Thy Day* was reviewed only by *Irish Times* and *Dublin Magazine* and I realise now that review copies were not sent to the other Dublin dailies. I may tell you that I wrote to them three times within the past month to send copies to *The Irish Press* and *Irish Independent*; they replied to my third letter to say that they had done so. You'll understand that I'd hate writing to them again with a few more suggestions; it was Teresa Deevy,[2] by the way, who told me that you hadn't got a copy. But I am sure they will waken up to the presence of *Irish Writing,* some day soon. I thank you.

I was indeed glad to hear that the story I sent you received much good comment from readers. I am writing a new novel at present but should I ever turn to the short story again I will give you first consideration.

* * * * *

[1] David Marcus, editor, *Irish Writing*, 1946-1954.
[2] Teresa Deevy (d. 1963), playwright.

To Jonathan Cape

I was glad to get your letter and to know the *Cornhill's* decision on the stories. I can well understand their desire to get "fresh" work, and should I write any short stories that I feel would suit them I will submit them to you first. Though I have a story coming in the next issue of *Irish Writing* and one in *The Bell* I have done little in that line since finishing *The Three Brothers*. To tell you the truth I am more interested now in novel-writing. It is true that I sent a batch of stories to Devin-Adair but it is also true that, with one or two omissions, they made the best selection, and what remains does not greatly interest me in the way of publication—they are early work and I think I can do much better.

The Irish Bookman are going to reprint "The Road to the Shore" and I told the editor to send you your percentage of the fee on publication day—you'll receive about one and a half guineas. The Macmillan people have agreed to the title *The Three Brothers*.

* * * * *

Belfast
20th April 48

To Father Joe Conboy *

Good poetry is very difficult to write, and before one can write it with any individual significance—the only significance that really matters—one must work off all the baleful influences of the schoolroom, all the stock responses to the conventional themes, all the echoes, verbal and thematic, from other poets, good and bad, that we have learnt either for examinations or under threat of the schoolmaster. From good poetry you can learn craft or technique—you can borrow these but you must

* Fr Joseph Conboy, friend of McLaverty family.

not borrow another's spirit. It seems to me that to be a poet you must face realities unflinchingly—for what is happening to you is happening to us all and when you express yourself—your real self and not a borrowed one—you speak for us all and thereby achieve the impersonality that poetry requires. But you must most of all try to gain freshness—a striking use of verbal imagery; a felicity that arrests the eye and the ear by its uniqueness, particularity, or individuality—something, we feel, that has arisen out of direct experience and hasn't been dragged from the poetic lumber and paraphernalia that clutters all our minds. I think of Gerald Manley Hopkins and this is a poet that you must grow to know and love; if you read him he will sharpen your approach to everything: nature, sin and holiness, the Cross and the Resurrection—the resolution of our spiritual conflicts. If I can get you to read him without sham appreciation I will be pleased and feel that this correspondence has been worth while. I say this because in a world so tormented as ours it is difficult to acquiesce in what we have been taught that "poetry is emotion recollected in tranquillity": such an attitude would produce poetry that is regressive in tendency like Yeats's "Lake Isle of Innisfree" or Hopkins's immature poem "Heaven Haven":

> I have desired to go
>   Where springs not fail,
> To fields where flies no sharp and sided hail
>   and a few lilies blow.
>
> And I have asked to be
>   Where no storms come,
> Where the green swell is in the havens dumb,
>   And out of the swing of the sea.

Such a life of accidie was not to be his and the expression of it in verse is, to my mind, bordering on the sentimental through lack of maturity and thought. But the words, like everything he wrote, are original. Compare this with the opening of his "Wreck of the Deutschland." (Read it aloud and give the vowels their full tonal quality):

Thou mastering me
  God! giver of breath and bread;
World's strand, sway of the sea;
  Lord of living and dead:
Thou hast bound bones and veins in me, fastened me
flesh,
  And after it almost unmade, what with dread,
Thy doing: and dost thou touch me afresh?
  Over again I feel; thy finger and find thee.

But to appreciate Hopkins you must not read him with the eye
but with the ear—this was his own advice and if you heed it
you will grow to love him in the way that I have done and you
will be a much better poet from having a long and deep
affection for him. "The effect of masterpieces on me" he said,
"is to make me admire and do otherwise." He strove for
singularity and he achieved it. Here is the stanza of the poem
that won me to him; it is entitled "Binsey Poplars" and he
wrote it after seeing a row of poplars being cut down. (Read it
aloud many times and your voice will follow its natural
rhythm):

My aspens dear, whose airy cages quelled,
Quelled or quenched in leaves the leaping sun,
All felled, felled, are all felled:
Of a fresh and following folded rank
  Not spared, not one
  That dandled a sandalled
  Shadow that swam or sank
On meadow and river and wind-wandering weed-winding
bank

Take a good breath for the last two lines and everything will be
easy. His poems are being re-printed and when they are
published I will have great pleasure in sending you a copy. At
first you may find him odd but as you grow to love him all the
oddities will disappear and you'll find him the most
exhilarating and exciting of poets. His words are sharp and

139

bleak—they cut where Francis Thompson would cushion.

> I wake and feel the fell of dark, not day

or again

> My cries heave, herds-long; huddle in a main.

He can express sorrow and physical and spiritual anguish in a
way that has been unparalleled in English verse. He not only
thought his thought: he lived it and because of his nervous
sensibility he was able to convey it to us in acute verbal form.

* * * * *

Belfast
13th May 49

To Jonathan Cape

I was glad to hear from you on publication day of *The Game
Cock*. The pre-publication sales seemed to me to be good—
good for a book of short stories—and I have a feeling that it
will just do as well as my novels. You'll not overlook the
Dublin papers when sending out review copies, and do please
send one to the new Irish quarterly, *Irish Writing*.

I know your newcomers, Kiely and Francis MacManus.*
Kiely is a near neighbour, a Tyrone man, living and writing in
Dublin. I believe firmly that he'll do some fine work for you;
he has a prodigious memory, an astounding knowledge of Irish
and Gaelic literature, and an ingrained critical correctness.
MacManus has written some good novels for the Talbot Press
but his best—a rendering of an urgent personal experience—
has still to come. He is one of the chief reviewers in the *Irish
Press* (Dublin).

I love the typography in *The Game Cock*. And by the way I
had a letter from the firm to-day regarding the inclusion of
"The Wild Duck's Nest" in *Choice*. I have never seen a copy of
Choice but I am sure it's a respectable journal (non-
sensational) and I have no objection. Good luck.

* Francis MacManus, (1909-1965) novelist.

To John Pudney *

Your kind letter of the 12th Dec. came in the Christmas rush and you must forgive me for not answering it before now.

I am afraid that I haven't anything that would suit you. I have turned my back on the short story and taken to the novel, and the short stories that I did not yet publish in book form are too short for your volume.

Thank you very much for asking me to contribute.

* John Pudney, editor of *New Writing*.

Night and Day: A Note on Literature

Text of talk delivered to Queen's University English Society

2 December 1949

Since literature is concerned with the penetration and illumination of life's experience, the critics and the creator's function appeals fundamentally to man's total nature. The achievement of a creative writer, poet or novelist, is appraised by the degree and depth of his experiences and by his manipulation of language in revealing those experiences to us. In human experience we are aware of a twofold quality: its night and day, sorrow and joy, sin and grace, or the "swift, slow; sweet, sour; adazzle, dim," of Hopkins; and in any radical response to literature cognizance of these correlations of opposites is valuable, for where one quality is missing or ignored we feel a sense of incompleteness or defectiveness, a lack of synthesis or ordering of experience. In the artistic metaphor we have "the intuitive perception of the similarity in dissimilars"—a reinforcement of the two so that they stand out with greater substantiality: an attempt to get at the essence of things.

In George Herbert's poem "Bitter-Sweet," this quality of experience is given an ethical significance:

> Ah, my dear, angry Lord!
> Since Thou dost love,—yet strike;
> Cast down,—yet help afford;
> Sure, I will do the like.
>
> I will complain,—yet praise;
> I will bewail,—approve;
> And, all my sour-sweet days,
> I will lament, —and love.

Such a resolution of opposites as expressed in this poem and such an integration of them are the reward of poets who seek after a philosophy that transcends the earth-bound and who continually strive to understand the complexities of life with relation to the decrees of God. This was Hopkins's quest, and here "the faithful waver, the faithless fable and miss." To a poet convinced of man's immortal destiny life presents a coherent pattern; life is neither tragic nor joyous—it is a mixture of both. He can find a meaning in the sorrow and misery of the world, in the sorrow and disappointments that afflict us, a realisation that suffering is designed to keep the soul awake. In the words of Donne: "Batter my heart, three-person'd God: for you as yet but knock, breathe" etc. A minor poet can record these experiences with power and beauty but if he desires greatness he must ascend out of them and relate them to a central philosophy.

At one moment Hopkins could point an accusatory finger at God:

> Wert thou my enemy, O thou my friend,
> How wouldst thou worse, I wonder, than thou dost
> Defeat, thwart me? Oh, the sots and thralls of lust
> Do in spare hours more thrive than I that spend,
>
> Sir, life upon my cause ...

at another moment he could cry:

> Not, I'll not, carrion comfort, Despair, not feast on thee;

and again buoyed up with the comfort of the Resurrection:

> Enough! The Resurrection,
> A heart's-clarion! Away grief's gasping, joyless days,
> dejection ...

In his mature work there is underlined this continual attempt to come to grips with the Night and Day of human experience, and it is to this truth to life—to the acceptance of the Cross—

143

blended with the original form and verbal freshness of his poetry that give it its meaningful significance. One of his commonest anthology pieces is a retrogressive little poem entitled:

Heaven-Haven
(A nun takes the veil)

I have desired to go
   where springs not fail,
To fields where flies no sharp and sides hail
   And a few lilies blow.

And I have asked to be
   Where no storms come,
Where the green swell is in the havens dumb,
   And out of the swing of the sea.

This poem, with its Lake-Isle-of-Innisfree attitude, was the product of his youth, but as such a life of accidie was not his his, for being nourished on St Ignatius and St Augustine he drew out of the simple lyrical and sought to reconcile "The Leaden Echo and the Golden Echo"—life's decay with the promise of eternal salvation:

> ...beauty-in-the-ghost, deliver it, early now, long before death
> Give beauty back, beauty, beauty, back to
> God, Beauty's self and beauty's giver.

In his longest poem, "The Wreck of the Deutschland," his poetic presentation of his thought and feeling is at its greatest: man is no longer "out of the swing of the sea"—here is no lace-edged portrait with the misery eliminated as it often is in poetistic verse; or a life of easy salvationism as that offered by Communist poets, to a Nietzchean portrait with its cult for an everlasting summer. Man in this poem is here in all his glory and misery; God is lightning and love, winter and warm.

Be adored among men,
God, three-numbered form;
Wring they rebel, dogged in den,
Man's malice, with wrecking and storm.
Beyond saying sweet, past telling of tongue,
Thou art lightning and love, I found it, a winter and warm;
Father and fondler of heart thou hast wrung:
Hast they dark descending and most art merciful then.

There is no extenuation in the poem—no desire to expunge the unpleasing characteristics of life; the sorrow and joy of life are in it, the acceptance of the Cross and the triumph of the Resurrection.

In a recent published poem "Natural History" the American poet, Thomas Merton, achieves a laudable fullness and altitude by a similar resolution of opposites. It is a longish poem beginning with:

There is a grey wall, in places overhung
With the abundant surf of honeysuckle:
It is a place of shelter, full of sun.

The poet sees the creeping things, in the wise diligence of an ascetic season, moving to this sheltered sunny wall to prepare their winter sleep and he adds:

…That this, the only thing they know, must cease,
And they must seal themselves in silences and sleep.
See with what zeal they wrestle off their ancient tawny life
And fight with all their might to end their private histories,
And look their days in the cocoon!

He ponders this miracle and contrasts our faithlessness and stubbornness with the wise obedience of these tiny creatures, and sees all creation teaching us some way of prayer. He develops and unifies the feeling in the poem and ends:

Here on the Trappist wall, beside the cemetery,
Two figures—death and heaven, and the night of contemplation—

Write themselves out before us in the easy sun,
Where everything that moves is full of mystical theology.
And we can learn such ways to God from creeping things,
And sanctity from a black-and-russet worm!

How we are taught to wrest our way
Out of the vesture of our ancient lives,
And kill the old tenacious Adam in us,
That we may die and sleep in the transforming Christ!

Run we, then, with like alacrity to our far sweeter
Figurative death,
When we at least have faith and Scripture telling us
The meaning of our metamorphosis!

Because George Herbert, Hopkins and Thomas Merton have endeavoured to comprehend life in terms that produce an integral apprehension—Man's destiny as seen in the light of Christian philosophy, their work has direction, unity and development. A poet cannot live on words alone: major poetry gives us something more than aesthetic pleasure, it helps us intuitively to see into the life of things; he may employ a fresh and arresting use of metaphor, a striking collocation of ordinary words, but if these are a substitute for thought the resultant poem, however beautiful, will be of a minor order. Art for art's sake, aestheticism, a verbal dexterity, will not continue to please those who approach poetry with a metaphysical spirit of mind; may please for a time but will not please for all time, will not reveal, at each rereading, something new. In major poetry matter and form are indivisible; there must be some reflection, some incidence of thought on the material, so that the experiences are unified and synthesised. In a play of Chekhov's, *The Seagull,* one of the characters, a writer, complains that his mind is a chaos of impressions and reflections without knowing the why and wherefore—he lacked synthesis. This lack, too, is characteristic of many of the Left poets of the 1930s and had made much of their work fragmentary, negative and directionless. It is a weakness displayed. It will be fatal, one feels, to the permanence of Yeats's work:

> ... All that I have said and done,
> Now that I am old and ill,
> Turns into a question till
> I lie awake night after night
> And never get the answer right.
> And all seems evil, until I
> Sleepless would lie down and die.

"We cannot become philosophic, our lives are too exciting"—
he quotes, in his Introduction to the *Oxford Book of Modern
Verse,* aware, I suppose of Spender's criticism: "Yeats's
poetry is devoid of any unifying moral subject, and it develops
in a perpetual search for one. Although he has much wisdom,
he offers no philosophy of life." At an earlier period AE wrote:
"The centuries have not yet brought us the philosophic mind"
(and in a recent lecture, a young Irish poet prefaced his
remarks with a quotation from Newman: "We live under the
lash.")

Because of this shilly-shallying, tasting one philosopher
after another, the whole corpus of his work does not reveal a
central philosophy with attendant ramifications.

It is about time, then, that our poetry underwent a change;
and since our poets have inherited and contributed to the
foundational stones of a lovely lyricism there is less likelihood
of their work degenerating into an abstract aridity when they
turn to resolve the Night and Day of human experience and
build the edifice of reason.

Added longhand note in author's hand
One could not deduce from Yeats's work a central
philosophy—a unifying principle growing upward like the
trunk of a tree and its attendant branches.

One cannot write lyrics continually and produce literature
but one must grow out of the lyrical—the fundamental stones
of poetry—in order to produce great literature—a literature
which speaks not only to the heart but to the mind of men as

well; in any race—the Irish for example or the English—where there is a living tradition of beautiful lyricism there is less likelihood of the degeneration into an abstract aridity when they resolve the Night and Day of human experience.

Journal 1949

26 December 1949

Went to the Quoile. The day was wet but mild. A little boy with a cowboy's hat cracked "caps" from his toy revolver at the back of the bus. The bus conductor was very tired. An old man in a new suit sat asleep on a window sill in Crossgar, his hands in his coat pockets, his knees jutting out sharply, his hat over his eyes. The boys rubbed the moisture off the windows in the bus to look out and smile at him. Terry met us at the Quoile Bridge.

I admired the oil portrait of their grand-uncle—the bald head the dark half-moons below his eyes, the sagging dewlaps, and the frizz of white hair around his ears. Peggy told of their old Dr. Murray who looked at these portraits. "This is the grand-père, I suppose," looking at the portrait on the opposite wall. "And this" pointing at the old uncle, "I suppose he's dead. Died of kidney trouble, I'd presume!"

The dog, "Paddy," was tired this year. He lay on the rug drying his wet paws and belly, and when he was dry he shook himself and the dust arose like chaff in a barn.

The boys played Ludo, the girls played the piano and sang.[1] The old people showed deep emotion when the Irish airs were played.[2]

[1] The author's children, Colm, Kevin, Sheila and Maura McLaverty.
[2] This is the record of a visit to the Nolan family, cousins of Mrs McLaverty.

Journals 1950-1951

1950
Frank O'Connor, and indeed many of the Irish writers, present simple-minded people. Many of Mary Lavin's people are people with refined intelligence. Her people contemplate cruelty and hate—(cf "Small Bequest").

* * * * *

1950
Art and Life.
There is more life than art in the Russian novels and we prefer that. In the French and in Henry James there is more art than life: we don't warm to them as much.

* * * * *

1950
After Reading Some Modern Novels
It is only the uncultured who nourish grudges because they have nothing else to nourish. That's what education should be able to do for a man—give him dignity of soul, tolerance, and an unbegrudging nature.

* * * * *

1 November—5 November 1950
Went to Killard with Colm and Kevin.
　　The sea-weed black, the bracken splashed of rust, the people in the fields gathering potatoes, the sun low in the south, swinging in a narrow arc from south of Isle of Man to its setting

behind the Mourne Mountains.

Frost at night.

During the day the fields covered with fine string of spiders' webs which when they caught the sun had a beautiful effect like a fish net spread out to dry.

Starlings bathed in a pool of water in a field, and the fine spray set up by their wings looked as if they were standing in the white smoke from a fire. They flew up to a neighbouring ash and as they spread their wings to dry in the sun they kept up an incessant chattering. A crow dried itself on top of a chimney. Grey linnets were in flocks feeding on the haws in the hedges. They sang sweetly. Wagtails foraged around the stones on the shore; an odd wren hopped in the lower bushes.

A smoke haze lay on top of the horizon but at night it had disappeared and the stars flocked out.

* * * * *

9 December 1950
Went this evening to an exhibition of children's paintings in the Art Gallery. I noticed that the younger children's paintings had a boldness of approach that the older children lacked. One felt the more they knew of technique the less free and flexible and sincere were their paintings—they were stiff and self-conscious, more near to poster work than to art.

* * * * *

28 December 1950
Reading Kiely's *Call For a Miracle*—he tries to show the loneliness and incompleteness of lives without God but somehow, his people (Irish Catholics) and his central idea do not coalesce—the same faults are manifest to me as *In a Harbour Green:* the absence of moral struggle. (Joyce had this presence, and so too had *Bird Alone*, but the absence of it in Kiely makes his Irish characters scarcely credible).

When he finally rids his mind of his influences—Joyce and O'Faoláin—he will write his best work, work that will endure.

With Father Peter and the influence of good that he conveys so easily around with him (cf. his influence on Mary and Christine) Kiely displays fine emotional power. But the introduction of the melodeon is a Graham Greene touch—a bit of meretricious humanity. In this novel Philomena is the Pat Rafferty of this story—good, honest, earth touched like us all with the shiverings of the flesh. Joyce's influence is seen in the technique, and in the story told about Dave's love which reminds one of Joyce's "The Dead."

I hadn't finished the novel when I had written the above. I admit that I spoke a half-truth when suggesting that there was an absence of moral struggle. *Christine's letter and her renunciation nullify this statement.*

The final pages are very moving but they carry with them like a too-full cargo the obvious influences of *Bird Alone*.

*   *   *   *   *

1950

The novelists are sick because the world is sick ... Where in the work is *Jubilate Deo*—Catholics and the Liturgy—Joy is prevalent—Even during the penitential season of Lent there is a *Laetare Sunday*—We would travel through acres of gloomy pages before we could come upon a page of exaltation in the modern novel. They are not in love with that which gives a spring step to life (Yeats and Geo. Eliot).

*   *   *   *   *

1951

If one can recall in later years particular but trivial incidents of a parent's anger it reveals that the parent was seldom angry. Day in and day out anger would produce in the mind an overall picture or tyranny—nothing really would stand out clearly, not even a trivial incident.

*   *   *   *   *

1951

Idea for a novel

Two families driven apart by passion, feuds, hatred are reconciled, united by a marriage of a son and daughter: harmony out of the hate.

* * * * *

1951

My grandparents had a reverence for bread—reverence in the baking of it, the handling of it, and the use of it; it was with a sense of shame that she made me ashamed if I left any bread on the plate.

* * * * *

1951

Idea for a novel

A man of forty-five has had one "shady" incident in his life: an unsuccessful love-affair with a married lady whose husband takes an action against our "hero." It is published in the paper.

When the novel opens we have him far away from the scene and 20 years ahead of it. He has tried to live it down; he is *good* at heart—he falls in love with a girl of *good* family; she knows there's something on his mind but she can never get to the bottom of it. When out with her mother she visits the town where our hero used to live. Mother tells of her daughter's forthcoming marriage. To whom? To a man called Joseph Doonin—"Joe Doonin"—he seems to recollect, then remembers the *incident,* says nothing, but leaves *mother and daughter* worrying.

Into their place arrives a teacher. He meets Joseph, and Joseph knows he knows, and knows also that he will tell. To ask him not to would be dishonourable. Arrives one evening and sees the teacher in the home of the girl he loves—the strange silence, strange looks, knows by the looks that the truth has been told about him. At the door the girl hesitates, walks with him: the truth he tells himself—the girl in tears; her love can't beat her pride—they part—he leaves but he's happy, happy in the happiness that revealing his past has given him.

* * * * *

1952
We are made whole by our loves.

* * * * *

1951
W.R. Rodgers is a physical poet. To be a great poet he needs to become metaphysical.

* * * * *

1951
When sorrow falls upon us we should not despair; we should accept it as God's loving plan for us, to keep us from wandering from him. We should say slowly the *Our Father* and emphasise the *Our*. Being our heavenly Father he will not wish anything for us but what is for our eternal good; he is more loving than all the loves of loving earthly fathers.

* * * * *

1951
Poetry and literature do not exist to give us information; they appeal to our sense of wonder and make the earth and the people in it more wonderful for us.

* * * * *

Tragedy experienced in the individual should be a means of softening the soul's hardness and allowing it to grow in wisdom—tolerance and sympathy.

* * * * *

1951
For Henry James I'd say that he saw in a story or novel an idea

that fundamentally changed the character. Most stories don't conform to his idea. Writers are content with showing a change of mood or content to describe a single incident.

* * * * *

1951
The meaning of art can be seen in the fresh approach of children's paintings—when they grow into adolescence their minds are less free, they are crippled by self-consciousness and logical ways of design.

* * * * *

1951
From a reading of Mauriac one would never conclude that there is a God of love. His work is *stratified* with thick layers of lasciviousness.

* * * * *

1951
Growth is the only evidence of life.

* * * * *

1951
St Thomas: "Sins of the flesh are less grave than sins of the mind, than pride and hatred and despair."

* * * * *

1951
When you desire to escape from anxiety and are doing all in your power to escape it, you are not being fully Christian.

* * * * *

1951
Treat everything and everyone with reverence because God made them. Have patience with the stupid—never humiliate

them for they are persons made by God. Respect an reverence God's infinite variety.

*   *   *   *   *

1951
Why do we wait to forgive a person when he is in his grave—forgiveness is easy then, and for that reason it loses its virtue.

*   *   *   *   *

It's not our actions that count but our motives.

*   *   *   *   *

Hopkins's poetry gives us more than aesthetic pleasure, it helps us to see into the life of things, and into the life of men in relation to our eternal destiny.

*   *   *   *   *

Suffering and pain and disappointment are used to keep the soul awake.

*   *   *   *   *

I would rather spend money on enriching my children's minds by travel and art; it is a richness that can't be taken from them. A display of wealth and grandeur never impresses me—what impresses is aristocracy of mind.

*   *   *   *   *

Control the will—do not pay lip-service to God, compromising the divine and the natural according to one's mood. God moves and breathes over everything: Listen to him always and not just the lip-service on Sundays. God is not mocked.

*   *   *   *   *

Learn not to dominate, to impose your will on others.

*   *   *   *   *

When one gives one should have no motive behind it beyond the benefit the giving brings the receiver. There should be no underlying motive.

*   *   *   *   *

1951
Suffering is the prelude to a deeper and fuller life.

*   *   *   *   *

1951
Those who carry daily the knowledge of their early death around with them seem to live their short lives intensely (cf K. Mansfield, D. H. Lawrence and Synge). Is it divine compensation?

*   *   *   *   *

1951
To combat evil by evil is to increase evil in the world. To be kind instead of malicious is to reduce the evil in the world. Drops wear away the stone. Kindness nourishes love, hate withers it.

*   *   *   *   *

1951
The stars like shining nail-heads in the sky.

*   *   *   *   *

Drops running in single file in the bucket.

*   *   *   *   *

157

Raindrops on the telegraph wire like a musical score.

*   *   *   *   *

Don't try to seize your theme. Let it possess you.

*   *   *   *   *

Live in time as if you were to die tomorrow.

*   *   *   *   *

Letters 1951-1952

Belfast
26th Nov. 1951

To Cecil Scott

You'll be sorry to hear that the novel grows slowly on paper;* I
carry it about with me in my mind, but have had no opportunity
or inclination to sit down to it, my wife being seriously ill for
the past two months. She is now home from hospital, and in
about two weeks time when she'll have re-gained her strength
the house will be back to normal and so will I, and so will the
book. I'll write to you in the Spring of the year and will let you
know then how it grows—the book, I mean.

* * * * *

Christmas 1951/New Year 1952

To Daniel Corkery

First of all thanks for your long letter—I didn't expect that, for
I know how letter-writing can become a drag on a man's
leisure. Thank-you also for the water-colour which will be a
fitting companion for your Dungannon scene. What a lovely
glow and depth you can get in colour! I remember seeking
another one of yours, of a house with the quiet glow of evening
rising round it; the new one has the same vivid richness. I like it
greatly. In my room at school I have the walls plastered with
the lads' attempts (the whole apparatus is supplied free and we

* *School for Hope*, published by Macmillan and Cape, 1954.

159

usually reserve Friday afternoons for the Painting Lesson).

Occasionally—when they depart from conveying stiff verisimilitude—a few can create a composition of colour that is a delight, and when I come in in the morning and see the dull room (it faces north) alive with colour, it makes me happy. The best we have are a street at night with lamps and dark houses, and a watchman's hut with brazier; a brickyard, a biscuit factory; a bill poster standing back to admire his advertisements, and two men playing cards in a club room with a dart-board and boxing notices on a wall that has gaps in its plaster. They're a fine lot of lads and I have always been very happy with them. I don't suppose I'll ever give up teaching— for one thing it makes me independent and keeps me safe from the raw ranks of hackwriters or professionals.

Teaching, besides giving me a salary, permits me to take my time. I can write in my own way, and give thought and love to what I do. I have sent you on a copy of my latest—it has just come out at this side but as the English edition is not as well turned out as the American, I've sent you on the latter.[1] The picture on the dust-jacket was made from a photograph of Rathlin Island. The American critics say it is my best, but I prefer *The Three Brothers*. I was at work on a new one, but since my wife's illness I had to put it aside. I tried to go back to it, last week to seize it, but, alas, nothing would come that satisfied me and I knew I must wait till I am *seized by it*.[2] I am more content when I am writing—but I'll have to get back to it soon or turn completely to a new theme. I am more content when I am engaged in a bit of work. My wife, thank God, is now up and around, and the whole house is drifting back to normal. Kevin and Colum return to school on Monday. They are building a 12ft. boat and hope to have her ready for the summer. Last year they built a canvas canoe (a kayak, they called it), complete with a centre board and a sail the size of a small tablecloth; they had grand fun in it but one stormy evening they had her anchored off-shore and an east wind flung her against the rocks and damaged her—she was never sea-

[1] *Truth In The Night*
[2] *School For Hope*

worthy after it and they lost interest in her and talk of nothing now but the twelve-footer.

Strange to say the cottage we have by the sea is in a similar position to your own; it is at the mouth of Strangford Lough, facing the open sea with a buoy darting its light in at the window at night. The East wind, and it usually brings rain, is our worst enemy, but we love it at all times and seasons and it is a relief to get down to it, even if only for a weekend. We get away from everything—our only neighbours are decent honest country people, who would close your gate if they found it open and drop you a card if a storm happened to rip off a slate. The nearest village is Strangford, 4 miles away. Fitzsimons and Denvir are the common names, old Norman stock, and hurley is their usual game.

I never went as far south as you are now. When I was in Cork in 1942 or 43, I cycled out away beyond Croomhaven: and was disappointed. But I got one thing out of it: on a long hill, a car-load of nuns had knocked down a cyclist, and from the incident I wrote the short story "The Road to the Shore." The long sail down that hill and the long climb back remain with me but Myrtlegrove has disappeared. I'll certainly seek you out if I go south again. It won't be this summer as I intend cycling in Northern Spain.

Every good wish to you and your sister for the New Year.

Journals 1952

1952

A note after reading the *Irish Times* review of *Truth In the Night*.

One wonders what is a reviewer's function. Surely he should get below the surface outline, "the story," and ask himself what is the theme—and having possessed the theme he should go on to elucidate it for the ordinary reader. In my case he should have realised that the book was written to uncover a moral truth, viz., that hate and spit, and anger (Vera's character), disrupt the individual soul and the soul of a small community. Charity, (the old woman's character), on the other hand, nourishes and harmonises and holds all things together, and that out of suffering comes wisdom—The Truth in the Night. Having discovered this he should demonstrate how this was achieved—"all works of art act their moral judgements" (Leavis); the moral significance is presented as a lived experience and not *stated* as in journalistic books.

Criticism of a novel in Ireland seldom goes further than the life or vitality in it. They delight in vivid characterisation but they never look for theme or pattern, the real reason for a novel's being. This approach is narrow and inadequate. F.R. Leavis's approach hasn't reached them yet.

*   *   *   *   *

6 June 1952

Discussion with Dan* on the Irish short story. We concluded that the Irish short story is an emotional one at its best and not

*Dan Clarke, Principal of St John's Elementary School, where McLaverty taught until 1958.

an intellectual one as in Henry James. Our history had engendered in us a capacity for portraying the emotional in life—that is why we can produce such emotionally intense short stories as "Going into Exile," "Guests of the Nation," "The Dead" etc., and plays like Murray's, Colum's and *Riders To the Sea.* The English are dulled to the depth of feeling which these stories contain, because of their history—they were always "invaders," don't know what hunger and hardship are, eviction and riots. An Irishman expects you to bring a sensitivity towards these things when reading his work; the English can't bring what they haven't got, hence the only Irish writers they take to are the satirical, the facetious (Gogarty's "Tumbling in the Hay," or M. Wall's "Leaves For the Burning"). For the same reason they can't understand the depths of feeling in the Italian writers who are writing out of "suffering."

Irish society is simple, but when it develops intellectually we will (due to our inherited emotional equipment), produce, probably, the greatest literature of this century (say from 1980-2000).

*   *   *   *   *

7 June 1952
My novels deal with the more grave sins: sins of the mind and not of the flesh, that common quarry of all novelists. Mine deal with anger, spite, love of money, lack of charity and their opposites.

Letters 1952

Belfast
29th April 1952

To The Editors, "Q'" Queen's University.

I have worked through the scripts and I enclose the result of what was for me a very interesting perusal. You may not agree with my selection and I wouldn't want you to. Cling steadfastly to your own judgment in spite of what I have said. I have never met two people to agree on the contents of any short-story anthology.

I will make a parcel of the scripts and leave it in the Queen's library (the hut) on or before Thursday and this will save you the trouble of coming up here. I was sorry I missed you when you called.

Good wishes to you,

Extract from a Commentary on
Q's Short-Story Competition

Published in Queen's University Student Magazine, 1952

Truth to life in all its manifestations is what is needed. The prevailing fault in most of the stories submitted was their lack of general truth. Large sections of Irish fiction, it may be added, are blighted by the same falsity: our common humanity smothered under portrayals of the freakish and the eccentric—romanticism masquerading in the borrowed robes of reality. Short stories with this falsity to common human experience (unlike, say, those in Joyce's *Dubliners*) do not wear well, for "nothing can please many and please long but just representations of general nature. Particular manners can be known to few, and therefore few only can judge how nearly they are copied. The irregular combinations of fanciful invention may delight awhile, by that novelty of which the common satiety of life sends us all in quest; but the pleasures of sudden wonder are soon exhausted, and the mind can respose only on the stability of truth." (Dr. Johnson)

Be artists of the normal; it is a difficult injunction to follow for it requires patience and may impose a limitation on one's literary output. But it is the normal that survives, and it comes from exploring the resources of your own people and your own environment—no matter how small the latter is, if it is deeply pondered the resultant work will overleap its boundaries and escape that niggling epithet "provincial" which seems to hang like an out-of-date calendar in every critic's workshop. The early O'Casey and Joyce were provincial, but writing as true artists of their own people they enriched the world's literature. They wrote of what was in their blood and did not practise

165

strange contortions of the spirit by frolicking after strange gods. Study other writers but be yourself: a writer or painter only develops when he realizes more fully his own potentialities and becomes something less when he gives himself over in imitation to those with whom he had no spiritual affinities, Kafka's problems were personal to himself and Slieve Donard is not Cezanne's *Mont Sainte Victoire*. One soon tires of the derivative and the polite borrowers.

> Selves—goes itself; *myself* it speaks and spells,
> Crying *What I do is me: for that I came.*

Become immersed in your work, surrender yourself to it and let it grow within you with the patient surety of the growing leaf; after a preparation of this kind the labour of writing comes easy—stories will be created and not manufactured, and the facile addiction to a formula avoided. Become deeply rooted: Katharine Mansfield's best stories are her New Zealand ones and Katharine Anne Porter and Eudora Welty, two of America's best short-story writers, are attached to regions in the Southern States, and Joyce's sole collection is aptly entitled *Dubliners*.

At the outset of your literary career attempt the small canvas and work over it to perfection: the single character, the single incident, the change of mood, the poetic memories of childhood—all those who help the growing writer to find his own personal equality of perception. We should not, however, be content with only scrupulous transcriptions of reality: art and life are not synonymous; the former postulates a selection and a synthesis and evaluation and uncovering of some truth. Work of this order we reread, as we do great poetry, for it modifies our attitude to experience by increasing our knowledge of human nature. Some short stories in this category that come to mind are: Henry James's "The Beast in the Jungle," James Joyce's "The Dead", Frank O'Connor's "Uprooted", J.F. Powers' "Lions' Hearts, Leaping Does", and Lavin's "The Will" and "A Small Bequest"—these are a few but there are many others. They all reveal human nature and add something to our understanding of it—we cannot ask anything greater from a short story than that.

* * * * *

Letter 1952

To David Marcus

About six weeks ago the students of Queen's University ran a Short Story Competition in their magazine *Q* , a copy of which I enclose. They asked me to do the job of adjudicating, and the stories I picked out as the best seem to me to be very promising. I am sending them to you in the hope that you may consider reprinting one of them; if you could do this I would stimulate interest in short-story writing among the students and draw attention to your magazine. But if the reprinting of stories is contrary to your policy I wouldn't wish you to alter it under any circumstances.

Journals 1952-1953

2 September 1952

After reading Henry James's "The Beast in the Jungle," I realise how patient we must be when reading him. He's a writer for the middle-aged. He begins ponderously, but as we persist in our quest he slowly gathers us around him and in the final pages he releases the *idea* of the story with such compelling force that we are not only affected by it but feel that our knowledge of ourselves and other people is fundamentally magnified.

* * * * *

3 September 1952

Have taken up my novel* again after a long lapse of two months. Convinced, now, that a novelist needs quiet so that his people grow according to their nature and not to contrivance. When I have thought out a scene, feel it and hear it, then I am ready to write it.

* *School For Hope*, (1954)

* * * * *

27 September 1952

Read Henry James's *Washington Square*—taut, economical— and (surprising for James) comical: at times his comedy led him into an almost damning facetiousness (laughing at them). Aunt Lavinia is outstanding but Dr Sloper and Townsend are stock-in-trade characters—they never surprise us but *she* does.

* * * * *

25 March 1953

In literature nothing fades so quickly as falsity and nothing wears so well as truth.

*   *   *   *   *

3 September 1953

Write a story of an old woman who has been ailing. Her sons and daughter persuade her to have an x-ray. The diagnosis is cancer but they tell her it's an ulcer. As days proceed she notices how they have all changed towards her. They rush to obey her every wish. From all these acts of kindness she guesses the reason—viz, she hasn't long to live.

*   *   *   *   *

7 September 1953

To search for a quality in life—a poetical quality—that is the purpose of a writer, poet or novelist. If this quality is absent from a novelist's work he is not an artist. It comes from long brooding, long thinking, reverence, patience, love—from these the quality is released. But having found it he should not shout about it, but treat it calmly. From the same fount springs his attitude towards his characters and their attitude to one another. By thinking deeply, by feeling, one gathers that out of suffering and sacrifice and unselfishness come happiness: the defeat of egoism, the futility of violence, the effect of kindness.

*   *   *   *   *

5 December 1953

As soon as a man begins to hate life, to wish to die, evil has entered his heart and soul. He is wishing to destroy the greatest gift that God gave him: the gift of life, the gift of the beauty of this lovely earth. "Glory be to God for dappled things." Yes, glory be to God for these things, and glory be to God for the sorrows and sufferings he sends to us, for it is these that give us the depth of feeling to appreciate the depth of beauty in this lovely earth: the beauty, not only of the fields and the trees, the sun and the rain, but the beauty, too, in kindness, in children at play in their great and abundant love of life. The beauty of friendship—real friendship; the beauty of youth and the loveliness of girlhood.

* * * * *

1953
"The Child on the Swing"
This little poem captures the joy and fear which the child experiences. Reality is not just a representation of the thing—it has a spiritual quality in it. If realists don't capture that quality they are not realists at all. True reality gets the deepest truth out of it. How has it its beginnings? K. Mansfield notes in her Journal: "Remember the bubbles from the stick when it was plunged into the aquarium tank"—or "How the basket squeaked at No 27." The reality then begins with something physical but it ends in being spiritual.

* * * * *

1953
Scott Fitzgerald in a letter to his daughter:
"The mind of a little child is fascinating, for it looks on old things with new eyes—but at about twelve this changes."
We can see this not only in literature but in their paintings—paintings that are full of colour, free and uninhibited. This changes about 16 or so.

* * * * *

1953
Novels and short stories should deal with the normal: normal people in truthful, not fabricated, situations. It is not a transcription of life but a poetic heightening of life; you do not transcribe; you transform. The life in the material must be given a poetic distillation or poetic aura. It's difficult to

describe this; we feel it—we know it immediately we are brought in contact with it. (Tolstoy, for instance, or Chekhov or K. Mansfield, or Joyce's "The Dead" or "The Sisters"). It was the absence of this poetic quality that made many of the proletarian writers in the 1930s so banal, so reportorial. A. Bennett is in the same category and so, too, Galsworthy. (cf. Middleton Murry's *Problem of Style* and his examination of this.)

* * * * *

1953
The writer should have love and reverence for what he is doing; if he becomes a "professional" novelist he can seldom give that love—"long looking"—the love that rouses his own flavour or personal vision.

* * * * *

1953
Hemingway
What we remember most from Hemingway is his power of simple evocative description: autumn, snow, heat, cold, etc. e.g. the old man of the sea leaning his cold back against the boat to warm himself.
His descriptions seem easy but should you try to emulate them you'll find extreme difficulty; Chekhov displays some misleading simplicity. And Forrest Reid at times.*
Hemingway's moral import we'll arrive at in a negative way— he'll show us, by implication, the futility of a life of hard-drinking, a gad-about life. But, unlike Tolstoy and Chekov, he shows us nothing affirmative (except in *The Old Man*, courage and patience). But with Chekhov and Tolstoy we have hints of a life that ought to be—they are great because of this.

* * * * *

* Forrest Reid, (1875-1947), novelist.

171

On Writing
1953

Out for a walk with a little boy: "The moon is like a silver snuff box." How to use words in a significant or an imaginative way. That is the beginning of the writer's craft: we'll not be able to write or to read well if we can't feel deeply. To wait—to contemplate—"That which teases the mind for years." How much good writing has come out of childhood memories: we all have them, buried deep, all have made an impression; to release that flow, to get the connection—the hunt for it.

Engulfed by experience: when we begin we imitate, but if we develop we'll come, by and by, to our real selves. How to get there? How to get as much in as the story will hold.

Words are the beginning only: Rodgers and "ululating." In time it can become a diction, a poetic diction, a sleight of hand—you see it in many of the modern poets.

Words are the beginning: in a normal human relationship—a superstructure of values: signification—attitude to violence of instance—uncovering of some truth: see the emptiness of violence: the harm done to a human soul that lives in spite and hatred—Love and reverence.

*   *   *   *   *

1953

Those who wish to hold tightly to what they have transfix themselves with misery. Bob in *The Three Brothers*, and Helen in *School for Hope*. In all my books I strive for opposites.

*   *   *   *   *

Letters 1953

To Cecil Scott

I had hoped to have the book* ready for you before I go off on vacation at the end of the month but it's just not to be. I just can't manage it, and my chief delayer in this respect is my own desire for perfection: perfection of phrase and consistency of mood. I could let my imagination run wild for awhile and so write easily, but then it would all be false, and falsity is, I hope, what no critic will ever accuse me of. No, nothing goes out of fashion as quickly as falsity and nothing wears so well as truth. Joyce's *Dubliners* is always there to confirm me in that.

If you would care to see the first 70,000 words of it I could send you the typescript out immediately and send you the remaining chapters after the holidays; I'll leave this to your own discretion, and I'll do what will please you best. As you have seen and like the first chapter I'm sure you will like the rest of the book—its whole mood is suggested in that opening.

My good wishes and thanks for your great patience,

*   *   *   *   *

Belfast
19th June 1953

I have sent on part of the book and I hope it will please you. At times I have misgivings that I am too restrained and the style too bare to produce the effect intended. I try to suggest, to hint,

* *School For Hope*

173

rather than make things obvious. The long apprenticeship I spent at the short-story because of its brevity induces a slow and relaxed response on the part of the reader, a response that the same reader seldom gives to a longer work written with the same compression of style. And since it is my creed as a writer to deal with the normal and the ordinary (the stuff of life that has general truth in it) I add to my difficulties. How much easier it is to write of the abnormal and the extraordinary—the warp and woof of most of our professional novelists.

I hope to have the remaining chapters of the novel ready for you by October. I could, however, send you out a respectable summary of them before then if you intend mentioning it in your early 1954 list. Unlike my last book it does not end in death—deo gratias.

* * * * *

Belfast
2nd November 1953

At the last moment I have decided to send the script by air mail.

It will probably be my most successful book though I wouldn't say it's my best. No book ever gave me so much trouble, I cut out thousands of words in an effort to preserve unity of scene and to use nothing that did not give point and piquancy to the main theme. If the reviewers read me slowly and with full attention they will see that each chapter is created with the same meticulous integrity that I'd expend on a short story. I hate contrivance; I love the natural gesture and the natural event—but these can only be achieved, it seems to me, by long and reverential contemplation. When one has learned the "tricks of the trade" it's easy to write a novel, but a novel of that kind would not be worth writing or reading. All this doesn't mean to say that I regard this present novel as perfect— I do not. I'm never fully satisfied with anything I do: something in it always defeats me. But I needn't hold up the script any longer on that account; when I begin to revise and alter I usually make a botch of it. I'll let it go to you as it is. You'll send me a set of proofs, and if there is any repetition of phrase, awkwardness of expression, or stale crust of observation I'll make short work of them. I enclose with this lot a revision of page 47. You have already in you hand 184 pages, and this lot begins with page 185.

*   *   *   *   *

Belfast
6th December 1953

Yesterday I signed up with Cape for publication at this side and I am looking forward to the arrival of your contract soon.

Cape like the book and are hoping that the Book Society will make it their monthly choice. But they don't care much for the title and should you feel the same I'll change it. Primarily it's a novel of conscience: the conflict of conscience with desire. But there's much more in it than that because the group counts as much as the individuals. And figuratively the title stands for the core of meaning in all my books: the white and the black, the joy and sorrow in life—and in this book light shines sharply out of it; this is specially true in the character of Mary. I loved writing of her and only wished she could have appeared oftener.

As an alternative title what would you think of *Conscience makes Cowards*—this has the virtue of directness and would save my book from misrepresentation by the too harried reviewer. I'll send a note to Cape about this new title and let you know what they say.

Drop me a line as soon as you've time. Good wishes to you.

*   *   *   *   *

Belfast
31st December 1953

Thank you very much for the cheque and the form of agreement.

175

A few days ago Cape asked me to indicate a few things that might help in preparing the blurb for my book. I am sending you a copy of what I wrote though I realize that the writing of blurbs is a craft for which I have no aptitude. You may get a hint out of it or maybe nothing at all. Here it is:

> Is it true that conscience does make cowards of us all? Should a sensitive young girl, who has come to teach in an Irish village school, allow the fact that her mother and sister have died in a sanatorium, to dominate her life? Should she obey the dictates of conscience by telling what might ruin her chance of marriage?
>
> In tracing her problems we are brought into contact with the school, her fellow teachers, and the lovely Irish countryside. It is a taut and fully integrated novel written with that curious quietude and assurance which critics have noted in the author's previous novels.

I suppose I'll hear from you soon about the title. We have settled on *School For Hope* for publication at this side. It was Cape suggested that and I think it fills the bill O.K.

* * * * *

Journals 1954

We realise our true selves only by suffering—our life grows and is fulfilled by that way only (of the Cross).

My Method in Writing Prose

I use words for their associative subtlety and depth, the exact word, the fresh word, but it must not draw attention to itself.

I try to find the "objective correlative" that would evoke the mood I desire or bring out by implication the inward mood of my characters.

Of Vera coming home from Mass on a Sunday: the *hot* sun, the *shady* bracken, *moist,* and *warm*, opening her coat, loosening her hair (sensual gestures).[1]

Or Helen coming for the last meeting with Nora: the bubbles like "frog-spawn," the "snail," the "scratching" of the briar ...

The dark fall of rain with Nora against the tree trunk—to those who read me with full attention surely that objective description accentuated her sorrow without my having to spend my time analysing and so destroying it.[2]

* * * * *

September 1954

If a novelist has an attitude to life and the book unfolds this the critics say he is a novelist with a "message" and proceed to condemn him. If, on the other hand, he puts "life" down in a pell-mell way, they say he had no direction and no aim, and

[1] *Truth in the Night*
[2] *School For Hope*

again the critics condemn him. Chekhov was condemned as an aimless writer by critics *in his own day*.

*   *   *   *   *

Sex: an innate modesty prevents us from speaking in detail about this in our own life. Why then, should a novelist *usurp* this inborn tendency and write in detail in a book?

*   *   *   *   *

December 1954
Read Albert Camus's *The Plague*—a fine human book. Disaster brings out the best in man, friendship and charity are induced because the characters share a common fear (cf. the change in people when the bombs were falling in Belfast. Convention and snobbery were killed by fear—everyone experienced kindness and tolerance). The doctor in it by just *being*—unselfish and working for others without complaining—he affects those whom he comes in contact. (cf. his effect on the journalist who wishes to escape the plague-stricken city to get to his wife). The doctor, whose wife is "outside," never complains or feels that he has done enough for the plague-stricken city.

Letters 1954

Belfast
9 August 1954

To Daniel Corkery

I read your kindly letter (and how well-wishing it is)—not once but many times, and when *you* say my book is thin that is sufficient for me and I strike if off as a failure.* Not that I thought it was that when I had written it. But you made me see why and where. The book in its original form was about twice its published length but I slashed at it in revising it, hoping to make it taut, actionless, but realise now I must have choked the life in it. I always strive after the normal, the ordinary—believing that the best fiction displays these qualities abundantly. If I have a creed in writing that is it; to be an artist of the normal. I want a thing to be true no matter how small it may be. It's a restrictive attitude, and I feel that I have reached a stage where restraint in the matters is serving me badly, has become a vice, and where a too finicky attachment to design has squeezed my quest for normal life into a rigid outline. Your fine letter has opened my eyes to that. I had hoped in writing that novel to suggest, by hints and nudges, far more than was on the page, but I see now that it hasn't come off and I'm sure Cape will lose on it and won't relish anything else I may send them. Of the small editions they published of *The Game Cock* and *Truth in the Night* they still have many copies on their hands. I haven't much of a public at this side, though in America I fare a little better.

* *School For Hope*

I don't know what to tackle next. I may try my hand at a play or some short stories. I'll read Conrad's stories this autumn. I have only read two of his books: *The Shadow Line* and *The Secret Agent*, one I liked for its absence of women and the other for its sinister atmosphere in the old gaslit London streets. Mauriac, whom you also mention, I have read but do not like. I recognise his great merits, but with the exception of *Vipers' Tangle*, which I read years ago in a translation, the people he creates are incredible, and I don't think one would come upon their like in Bordeaux or in any other country for that matter. One can't relate his people to real life. I would have been better for the life of his books and the life in them if F... had remained in the land instead of gallivanting about taking the train to Paris.

If we take Tolstoy, one believes immediately in his creation.

*   *   *   *   *

A Note on Katherine Mansfield

published in *Belfast Telegraph*, 15 January 1955

She was completely dedicated to her writing, striving to make each story better than the preceding ones, but never entirely satisfied with anything she had done.

Katherine Mansfield was born in Wellington, New Zealand, and in her early teens was educated in London. She returned to Wellington at the age of eighteen, but two years after, feeling that she was only paddling in a parochial puddle, she left again for England.

She was never to return to her own country, and after a long and courageous struggle with ill-health she died in Fontainebleau, France, on January 9 1923. She was then thirty-four. She never wrote a novel, and her fame rests securely on her short stories.

Her journal has just been reissued by Constable, the publishers, and it displays better than any outside criticism her intentions as an artist and her attitude to life. She was completely dedicated to her writing, striving with each story to make it better than the preceding ones, but never entirely satisfied with anything she had done. Some blemishes in her work, that she might see and others not, baffled and depressed her. And in spite of her constant ill-health and her struggles with composition she was never easy on herself and never gave sloth root-room.

In a letter to her husband, John Middleton Murry, she says: "My work excited me so tremendously that I almost feel insane at night, and I have been at it with hardly a break all day." Entries in her Journal convey the same unflinching absorption: "Finished 'An Ideal Family' yesterday. It seems to me better than 'The Doves' but still it's not good enough. I worked at it hard enough, God knows, and yet I didn't get the deepest truth out of the idea, even once ... It took me a month to 'recover' from 'At the Bay'."

Like a true artist she is not in competition with anyone except herself. She is her own severest critic and complains about some of her stories "being a little bit made up and not inevitable." Early in her career she realised one empirical truth about a short story: that there's a lot one would like to put in, but a sacrifice must be made. Humbly admitting to herself that she was not a good writer, she strove to write more simply and fully and freely from her heart, and she would not care about success or failure, but just keep going on, quietly perfecting her work.

A few writers find their own voice immediately, but the majority have to work hard to find it. Katherine Mansfield was one of the majority, and it was through suffering and misfortune that she was brought to self-realisation and enabled to slough off the influence of Chekov on her work and reveal her own individuality.

She had written many stories with a London or Continental background but, competent as many of these are, they lack the love and warmth that radiate from most of her stories that have a New Zealand background. These stories, I feel, transcend their place and time because a unifying spirit informs them—a spirit engendered by long and loving contemplation of her material.

Reading her journal, one wonders if she would ever have written them but for a visit her brother paid to her London home on his way from New Zealand to the front in the First World War. That visit is described in her journal, and save for one obvious lapse of unexamined feeling, it is the finest entry in it.

They are walking up and down her London garden in the dusk of an October evening. A small round pear, hard as a stone, falls to the ground and her brother picks it up "and, unconsciously, as of old, polishes it on his handkerchief." Intimate memories crowd back to both of them, memories of their New Zealand garden and of the wobbly seat with the marks of a snail line on it.

> "And do you remember the enormous number of pears
> there used to be on the old tree?" they asked one another.
> "They were so bright, canary yellow—and small. And the
> peel was so thin and the pips jet—jet black. First you pulled
> out the little stem sucked it. It was faintly sour, and then
> you ate them always from the top—core and all."

With memories such as these, gathering a poetical aura
around them the more she pondered them, her brother leaves
her for the Front and a short time afterwards she gets news of
his death.

She felt his death keenly, and in memory went back to New
Zealand and to their growing up in childhood together. Sorrow
releases in her the hidden springs of true feeling, and with love
and reverence and humility she decides to write about her own
country.

"Not only because it is a sacred debt that I pay to my country
because my brother and I were born there, but also because in
my thoughts I range with him over all the remembered places.
The people we loved there—of them, too, I want to write ... Oh,
I want for one moment to make our undiscovered country leap
into the eyes of the Old World."

And so she came to write "Prelude"," At the Bay", "The
Doll's House", "The Garden Party", "The Voyage"—stories
that are a permanent contribution to the literature of the short
story. In these she is an artist of the normal. There is nothing
bizarre about them, nothing in them to strain our credulity.

In "Prelude" and "At the Bay" she takes the Burnell family:
husband and wife, the children, grandmother and aunt, servant-
girl and neighbours. Her acute perception seizes the small
things that make up their day-to-day existence, the small things
that cause sorrow or joy or frustration in every family.

The father in a hurry out to his work in the morning chivies
everyone around him, and has no time to be polite. And, then,
the difference it makes to the whole household when he's gone.
The joy to have a man out of the house: "Their very voices are
changed as they call to one another; they sound warm and

loving, and as if they shared a secret." It is, I think, in her revelation of these small things and their effect on human character and human relationships that she manifests her specific individuality.

She has a specific grace, too, when writing about children (read "The Doll's House"), for she is able to write of them with complete naturalness and unsophistication—a gift that she shares with Mary Lavin, Katherine Anne Porter and Mary Beckett. Her work abounds in delightfully fresh observation of childhood:

> That afternoon they were allowed to cut jugs and basins out of a draper's catalogue, and at tea-time they had real tea in the doll's tea-set on the table. This was a very nice treat, indeed, except that the doll's tea-pot wouldn't pour out even after you'd poked a pin down the spout and blown into it.

Or this from "At the Bay":

> "Oh, Kezia! Why are you such a messy child," cried Beryl despairingly.
> "Me, Aunt Beryl?" Kezia stared at her. What had she done now? She had only dug a river down the middle of her porridge, and was eating the banks away.

Freshly observant as she is to externals, it is not her greatest endowment. We remember her most for her knowledge of the adult world: her ability to capture the subtle gradations of mood and the emotional complexities that spring from trivialities. We remember her, too, for her poetical evocation of the New Zealand background, and when this background is in organic relationship with her characters, as it always is in the case of Aunt Beryl in "At The Bay" and "Prelude," her work is at its finest.

She is not everybody's writer. Her stories are almost plotless, concerned with mood rather than incident, with subtlety rather than the obvious, with sensitivity rather than the bareness of fact. If she had lived longer she would, I feel, have probed deeply into the corrupting influences of petty jealousies and hates and absences of love that surround ordinary lives.

Journals 1955

April 1955

I can't understand how it is that in some quarters my novels are regarded as thin or insubstantial. Is that the fate of all artists who hint and suggest rather than state and state concretely and abundantly? To be popular, a writer must leave nothing to the reader's imagination—give the poor reader everything and tie up everything in a neat parcel. Leave nothing in doubt. Write always on the surface.

* * * * *

1955

To reveal the stupidities of people: the violence they do to their own nature and to other people by their hates and angers and jealousies and avarice, is my aim. Our corrupt tendencies are, I hope, made manifest in my work. And the obverse side of this is the manifestation of kindness and affection: the flowering of charity and its withering. As a writer that is my aim. And there is the conflict. A good novel increases our sense of living, our sense of right and wrong—it is an increase in our knowledge of ourselves and of other people.

"Mr. Lionel Trilling said the greatness of a novel lay in its work of involving the reader in the moral life." (quoted in *Listener*, April 21, 1955, by T. R. Fyvel).

* * * * *

14 May 1955

Digging in the garden I notice that the weeds grow strong in the silence of the shade; they do best when out of the light from the sun. (Man's evil grows strongest in darkness when out of the *Light*).

* * * * *

A snail leaves a slime behind it, so too does Evil.

* * * * *

31 May 1955
Man's unhappiness is due to his failure in understanding the meaning of the Cross. He cries out against disappointment, against suffering. If he would only accept it, synthesize it as God's given plan for him, realise the pain and ask God to give him the strength to bear it without whining. God loves the courageous man and it is to him He gives His grace, His love.

Man strives to live for himself alone. He is the centre of all things—such an attitude disharmonizes life and produces unhappiness.

* * * * *

3 June 1955
"A contented man," says Pascal, "is one who is not at war with God and Nature."

We must harmonise the spirit and the sense; we bring disruption and disquiet to ourselves when we try to live without the spirit, as the modern world does, or when we try to live without the senses as some ascetics do. Hopkins had this struggle for harmony and it was Duns Scotus ("who of all men most sways my spirits to peace") who helped him not to stifle or smother his love for all created beauty. The beauty of God's creation, loving it, makes us feel the presence of God.

* * * * *

4 June 1955

Walk along the Lagan: the leaves of the water-lilies lie flat on the surface of the water. Raindrops lay on them like blobs of grease. The leaves were shaped like trowels.

* * * * *

14 June 1955

Reading a few stories in *Types of Literature*. Read Hemingway's story, Eudora Welty's, Graham Greene's and *Dostoevsky's* and E. Bowen's. Dostoevsky's story has heart and feeling. The others are cold, scientific, inhuman in comparison. All head. Irish stories, when they are good, have this kinship with the Russians: feeling, love humanity. "The Dead", "Guests of the Nation."

* * * * *

26 June 1955
The Short Story

I have just heard adjudicators' reports on a short story competition run by Radio Éireann. They found that the short stories dealing with childhood were the best. A pity they didn't try to give a reason why this should be.

Why? It is the emotional aura that surrounds childhood reminiscences that engenders the "good"—the emotional capacity of the theme sets the writer on the right key: having got that he will write above his accustomed pitch. There's an urgency behind the work, truth to reality. They live, are viable, and so they shine out above the fantastical nonsense and unreality.

* * * * *

1955

There is something lacking in the Irish short story when we compare the best of our products with "The Death of Ivan

Ilych," "Ward 6," even Power's "Lion's Hearts, Leaping Does." In this latter we reach a different plane of feeling and understanding. In Tolstoy's great story we are in the world of values and are aware of some judgement, some criticism of life. Our spirit is moved, is shaken. "To live for others," Tolstoy shows us, is the *real* life. In "Ward No. 6" a man refuses to fight against evil and is ruined by not doing so. Powers' story is one on *selfishness*. We meet the same in James's "The Beast in the Jungle." The nearest we get to these in Irish work is Mary Lavin's "A Small Bequest," "The Will," Joyce's "The Dead."

The Irish story at its best is full of feeling but it seldom reaches the high plane of spiritual values set by "The Death of Ivan" etc. The great story sets us reflecting.

Anton Chekhov

published in *Belfast Telegraph*, 5 November 1955.

"Life has gone by as though I hadn't lived." That sober reflection, one of the saddest Chekhov ever penned, forms one of the concluding sentences of his play, *The Cherry Orchard*.

It is a sentence that distresses many a man as he realises that the years have stolen upon him and all the things that he intended to do are left undone. But Chekhov, weak as he was in health (he died from tuberculosis), did not allow the years to sift away unused and unnoticed.

Into his short life of forty-four years he packed a lifetime's work: as a doctor, a playwright, and a short-story writer of unsurpassed merit.

His letters have long been out of print and a new selection has now been published with an admirable commentary and introduction by Lillian Hellman (Hamish Hamilton, 21s).

A young writer will gain much from them, not only worthwhile advice on writing, but also an insight into the character of a fascinating humanist: a man of spacious sympathies, absolute fair-mindedness, and gifted with self-criticism and a gentle ironic humour.

His life was never an easy one at any time. He was born in 1860 in Taganrog, in Southern Russia, and after matriculation from the local grammar school, Anton entered the University of Moscow in the faculty of medicine and there, to support himself and his thriftless family, he began to write shoals of humorous stories under a nom de plume.

Written out of economic pressure and not from the impulsion of themes that engaged his deepest sympathies, he later decried them, and it wasn't until he became a doctor that he turned away from such frivolous dissipations of his gifts to take a serious interest in literature.

"My work in the medical sciences," he wrote in a letter, "had undoubtedly a great influence on my writing: certainly it widened the area of my observations, and only one who is himself a doctor can tell how valuable the training has been."

His fame was rapid and he was awarded the Pushkin prize for literature before he was thirty.

Lack of money and impoverished health incessantly worried him, and yet we read of him doctoring patients without payment, building three schools with his own money, and setting out on a voluntary journey across Siberia to expose in writing the inhuman condition in the penal settlement at Sakhalin.

He spent three months on Sakhalin, made a census of the entire population, witnessed a flogging that gave him nightmares, and spoke with convicts chained to their wheelbarrows.

After the journey is ended he remarks in a letter: "God's earth is good. It is only we in it who are bad ... We must work, the hell with everything else. The important thing is that we must be just and all the rest will be added on to us."

Throughout his life he continually stressed this importance of work and often chided himself for his idleness.

In his play, *Three Sisters*, characters' opinions are often consonant with his own: "A man ought to work, to toil in the sweat of his brow, whoever he may be ... The reason we are depressed and take such a gloomy view of life is that we know nothing of work ... If only for one day in my life to work so that I come home at night tired out and fall asleep as soon as I get into bed ... Workmen must sleep soundly."

A play like his *Three Sisters* or his volumes of short stories will never be popular: for he writes with compactness, writes by the line and not by the chapter, making no concessions to the skimming reader.

His stories have no swift and vigorous action, no accentuated plot or mechanical devices that would sever the life in them. He tosses off pivotal sentences with an air of careless casualness and often renders the feelings of his characters by means of a lyrical atmosphere—an artistic device that Mauriac is praised for at the present time.

His best stories are conflicts of the spirit, his drama taking place within the life of the mind. He avoids the exceptional in life and eschews all flashiness and falsification, the precious bane of many Irish writers.

"Bear in mind," he writes to a critic who called him unprincipled and directionless, "that writers who are considered immortal or just plain good and who intoxicate us have a very important trait in common: they are going somewhere and beckon you with them—the best of them are realistic and paint life as it is, but because every line is saturated with the sense of life, you feel, in addition to life as it is, life as it should be, and you are entranced."

A contrast between "life as it is" and "life as it should be" forms the fine-edged fulcrum of many of his stories.

"The Bishop" is a convenient example. An old mother with her little grandchild, Katya, pays a long visit to a monastery where her son is a bishop.

He is in poor health; they meet occasionally in his room and at each meeting his inmost desire is that she will talk of home and his beloved village. But she is constrained and formal in his presence, speaks artificially, and being embarrassed at sitting before him, makes excuses to stand up and get away.

Inwardly he is vexed and hurt, but out of delicacy of feeling says nothing, and later hears her talking freely with the lay brother in the adjoining room.

Katya, the child, slips in to see him, and her directness and naturalness contrast with the stiff formality of the mother:

> "Is that you, Katya?" he asked. "Who is it downstairs who keeps opening and shutting a door?"
> "I don't hear it," answered Katya; and she listened.
> "There, someone has just passed."
> "But that was a noise in your stomach, uncle."
> He laughed and stroked her on the head ...

191

As she is telling him about the death of her father, her cousin, and the wretched conditions at home, the mother comes in and takes her hand: "Come along, Katya; let his holiness sleep a little."

A few days later when the bishop is dying the mother is natural with him for the first time, but by then he is beyond consciousness and her feelings are lost on him.

A similar ending pervades his well-known story, "The Grasshopper," a story of marital estrangement: "Life as it is" and "Life as it should be."

But deeper than either of these is "Ward No 6," a story of rich moral complexity that exemplifies his greatness as a short-story writer.

"All works of art," says F.R. Leavis, "act their moral judgments." This, too, was a specific creed with Chekhov. He never judged his characters: by deft strokes of implication he presented the moral problems and left the judgement to the reader.

It is this moral involvement, the touchstone of the greatest fiction, that makes his stories so difficult to summarise or retell orally. His stories are experiences that we relive at each rereading and are not memorable in the manner of heavily actioned stories with climactic endings.

Though the conditions prevailing in provincial hospitals have changed since he wrote "Ward No. 6," its essential theme—a good man's misunderstanding of the true nature of meekness—remains unaltered. And as soon as the reader perceives this submerged theme the whole story explodes with meaning.

Dr. Ragin is appointed to a job in a provincial hospital. He is gentle, refined, unmarried, and lives a life of unruffled habit. He reads much and with understanding, and has a theory that man's peace and contentment depend on himself and not on outside circumstances.

It is this theory that receives a cruel and devastating demolition before the story ends. He sees the cooked accounts he has to sign, and is aware of the polite dishonesty of the superintendent and the roughness of some of the nurses, but he hasn't sufficient moral strength to oppose or expose these and other evils.

Bit by bit his placidity and negative sense of justice are undermined by external forces, and his spiritual and physical ruination are revealed in pages of heart-breaking intensity.

Chekhov's innate gift for selecting the right incidents to counterpoint his theme has never been so magnificently manifested as in this story.

This gift he would have generously presented to other writers if he had been able. But it was, I suppose, a mystery to himself as it is even to those who read him with the same care and attention by which he wrote.

To other writers he could and did give valuable advice, and some of these critical letters, especially those to Gorki, are included in this volume of Lillian Hellman's.

Journals 1956-1959

2 June 1956
Read Frank O'Connor's story, "The Train," in the *Atlantic Monthly*. It has an O'Casey influence but it has no love. It's written in a comic vein for the consumption of outsiders who think the Irish a "queer" race. Its attitude is Ascendancy—"the natives are indeed comic!" But the situation is a lie to begin with.

Comic exaggeration—the bane of Irish writers. Joyce doesn't fail in this respect.

* * * * *

For Dan*
From Heraclitus: "I wept when I remembered how often you and I/tired the sun with talking and sent him down the sky."

* * * * *

1 January 1959
You can't dissolve suffering but you can transfigure it.

* * * * *

* Dan Clarke, died 1956.

Letters 1959

Belfast
23rd January 1959

To John McGahern [*]

I was greatly pleased to get your letter and pleased too to hear that you admire Corkery's beautiful story "Vision." I remember reading reviews of "Earth Out of Earth" and not one critic gave "Vision" as much as a line of praise. Years later I met Corkery and I told him I thought "Vision" his best story and he smiled in his own quiet fashion, glad to hear that I had loved it. You are fortunate as a teacher starting out on your career by reading stories of such quiet power to your pupils. You'll enjoy your work and your pupils will enjoy school. May I suggest that you also read to them Seamus O'Kelly's "Billy the Clown" and if you can act it, as you read, their enjoyment will be a memorable one. Others that you may find effective are Mary Lavin's "The Sand Castle," Chekhov's "The Runaway" and "Kashtanka," Katherine Mansfield's "The Doll's House" and "The Voyage." And for your own private enjoyment Mary Lavin's "The Small Bequest" and Tolstoy's great, great story "The Death of Ivan Ilich." Of O'Connor's I'd suggest "Uprooted"; he has also written one called "The New Teacher" but it's so silly, so palpably unreal, I often wondered why he enclosed it between the covers of a book.

I don't teach any more and I regret that greatly. This past eighteen months I'm head of a large secondary school in the city and though the salary is good the administrative work is

[*] John McGahern, (1934-   ), novelist and short-story writer

195

unrewarding and it leaves me with no time and no energy at the end of the day. *The Choice** was finished two weeks before the school opened and except for a little story, not a good one, written during the Christmas holidays, I haven't had time to write or even think of writing, and the thinking is more important than the actual labour of writing. But as each week passes I always hope that the burden of school will lighten and leave me time to follow the heart's desire. Strange to say, my literary work has no following in Ireland, and the novel about the school sold poorly here and yet was a success in Italy where it still sells moderately after two or three years in print. But of all my books I have the deepest affection for *The Three Brothers* and *In This Thy Day*.

You'll be interested to hear that my greatest friend Dan Clarke (he died three years ago) was married to a Roscommon lady, a Fellon from Castlerea. She is still living here in Belfast but since her husband's death and for me too this place is not the same.

Good wishes to you always, and may you enjoy teaching as much as I did. One word more: now that you have written to me you should write to Corkery about his "Vision;" he'd be very pleased. He lives with his sister near the entrance to Cork Harbour.

Professor Daniel Corkery, Roberts's Cove, Co. Cork, would be sure to find him.

*   *   *   *   *

Belfast
22nd April 1959

To Mary Harris

Well, here I go again to thank you for *The Wolf* and to send you a few of my own books. I am sorry I haven't a copy of *Truth in the Night,* a book I think you'd like and one that *Time* magazine gave a whole page to. The volume of stories was well reviewed both at this side and in America and the B.B.C. Sunday critics

---

* *The Choice*, published 1958 by Macmillan and Cape.

did it over the air, Walter Allen having selected it that week. The last story in the book I like best but I have written others since then, and one of them, "The Circus Pony," about my own nieces I'll send to you when I get my hands on it. Others have been translated and I have been lucky too in getting a novel into Spanish, one in Italian, and the last one, *The Choice,* is coming out in German this year. I don't employ an agent, for I'm not a professional writer, and I like the personal touch that one gets when working alone. I do believe you'd fare better with *The New Yorker* if you by-passed your agent and sent one on your own steam.

I wrote to Chatto but, unfortunately, your book is out of print. I'm reading it slowly for the second time. And time and again I've raised my eyes from the page and shaken my head over the stupidity of the reviewers. Why do they steeplechase through an artist's work, hopping and skimming and getting to the heart of nothing. Your book's so genuine I'm annoyed it didn't get the success it deserves. The unspoken jealousy in it, the young girl's life withering for affection, her sense of guilt, her docility, the fresh and unified characterisation, and the theme splendidly converging in that final chapter and opening out again after we close the book. Any of those qualities would make a good book but their combination makes for an unique one. And yours is surely that. If one dwells on the style on any page an artist's hand has worked reverently over it: no down-at-heel phrases, no verbal extravagance, no intellectual posturing, nothing but coolness, precision, and noble dignity. There are times when that old gargoyle Flora is cross-questioning the child that you make one cry out in anger: "Flora, for the love of God leave the child alone!" You make a reader physically present at what you describe; and then the fresh and compelling details charged with emotional significance—"the threading of the needle ... and the old brass knob on the bed-post." Chekhov would have loved them and Henry James would have admired the beautiful working out of the theme. But what you don't say is even of greater import: it's all there as we read it but you haven't expressed it. Flora was there in every chapter even if you didn't mention her name.

One knew she was going through Mrs Randolph's things long before you told us so. I don't think I'm making myself clear but one can't really analyse the atmosphere of a book; it's an experience that we enjoy when we read a book. It's achieved not by piling up words but by leaving them out. Some of the American books need a lawn-mower at them and not a pruning knife. There's a little word you are overfond of and that you overwork and I'm not going to draw your attention to it in case you'd think you had put a blemish on a page—and you haven't.

Where will I go next? Yes, Forrest Reid. He, too, was an artist. But of all his books the one I have read twice is *Brian Westby*. I prefer that to his trilogy. Do you know that he lived alone? When we lived at the other side of the city I used to see his washing out on the line on my way from the school on Monday afternoons. I'd see his shirt, two collars, a pair of socks and a couple of handkerchiefs taking their fill of the breeze, and in the evenings I used to see him going or coming from his walk. But I never spoke to him. I was too shy at that time and had never written a line and for that matter I had little or no sense of literature. I was interested in it but that's not the same thing. You see I had done science at the university and was only a semi-educated savage. It was about that time that I read *Memoirs of a Midget* but I must say I never finished it; your letter is going to send me back to it. I did read some journal of Julian Green's years ago but I can't say that I had ever any yearning to return to it. I looked for *The Closed Garden* today in the library but found *The Transgressor* and I have it home with me and *The Little Ark* by Jan de Hartog. I never read anything of the latter's.

I suppose you know James's *Portrait of a Lady*. And do read Mary Lavin's story "A Small Bequest" and "The Cemetery in the Demesne." Her last volume is not so good: "Chamois Gloves," a story about a young nun and "A Meeting" are to my mind the best things in it. Macmillan in America are bringing out a selected volume next month. When she's good she's really good and when she's not … well, that's a different story. Of K. Mansfield I find her handful of New Zealand stories her best: her heart is in them and but for the death of her brother she might never have written them and would probably be now forgotten. Read K. Anne Porter's "Old Mortality"—to my mind it's America's best.

(30th July 1970)
Author's note on Mary Harris
Mary Harris wrote some lively books for children (girls of fourteen plus would love them). She wrote two novels and her first *My Darling from the Lion's Mouth*, I picked up among "remainders." It impressed me greatly and I wrote to her about it. Crowell in U.S.A. published it. Her second novel I disliked but didn't write to her about it. She was a convert to Catholicism and died about 4 years ago (R.I.P).

*   *   *   *   *

30th January 1961

To John McGahern

I am sorry to hear of the death of your friend. Last time, some six or seven years ago, when I was speaking to Corkery he mentioned your friend and, I think, his sister. With them he included the poet Sean Ó Riordáin whose work he said had fine possibilities ... I can't read Irish, I'm sorry to say, but I do recall reading translations of some of Ó Riordáin's poems in the *Dublin Magazine* which seemed to me to be in the Hopkins manner: not in the metre but in the associative depth and freshness of the images chosen. They set up wide ranges in the mind; they had body and strength ... and not superficial or secondhand in the manner of, say, Betjeman, as exemplified by a poem of his which I have just read in a recent *New Yorker*, a poem about toast in the mornings and bicycling excursions in the summery afternoons. It had as much freshness in it as the lower Liffey after a summer drought.

How are you? I take it that the typewriter is a good sign of work to come. Keep at it. Have you called on Mary Lavin again? You should keep in touch with her. You'll find her a great help and stimulus. I'm working away at a novel but can't really get time to get my teeth fully into it.* The school is a burden, and there's no let-up in the foreseeable future except I gave it up entirely. I would do that if my family were free.

*   *   *   *   *

Belfast
23rd March 1961

I'm sorry for having kept your magazine for so long. I have been very busy of late, both in the school and out of it, and though I read your work as soon as it arrived I hadn't time to write to you.

Your work afforded me the same rush of delight that used to come over me when I saw my algebra teacher write on the board Simplify. To read your work and Chekhov's and Tolstoy's is to convince me that simplicity is the finest ornament of any style: the few words, the right words, chosen for point and propinquity. It was this fine control that fascinated me, for the young are too prone to have the loud-stops full out. Not so with you: each sentence was sharp and effective, each incident achieved without fuss, intimate without being laboured. Indeed the style in that first section had the sting and clarity of an early morning in October.

There's a lovely paragraph beginning: "It was a dark night." And then those vivid touches: of the the light fumbling in the hills; the wet clay and the spuds; the waterbarrel overflowing; the coiling of the string to put in the empty tea-canister—all these suggest far more than what is on the page. They give the piece substance for they are the right details in the right places, something that is never learned in a correspondence school. They are the individual touches, God's gifts, poetic and not enumeration. How they reminded me of Chekhov's famous advice to a young writer as he urged him to cut out and simplify: you evoke a moonlit night by saying simply: "A star-

* *The Brightening Day,* published by Macmillan, New York, 1965.

point flashed from the neck of a bottle floating on the mill-dam." Saturate yourself in the material and the quintessential will take care of itself.

I only boggled at one phrase—"on the tussocks in the frost"—I thought it unnecessary, a blurring of an effect already achieved. But one couldn't boggle at the people: they were alive and biting as a chapped finger in a frosty wind. You felt them, not one-sidedly but compact with feelings that had the human ferment of black and white.

Don't be stampeded by any letter from a pressing publisher. Take your time and let your work ripen and fall of itself. You have your teaching job and you haven't to write in order to live. Now that you have a foothold in *X* let them publish you for another while till you are firmly established.

I was sorry I didn't see you during my few hours in Dublin. If you had come into the hotel we could have walked together to Amiens Street.

* * * * *

Belfast
15th May 1961

To Sybil Hutchinson *

"The Wild Duck's Nest" is one of the first stories I ever wrote. The first draft was written during an English class in the school where I was teaching. It was always my policy to interest the English class in creative prose rather than in the factual or the commentative. And to develop this attitude I would give the class an opening sentence and asked them to enlarge upon it.

Sentences like: "It was growing dark and the old man, too tired to switch on the light, sat quietly by the fire" or "The two boys had spent all their money, and as the snow began to fall they watched the last bus leave for the outskirts of the town

* Sybil Hutchinson, a Canadian academic who approached the author for information about his method of writing.

where they lived." One day as the class were engaged on writing a story beginning with the sentence "The boy watched the lone wild duck circling over the mountain lake" I thought of Rathlin Island where I had spent much of my childhood and from that memory there slowly emerged "The Wild Duck's Nest."

From my experience of teaching children I find that they can write well on any subject that has moved them, providing that they brood over it and let it ripen slowly in the mind. In the initial stages they should not think of plot or climax. Their minds should dwell on character and atmosphere, and in this way they will write naturally and without fuss or stiff contrivance. They should write truly and write about their own people and their own experiences. Katherine Mansfield only found her own voice, her true voice, when the news of her brother's death in World War I awakened her to the life they had both lived as children in New Zealand. From that sudden heartbreak came those stories, stories with a New Zealand setting, by which she proclaimed her status as a real artist: "The Doll's House," "At the Bay," "Prelude," and "The Voyage." They have unity and universality because she didn't strive for those qualities. She achieved them because those stories were written out of deep love for her brother and her homeland. As Yeats says: "To this universalism, this seeing of unity everywhere, you can only attain through what is near you, your nation, or, if you be no traveller, your village and the cobwebs on your walls."

*　*　*　*　*

To Sister Mary Edna *

Your kind letter has set me a problem, a problem that I'll not answer in my direct way, for I dislike theorising about my work, believing that it would only entrench it in a hard mould and spoil the freedom and freshness that works of art should manifest. But on hunting through old papers I came across two critical articles that I had written on Chekhov and Katherine Mansfield, and on rereading them I felt that what I had said about their work could by easy transposition be said about my own endeavours–not, mind you, that I am putting myself in the same category as those two artists. And along with the articles I came across a few reviews that may interest you. When you have perused them you may send them back to me for they may give some pleasure to my own children after my days are spent.

Other things that you may look up or have seen are a critical essay on my work published by a Dominican Sister in January 1959 issue of the American magazine *Today* and a few pages towards the end of Blanche Mary Kelly's book *The Voice of the Irish* published by Sheed and Ward in New York. I could send you some American reviews of my books, but I presume you have seen them and I don't wish to burden you. The quote you are looking for I can't remember when I wrote it: it was probably written in a letter to my publishers and they fished it out and printed it on the dust jacket of one of my books.

I am sorry you didn't mention *In This Thy Day* for I feel it is one of my best books. And when I tell you that *Truth In The Night* was originally entitled *Let Not the Sun Go Down,* and had as epigraph (deleted while I was correcting the proofs for I thought it would put people off) Hopkins's line: "Hast thy dark descending and most art merciful then," I have revealed a great deal.

* Sister Mary Edna, a member of the Mercy order, in Milford, Connecticut, had written to McLaverty in late 1961 to ask his help in a research paper she was writing on his work.

I have a predilection for the ordinary in life, for the normal, for the small talk that leads to sudden changes in mood, for the ambience of evil that arises from spite, discord, anger, hatred, revenge, hardness of heart—in short, for the absence of charity. Charity holds people together, its absence is a destructive force that many people live by without realising it. The old woman in *Truth in the Night* holds all things together while Vera's spite tends to destroy not only herself but even the small social fabric of the island. Her pride is her undoing and God batters the hard heart to gain entrance and win it salvation. In *In This Thy Day* toward the end of the book Mrs Mason is neighbourly for the first time and something has touched her. Chekhov and Tolstoy have explored these human traits with much greater pungency and power than I have done or ever hope to do. Mauriac has also done it, superbly in *The Tangle of Vipers,* but inhumanly in many of his other books. There's no joy in the man; to read him you wouldn't think that the word had become flesh and dwelt among us.

I am greatly pleased that there are still some readers who can read me in a quiet place and read me slowly the way that I wished to be read for it is the way I write. But it is a pity that much of the humour in my books does not carry across the Atlantic. When Kate O'Brien reviewed *Lost Fields* she said I sacrificed too much to humour, while in America they regarded the book as gloomy and depressing.

You will be glad to hear that most of the short stories have been translated into many languages. Of the novels *The Choice* and *Lost Fields* appeared in German, *School for Hope* in Italian, and *In This Thy Day* in Spanish.

I am sending this letter by air-mail and I'll send the clippings by sea.

Good wishes to you and remember me daily in your prayers. I haven't time to pray these days. I became headmaster of St. Thomas's Secondary School, a new school, some four years ago and I am hard-pressed daily. I am half-way through a new novel and if you keep up the prayers I may be able to finish it this year.

Tell your companion that Lady Street is at the side of the

city, a quiet street that I used to pass by daily when I lived at that side myself.

One word more: the island mentioned in *The Three Brothers* is not regarded as the burial place of St. Patrick; there's a well on it connected with his name. It's quite close to Lough Neagh and has no connection with Rathlin.

I have answered some of your questions, and God forgive me for side-stepping most of them.

* * * * *

To John McGahern

Belfast 9
27th September 1962

Alas, I'll not be able to make for Dublin this week-end. I have just returned to school today after a heavy bout of 'flu that kept me in bed since last Saturday. Though I'm not a hundred per cent fit I feel much better to be out in the air. But I will go up some Friday or Saturday and we'll have a long chat.

I saw where you had a piece in the new *Dolmen Miscellany* and I ordered it direct from Easons in Dublin and read some of the contents during my sojourn in bed. Your new extract is the best yet. You write with extreme care and that quality alone should attract and hold the serious attention of even the most hardened of the hop-skip-and-jump reviewers.

There were one or two places where my Northern eye or ear stumbled, found the rhythm upset, or the object blurred. I tripped off "blinded windows" and would have preferred "that beat on the slates and on the windows." And in the dialogue found that the addition of "on us" knocked off balance the line "rich Americans didn't run off with a girl like you." And a point that seemed to me to lack *general* truth was Regan's use of "bejasus" in front of his children. The rest was a thing of real beauty: the intimate atmosphere, the children, and above all the quiet power of Elizabeth who says so little and yet floods the whole scene with her presence. "Feeling the shirt for dampness" is a delightful stroke. More power to you.

I read a few of the other pieces; found Plunkett's a skillful bit of padding and Moore's old-fashioned despite its modern dress. Kinsella's "Country Walk" disappointed in places because of secondhand stitching and that crippling poetical cliché of Paudeen and his greasy till. It wasn't a patch on his lovely poem of his sweetheart in the hospital with the "air like a laundered sheet," "the world a varnished picture," and the airy spaces of sunlight on the walls of houses seen from the window. I quote from memory as Roy McFadden got the loan of it over a year ago and I must get a spaniel out to retrieve it for me. It would be tragic if Kinsella's gift would turn fierce in face of the critical terriers of Dublin.

Did I tell you I'm now provided with a secretary for the school and I feel now my evenings opening out in freedom. This winter, please God, my pen will not be employed in an official capacity. Don't blame this typing on her—I did it.

P.S. You'd love Muir's autobiography.

*   *   *   *   *

Belfast 9
25th November 1962

You'll be glad when your book like a true homing pigeon has come back to its roost. I'm sorry to have kept it so long. I read two of the stories, "Bartley" and "Billy Budd," the latter, I feel, the better and would repay re-reading. Barley is fascinating on a first reading, but I'd doubt, since it leans too much on the element of curiosity, that I would enjoy it as much on a second reading.

I fished out some of Elizabeth Cullinane's stories from past *New Yorkers*.* (By the way she is a lovely sweet girl and I was glad to meet her.) Her stories are good. They are cool and calm and precise. She takes endless pains to tell the truth and shirks

* Elizabeth Cullinane, American short story writer

the easy line of falsification or comic entertainment, a line that we are all too familiar with. The best of her stories was "The Power of Prayer" which I've since sent on to Teresa Deevy. But what she seems to lack is the facility to distribute emphasis in the proper places. She'll raise our interest on a particular thing and then suddenly, and without an excuse, she'll drop it and then lead us to the real heart and hinge of the work. I haven't her stories beside me as I write, but from memory I can recall a girl in one of the stories coming upon her father slumped asleep in a cloakroom and she leaves him there as if he were a bundle of old clothes. Again there's something about a note being passed across a classroom and we yearn to know what was written on it but she doesn't tell us. In another story there's a lovely sensitive description of an icy pond and a frozen scarf on the bank and when we are thinking that this and the gardener are going to have some significance she leads away somewhere else. I'm describing myself badly and should really have written a comment after each reading and made myself more specific. But in one so young she had a remarkable capacity of conveying the truth with grace and refinement and this will stand to her success when spread over a longer work where strict sharpness of line is not an necessity. I'm sure she'd love "Family Happiness," and if she's still in Ireland over Christmas you should ask her to get *My Darling from the Lion's Mouth* on loan from Mary for I'd love to know what she would think of it.

In another parcel I'm sending you a copy of Edwin Muir's *Autobiography*. I didn't put your name on it in case you don't like it. But I bought it for you and Muir's widow will be the richer by a few bob.

* * * * *

Belfast
Sunday 26th May 1963

You couldn't have selected a better day than the 19th. The exams will be in top gear, the place as quiet as a Trappist monastery, and I'll be at peace to have a chat with you. I usually leave the school around 4.30 and you could come home with me then and have a substantial meal before setting out again.

There's a chap on the staff I'd like you to meet. He has a first class hons in English and though that may suggest to you that he hobbles through literature on borrowed crutches it's not so in this case. He is creative and is endowed with taste and discernment and has read and reread passages in your book with unstinted admiration for its style and quiet power. In September he leaves us and goes to the training college as lecturer in English.*

I'm glad you are with Macmillan and hope you are in direct touch with Cecil Scott. Don't be too sanguine about high U.S. sales for only a small section of that immense population are readers and only a small section are book-buyers.

I have typed nothing at the novel for the past months and won't be able to look at it till August. I just can't write while I'm harnessed to the school. If Maura were finished I'd kick over the traces in thoroughbred style, I'm telling you!

You sound a bit depressed; we all do—and writers more than most. In spite of it force yourself to be gay, seek cheerful company and go for a long tramp over the Dublin hills.

Hope your wee boys get a day with plenty of sunshine.

*   *   *   *   *

Belfast
29th November 1963

To Brian Friel

I wrote a note to you today in school, but with the constant interruptions that are now my daily round that note has gone astray.

What I want to say is this: your play[1] last night moved me as no other play since hearing *Autumn Fire* broadcast from Dublin, a few years ago. There were many beautiful touches in

* Séamus Heaney

208

your play: the birds alighting on the roof of the cell, the yelp of the dog that was kicked, the tin plate pushed under the door, and the Burmese face at the grille—this last touch emphasised for me Hopkins's line: "To the Father through the features of men's faces." The ending of your play was a poignant as Murray's *Maurice Harte*, a play rarely seen nowadays.[2]

I must also add that your "Foundry House" is one of my favourite short stories; I read it in *The New Yorker* and it moved me greatly—the decay in one house and the growth in the other. In one or two sentences you have given us as much as many a good writer would do in a page or two; I think particularly of the child's damp hand on the mother's blouse and she saying: "Put this divil to bed."

Good wishes to you and your good work.

* * * * *

5 May 1964
To write well one must feel deeply. Each section must be well thought out—it is easy to write after lone contemplation.

One has arid periods: better, then, to seek bright companionship. "If you leave your art for a day, it will leave you for three."

Don't wait for inspiration—sit down and write and the ideas will flow.

After wakening in the morning after a long sleep begin to think about what you intend to write that day.

Keep going. Sometimes what you re-read of your own seems dull and insipid. Don't destroy it—read again in a better mood.

* * * * *

[1] *The Blind Mice*
[2] T. C. Murray, (1873-1959) playwright.

To John McGahern

Before your note arrived this morning you had been on my mind quite a lot and I intended to write to you next week and arrange to meet you when I go up at the end of September to see Friel's new play. Since falling in love with his "Foundry House" I'm greatly interested in his work.

Glad to hear about your new novel. I hope it will be brimful with your wonderful gift for intimacy. Did you ever think of writing a play about a barracks? The last scene in your book is an act in itself and would be strong and compelling on any stage. Watch your health and take a long breather before embarking on new work.

My own novel, *The Stranger,* it is called, has been taken by Macmillan (New York). I'm not sure about Cape. My last four books were remaindered and I suppose Cape's patience is exhausted. I've suggested they buy sheets from Macmillan.

See you I hope at end of September. I haven't been in Dublin since February 1963. I'll drop you a card later and hope we'll meet for a long chat.

*   *   *   *   *

I got your very welcome letter before Christmas and would have answered it before this only I was laid up for a short spell, and when I was on my feet again the proofs arrived from New York and I worked hard at them and returned them to Scott in record time. The book is to be called *The Brightening Day,* Cecil Scott having discovered that there was already a book published in the States with the title *The Stranger*. The new title seems to me a better one: it's an optimistic one that may attract a few extra readers. I told you in a previous letter that Cape turned the book down, and now that my staunch friend

Jonathan Cape is dead his successors reminded me that my last four books were remaindered and didn't think the new book would do any better. I don't blame them one bit and we parted good friends and still correspond with one another. After receiving Cape's decision I offered the English rights to Macmillan in New York; their London office will distribute it over here. It may not have been a wise move on my part but it's done now and I needn't grumble.

I would extend this letter if I were sure you'd get it, but since you told me you'd be on the move in Northern Europe I'll wait until you have a permanent address before writing further. Mary Lavin I haven't heard from for a very long time. But she's still on the go as usual and I hear she's going to the States again on a lecture tour. She's wonderful and God has endowed her with tremendous energy. I go to the Galway Literary Society in March to speak about her and Katharine Anne Porter.

I haven't really settled down yet since I retired and find it no easy thing to do. I'm told it takes a year or more to adjust oneself to a new routine.

John, the few sentences you wrote to me about your new novel have saddened me. More anon when I hear from you.

A very happy New Year to you and may God keep you and guard you in all your travels.

Hope you still correspond with Elizabeth Cullinane.

P.S. My wife is in good health and sends good wishes to you for the New Year.

Notes for a Talk on K. Mansfield and K.A. Porter

March 1965 Galway Literary Society

The Short Story

What a short story is I do not know. A critic said it could deal with anything from a girl's first love affair to the death of a horse. I'm wary of definitions where literature is concerned for they only confine and restrict a writer's freedom—his freedom to go his own way, unhampered and uninhibited by a conventional structure or architecture.

This evening I am concerned with stories that will, I feel, endure the pressure and erosions of time. They deal with what is permanent in the heart of man. And what is permanent are the normal characteristics in our day-to-day lives, in our personal relationships: our joys and sorrows, the permanent see-saw of life.

The most difficult thing in writing is to tell the truth. Writers when they are in a hurry to make a living, professional writers, take the easy way of falsehood and exaggeration. It is easier to write about the abnormal, the grotesque—all we need is a lively imagination; but to create truth, to write of ordinary sane men and women, we need imaginative insight, which is quite a different thing.

Nothing will please many and please long but just representation of human nature.

Tolstoy had this gift to a marked degree; and the three writers whom I am going to speak about also have it, not in all their stories but in many of them.

Katherine Mansfield was brought to the realisation of her

truest self by the death of her brother. Prior to his death she had been writing stories about London and cosmopolitan life: stories that are dry, brittle, malicious—written by the mind only; the heart had not been touched by them. The stories were neat, clever, well-wrought but our minds don't return to them—we can only repose on what is stable, the stability of truth. She suffered from ill-health all her life, died at the age of 33 and kept a journal, mainly about herself and her reaction to people, to books, to climate, to writing, and to ill-health. Many of the entries display how a writer sets to work: what trivial scene or incident, what chance remark sets him in action. We gather from her remarks that she was never satisfied with her work, that she failed to get the deepest truth out of an idea. She strove to create background, atmosphere as much a possible; she felt that we don't know people fully unless they are seen against their environment. Unlike Jane Austen she took a long look out of the window at the weather; but this wasn't for mere description, it was used to heighten atmosphere; it was usually consonant with a mood, blended with the characters.

Exile; the pang of exile: Russians: Chekhov: homesickness. Wrote naturally about children: a difficult thing to do: we need detachment here: let them speak in their own fresh way; we must not feel the presence of the adult mind. "These kids are real." Exploring them for their own ends and not manipulating them for the author's.

Katharine Anne Porter:*

I find my writing reveals all sorts of sympathies and interests which I had not formulated exactly to myself ... My whole attempt has been to discover and understand human motives, human feelings, to make a distillation of what human relations and experiences my mind had been able to absorb. I have never known an un-interesting human being, and I have never known two alike.

A short story needs first a theme, and then a point of view, a certain knowledge of human nature, and strong feeling about it, and style—that is to say, his own special way of telling a thing that makes it precisely his own and

* Katharine Anne Porter, in *The Days Before*, New York, 1952.

213

no one else's ... The greater the theme and the better the style, the better the story.

Advice to writers
First, have faith in your theme; then get so well acquainted with your characters that they live and grow in your imagination exactly as if you saw them in the flesh; and finally, tell their story with all the truth and tenderness and severity you are capable of; and if you have any character of your own, you will have a style of your own; it grows, as your ideas grow, and as your knowledge of your craft increases.

The artist can do no more than deal with familiar and beloved things, from which he could not, and, above all, would not escape. So I claim that I write of things native to me, that part of America to which I belong by birth and association and temperament, which is as much the province of our native land as Chicago or New York or San Francisco. All the things I write of I have first known, and they are real to me.

The Short Story
Couldn't think of a definition than would embrace all the kinds of short stories that we know.

Time-element: Flaubert's "A Simple Heart" and Chekhov's "Darling" would not fit in.

The general run fit into a single situation leading to a climax: "First Ball," "The Doll's House," Mary Lavin's "The Will." But some of the best don't fit in: Katherine Mansfield's pictures of family life in "At the Bay," "Prelude" (a series of climaxes rather than a single climax) K. A. Porter's "Old Mortality," Chekhov's "The Steppe."

Henry James "the beautiful and blessed novelle." His are long, some intrigue working itself out and leaving people changed in themselves and in their circumstances.

But a short story does not need to be of any great length in order to be beautiful and enduring: Mansfield's "The Apple Tree," Bate's "Fishing, " Corkery's "Vision."

To write well you must *love;* "Feeling," love in particular, is the great moving power and spring of verse." (G.M.H)

"Long-looking, long-loving, long-desiring reaches other inner essence of a thing."

The heart must be touched: Friel's "Foundry House."

Love of New Zealand made Katharine Mansfield into a writer: Extracts from *Journal* after hearing her brother's death; Read "The Apple Tree," parts of the Doll's House.

And when Friel was not out for a laugh at any price love made him write "The Foundry House."

Nothing wears as well as truth and nothing fades as quickly as falsity.

You can fake many things in a short story but you can't fake psychology and get off with it. Joyce's stories are still the most alive that we have because the psychology is not faked. He's true to his people's ways and opinions. Furniture dates and in the long run does not matter. What matters is psychology. That is why Tolstoy is still the greatest novelist.

Many writers abhor clichés of language but don't abhor clichés of situation—a pity.

K.M. talked of the public's dreary interest in the promiscuous; Take "The Death of Ivan Ilych," "The Steppe", "Easter Eve".

K.A. Porter's "Pale Horse, Pale Rider"—a love story, tender and beautiful

Katherine Mansfield
When an author drives his characters at a tremendous pace she complains:

> Why will he not see that we would rather—far rather—they stay at home, mysteriously themselves, with time to be conscious, in the deepest richest sense, of what is happening to them ... Then indeed, as in the stories of Chekhov, we should become aware of the rain pattering on the roof all night long, of the languid, feverish wind, of the moonlit orchard and the first snow passionately realized, not indeed as analogous to a state of mind, but as linking that mind to the larger whole.

This is her own method and nowhere in her stories is it more surely used than in her portrayal of the adolescent girl, Beryl, in "Prelude" and "At the Bay"—with her dreams and her languor, or with Linda, the mother of the children.

And in "Prelude," in a couple of symbolic paragraphs she can capture with admirable reticence the relationship between Linda and her husband, thus:

> She was really fond of him; she loved and admired and respected him tremendously. Oh, better than anyone else in the world. She knew him through and through. He was the soul of truth and decency, and for all his practical experience he was awfully simple, easily pleased and easily hurt.
>
> If only he wouldn't jump at her so, and bark so loudly, and watch her with such eager, loving eyes. He was too strong for her; she had always hated things that rush at her, from a child. There were times when he was frightening— really frightening. When she just had not screamed at the top of her voice: "You are killing me." And at those times she had longed to say the most coarse, hateful things.
>
> "You know I'm very delicate. You know as well as I that my heart is affected, and the doctor has told you I may die any moment. I have had three great lumps of children already."

Her reticence, using one sentence where many an author would take a few pages. In "At the Bay", "Beryl felt that her mind was being poisoned by this cold woman, but she longed to hear."

* * * * *

Letters 1965

Belfast
23rd May 1965

To John McGahern

I have read your novel and was greatly impressed by its painful sincerity and its pared-to-the-bone style, a style that has caught the essential and has left the verbal flotsam and jetsam to the best-selling novelists. In spite of the pressure upon me of the fine reviews it has received *The Barracks*, because of its wider scope of characterisation, seems to me the better book. Still, *The Dark* could be read as a continuation of *The Barracks* with Regan and Mahoney one and the same person.

I haven't the book beside me as I write, but when I recall it there stands out: the fishing on the river, the throwing of water round the screeching holepins, studying for exams, thoughts engendered by two old boots on a hearthstone, and the rain-damp atmosphere of an old garden. It would be difficult to analyse how you achieved this and to attempt to do so would be to kill it—it's your own natural gift as a writer and if you were fully conscious of it it would blemish the ease and inevitability of your style. The book rings with truth at every turn and it must have been a heart-breaking and exhausting book to write. I recoiled from one or two pages (a priest's thoughts) and wishes they hadn't been there, though I realise that not a line of it was written out of a weakness to shock or degrade. The final chapters, which I found compassionately moving, do justice to Mahoney as a father and as a man and demonstrate that you have the maturity and fair-mindedness of a true novelist.

Hope you and your wife have had a good holiday in Spain and that we'll meet next time you are in Ireland.

*   *   *   *   *

Belfast
Sunday 13th March 1966

To Cecil Scott

Thank you for your encouraging and friendly letter of the 18th February. I have been very busy and very happy lecturing on the teaching of English to the postgraduates in the College.*

They are now out in the secondary schools in the city doing their practice of teaching, a practice that will last four weeks and keep me busy from nine until four each day supervising their work. Into the bargain the Professor of Education and myself are engaged on a prose and poetry book for schools. We are both tired looking at the stale and uninteresting stuff that's in the prevailing schoolbooks and we've decided to embark on this venture and include mainly the poetry and prose of the modern writers. I am interested in the poetry of Norman MacCaig, a man from your old country who has written a few books of poems, a couple of which has impressed us greatly: *Rain on a Wire Fence* and *Dipping Sheep* for instance.

But this is really what I wish to say. Would you think of publishing a volume of short stories? I know that publishers hate the sight of them arriving in their office for they scarcely ever sell more than 2,000 copies. The late Jonathan Cape told me that though he published such great short stories as those of Katharine Anne Porter they didn't pay him to do so; she had no public, he told me. *Flowering Judas*, her first volume, didn't sell a thousand copies, and so when publishing her second volume *Pale Horse, Pale Rider* he imported sheets from New York and had them bound in London. That book was also a commercial failure. It was sad to hear that from Cape, for I

* St Joseph's Training College, now St Mary's College, Belfast, where McLaverty lectured, part time, in the mid Sixties.

considered the three stories in that book to be the greatest that has come from U.S.A. this century. I don't know how many times I've read them and I only wish I had written them. They are word perfect and are true and true throughout their entire length. There's only one way to be new and that is to be true, and that's the reason why *Pale Horse* will live and the reason why *Dubliners* will live. Three-quarters of O'Connor's are false and will fade into a deserved oblivion but such stories as his "Uprooted," "The Long Road to Ummera," the title story in *Guests of the Nation* and a few others will live. O'Faolain has written two fine novels in *A Nest of Simple Folk* and *Bird Alone*, but the majority of his short stories are faked and, I suppose, were written with an eye on the market. "Admiring the Scenery" is the only short story of his that will survive. Having said that I must add that his book on *The Short Story* is a very good one indeed. In Ireland we laughed at the way American critics praised O'Faoláin's "The Man Who Invented Sin," one of the silliest stories and the most fabricated he ever wrote.

I have wandered from what I want to say. I have about twenty stories that were published in magazines and I do believe that at least fourteen of them are worth publishing in book-form.

"Six Weeks On and Two Ashore" was published in the London edition of *The Game Cock* but not in the Devin-Adair edition as I hadn't it written when submitting my stories to that bunch! It has become world-famous since then and has appeared in three anthologies on the continent and has been broadcast many times. It's a story about marital maladjustment told with tenderness, subtlety, and without disgust. I am sure you remember it for it is in *The Game Cock* volume that I gave you when you were in Dublin. But I have others in the new collection equally good: "The Circus Pony" (John McGahern who loves my work and had read *Truth in the Night* three times thinks that "The Circus Pony" is the greatest thing I've ever done), "Uprooted," "The Half-Crown," "Mother and Daughter," "The Priest's Housekeeper," and possibly, "The Steeplejacks" (I'm not too keen on this one but Séamus

Heaney, who lectures in English in the College and who has a book of poems coming out from Faber next month thinks very highly of it and since he's only a young man of 27 I'd defer to his judgement and include it in the new volume). If you decide to take the collection I would be willing to take a small advance royalty and a lower percentage on book-sales. I would also be willing to have Collier-Macmillan distributing it over here. *The Game Cock* sold about 1500 copies for Cape but in U.S.A. the Devin-Adair company sold 6,000; Garrity wanted me to sign up with him some years ago for another volume but I didn't do so and I'm glad now I didn't.

To get back to the new volume of stories: when you have read that and you decide to publish them I'd love to write an introduction to the book and tell how the inspiration for each story came to me—an introduction like that would attract students to the book.

Before I end I must say this: the blurb on *The Brightening Day* shouldn't have put a Catholic label on me, as the majority of my readers in Northern Ireland are Protestant and I am proud to number them among my friends; the book, too, is set in the Northern-East corner of Ireland and not the West. Your London branch should have pasted a 25/- sticker over the 4.95 dollars—if they had concealed the fact that the book came from the States the English papers might have reviewed it. I don't blame the English papers for not having reviewed it as they haven't space enough to review all the books sent to them by London publishers.

Hope to see you and Eleanor in Ireland this year. I'd love to drive you round the Mourne Mountains and show you the lovely places in this loveliest of lands.

I read John Updike's novel *The Poorhouse Fair* and thought it the best that has come from the States in the last 30 years.

Notes for a talk to a Young Writers' Group, Monaghan, 24th July 1967

Beginnings:

I have often been asked how I came to write—that question is usually asked in a note of surprise because I was a Science student and not an Arts student when I was at Queen's. I was a rather shy sort of student and when I used to go to the Students' Union for a cup of tea and a bun I always sat, if I could manage it, at the same table and always by myself. At another table near me three Arts students usually arrived about the same time, and as I drank my tea, looked out the window, I often eavesdropped on their rather loud conversation. I heard them discuss Wordworths "Prelude" and denounce rather vehemently a lecturer's notes on *King Lear*. I knew nothing about either, and I decided that I was an ignoramus and must fill up the gaps in my education when an opportunity arose.

I must say that I look back on my schooldays not in anger but in gratitude. I was happy in St.Malachy's College and I only wish that we had had enough wit and decency to listen to a Father McCloskey who tried valiantly to teach us English for our Senior. We all thought he was cracked for he used to enter the room saying: "By the waters of Babylon there we sat and wept remembering thee, O Sion!" ... Beautiful language, gentlemen, beautiful language." I remember also his saying aloud one day as he came into the classroom Turner's "Romance;" he read aloud one day a passage from Joyce's *Portrait* (he didn't tell us who wrote it for Joyce's name at the time was taboo) and it was many years later when I was reading the book for myself that I came on the passage and remembered Father McCloskey's reading of it. I remember also that *Macbeth* was the play we had to study and

221

I can recall Father McCloskey's heartfelt pity for Macbeth when he says after the murder "Wake Duncan with thy knocking! I would thou couldst!"

Recalling these things makes me realize how important it is for teachers to read aloud and to read things that are not on the prescribed course. Our teacher, poor man, did, but we in our ignorance blamed him for it and I only wish he were alive now so that I could talk to him in the intimate way that I am now talking to you.

After doing Science at Queen's and learning the names of authors, poems, and plays from the three Arts students in the Union, I made up my mind to do a bit of private reading. I went as a one year student to St. Mary's Teachers' Training College in London. I was only supposed to do the Principles and Practice of Education but being aware that I was a bit of a gom where English was concerned, I asked for permission to attend the English lectures. The lecturer hadn't any of Father McCloskey's idiosyncrasies or genuine enthusiasm and I can't recall any of his lectures except that we studied *Antony and Cleopatra* and a book on Wordsworth by, I think W.H. Hudson. Since I hadn't any examination to do I could read the books for enjoyment and that I proceeded to do.

Reading

To write well we must first of all know how to read well—to read, that it, with discrimination and taste. And a few years after leaving St. Mary's in Strawberry Hill I came across a little booklet *How to Teach Reading* by F.R. Leavis. That little book is no longer in print but, fortunately, it is incorporated as an appendix in his book *Education and The University*. It is an invaluable little essay and all young and aspiring writers and teachers should read it and, in consequence, they will be able to read Shakespeare with a new vision and if they have a mind of their own they'll be able to handle language in a fresh and compelling manner.

Another book I would recommend is J.M. Murry's *The Problem of Style* and particularly the chapter on *Creative Style*.

Those two books I hope will help you to enjoy your reading.

Reading, like writing, is also an art and we have to become apprentices both in order to enjoy life, enjoy reading and enjoy the art of writing. To reach maturity we must read widely and wisely.

Read poetry, especially Shakespeare, and read and reread him every ten years, and what he has to say will ripen with our maturing years. You'll find he's always in advance of us.

Why read poetry? Because poetry in its purest form is the outcome of deep and genuine emotion, and without emotion writing is dead and becomes a record rather than a revelation.

My own favourites, after Shakespeare, are Yeats, Edward Thomas, Hopkins, John Clare, Edwin Muir, and the poets of my own country. Seamus Heaney is a young man to read and watch develop. I read as many of the young poets as I can find! Norman McCaig, for instance.

An experience of complete realization comes over us when *John Clare* writes about the hare:

> Where squats the hare to terror wide awake
> like some brown clod the harrows failed to break.

or *De La Mare* and his Snowdrop:

> Beneath the ice-pure sepals lay
> a triplet of green-pencilled snow.

or *Yeats* and the Swan:

> So arrogantly pure, a child might think
> it can be murdered with a spot of ink

Rodgers

> each one bright and steady as a frog's eye.

Kavanagh

> And the New Moon by its little finger swung
> From the telegraph wires.

Norman McCaig: Rain on a fence wire

> What little violences shake
> The raindrop till it turns from apple
> To stretched out pear ...

Coleridge the eave drops fall

> Heard only in the trances of the blast,
> For if the secret ministry of frost
> Shall hang them up in icicles
> Quietly shining to the quiet moon ...

Edward Thomas: "The Cherry Trees"

> The cherry trees bend over
> And are shredding on the old road
> Where all that passed are dead
> Their petals strewing the grass as for a wedding
> This early may morn when there's none to wed.

Writing (Short Stories)

There is no great writing without emotion and no satisfactory reading unless our deepest sympathies are engaged. Unless you feel deeply your writing will have no incandescence and leave no afterglow: it will be factual, arid, and dull.

"Feeling, love in particular is the great moving power and spring of verse." It's also the great spring of prose. No knowledge of technique—the scaffoldings of literature—will ever be an adequate substitute for the absence of genuine feeling. And you may be sure (granted that you are mature and reflective) that a story or novel or poem that doesn't awaken within you some dormant feeling isn't a good one. That is the primal test.

To write well you must feel deeply and those feelings are the most deep when you are writing about your own homes, your own people, your own backyards. The parochial, the local (the national in this sense), if seen and lived deeply enough is the world. It will jump across its boundaries and become universal. Yeats, when a very young man, reviewing Allingham's poems said truly:

> There is no fine literature without nationality. Allingham had the making of a great writer in him, but lacked impulse and momentum, the very thing national feeling could have supplied. Whenever an Irish writer has strayed away from Irish themes and Irish feeling, in almost all cases he has done no more than make alms for oblivion ... to the greater poets

everything they see has its relation to the national life, and through that to the universal and divine life; nothing is an isolated artistic moment: there is a unity everywhere, you can only attain through what is near you, your nation, or, if you be no traveller, your village and the cobwebs on your walls.

*   *   *   *   *

Letters 1969

Belfast
27th May 1969

To Elisabeth Schnack*

Cape sent me on your letter a few days ago. Yes, I'll be delighted to meet you should you come this way. The College closed at the end of June and we usually spend the summer in our little bungalow about thirty miles from here. The address is Killard, Strangford, Co. Down; and we stay there until the beginning of September. If you have read my last novel *The Brightening Day* you will get a full description of the bungalow and the sea and the surrounding countryside. By the way if it is a TV programme you are thinking of when you visit us I suggest that you *do* Seamus Heaney. His new book of poems comes from Faber and Faber on the 4th June and I think it will enhance his reputation and gain for him as many prizes as his first book of poems *The Death of a Naturalist*. With his Somerset Maugham award he has to do some foreign travel with the cash but he'll be back again from his travels before you'd arrive here, presuming of course that you're not setting out for Ireland right away.

There are many questions I'd like to ask you but I'll content myself with two. Was it you who translated my story "Six Weeks On and Two Ashore" for the German anthology *Europa Heute*? Would you ever think of translating my last novel of *School for Hope* which is still selling in Italy at about six hundred copies a year although it was translated some seven or eight years ago? Marion Von Shroder Verlag who published

* Elizabeth Schnack, German translator.

The Choice has folded up, I hear, but Rex Verlag Munchen has still *In This Thy Day* on their list under the title *Zu Ihren Lebzeiten*. I hope Muchen radio got in contact with you before they broadcast The Schooner last August; I told them to. But I must stop.

I hope the weather is good for your visit. Ireland in good weather is the loveliest and freshest country in the world.

Should I not go on a TV programme for you Séamus Heaney will; I think he is the best poet we have in Ireland at present. The BBC asked me a few times to appear on TV or the radio but I declined with thanks.

*   *   *   *   *

Belfast
5th June 1969

It was pleasant to hear from you again and so soon. A pity I can't get to Dublin to see you and the Brian Friel play. If you haven't read Friel's story "The Foundry House" (it's in his *Saucer of Larks* book) please do. I only wish I had written it! I am sending you a magazine with a good one of his in it and one by myself, one that I am really proud of. It had been published before in *The Dublin Magazine* and also in U.S.A. The BBC gave it a couple of trots but, unfortunately, they take pieces out of it in order to squeeze it into a 15 minute programme. I have about eight or nine other good ones but not enough yet to make another *Game Cock* volume. But I hope to write two stories and a children's book during the College holidays, about ten weeks in all.

At this time of the year the final year students are out on teaching practice all over the county and though I enjoy the work and love driving I find myself pretty tired when I return in the evenings from my journeyings. I hope you'll get good weather during your stay; our country is simply wonderful at this time of the year. While you're here you should take a run out to see Mary Lavin in Bective near Navan. She'd be delighted to see you for I heard her speak of you with great admiration and referred to you as "the *great* German translator." I told her you had translated some of mine including "Father Xmas" and "The Schooner."

I must end. I hope you'll enjoy your stay. Please read "The Foundry House"—horrible title for such a lyrical story; Chekhov would have called it "The House in the Demesne." Did you ever read Giuseppe Berto's story "The Works of God?" A beautifully tender piece of work. I told my publishers in New York (Macmillan) about it and they declared it a masterpiece and were giving it pride of place in an anthology I was to edit for them. I must stop or I'll go on and on like an old woman.

Autobiographical Fragments

1978

"The Wild Duck's Nest" is one of the first stories I ever wrote. The first draft was written during an English class in the school where I was teaching. It was always my policy to instruct the English class in creative prose rather than in the factual. To develop this attitude I would give the class an opening sentence and ask them to enlarge upon it. Sentences like: "It was growing dark and the old man, too tired to switch on the light, sat quietly by the fire"; or "The two boys had spent all their money and as the snow began to fall they watched the last bus leave for the outskirts of the town where they lived." One day as the class were engaged in writing a story which began: "The boy watched the lone wild duck circling over the mountains," I thought of Rathlin Island where I had spent much of my childhood, and from that memory there slowly emerged "The Wild Duck's Nest."

From my experience of teaching children, I find that they can write well on any subject that has moved them, providing that they brood over it and let it ripen slowly in their minds. In the initial stages they should not think of plot or climax, but let their minds dwell on character and atmosphere. In this way they will write naturally and without fuss or stiff contrivance. They should write truly and write about their own people and their own experiences. Katharine Mansfield only found her own voice, her true voice, when the news of her brother's death awakened her to the life they had both lived as children in New Zealand. From that sudden heartbreak there came these stories, stories with a New Zealand setting, by which she proclaimed her real status as an artist: "The Doll's House," "At The Bay,"

229

"Prelude" and "The Voyage." They have unity and universality because she didn't drive for them. They were written out of deep love of her brother and her homeland. As Yeats says: "To this universalism, this sense of unity everywhere, you can only attain through what is near you, your nation, or, if you be no traveller, your village and the cobwebs on your walls."

*   *   *   *   *

"Four Ducks on a Pond"
Preliminary notes for an autobiography, 1982

I was born in Carrickmacross, Co. Monaghan, a town noted the wide world over of its beautiful lace-making, some of which is to be seen in Buckingham Palace where the Queen of England lives. I was only at school in the town for one day—probably at the age of five. I could check that but I haven't been long out of hospital and I'm too tired to rise from the typewriter, or I might take up my pipe and fill it with tobacco and have a long delicious smoke like Compton McKenzie whom I met on the Catholic island of Barra many years ago. If God gives me the strength I'll return some day to the outer and inner Hebrides and maybe meet another Canon McEwan, who is now too old to sing, and instead enriches a party with his lovely speaking voice and good looks. A pity Roy Plomley doesn't put him on his *Desert Island Discs* programme—maybe he had heard that he sails a little yacht which he wants to take with him. If my namesake on Islay* has a yacht I'll call to see him and maybe take in the Orkneys where that lovely Christian poet, Mackay Brown, lives alone and writes his wonderful books. Seamus Heaney, that genius, who once graced the school where I taught, should swop homes for a while and gaze longingly at the paps of Jura or the mountains of Colonsay which Colmcille climbed before pushing on to Iona with its ruins of churches and bee-hive cells. If you go there, and you are a Catholic, you'll have to come off it before a Sunday to hear Mass in Oban's truly beautiful cathedral which Sidney McEwan's

* Bernard McLaverty, (1945-   ) novelist and short story writer.

230

charity concerts helped to pay for. Sidney McEwan also helped to build Galway's cathedral, and when he wasn't asked to its opening he was grievously hurt. In Ireland we have long memories of some things, and short memories where gratitude is concerned. The farmers are always fighting, squabbling over land and bringing one another into court, and falling out with their nearest and dearest and not speaking to one another for years. What a waste of energy would that be!

Michael McLaverty
1982

Bibliography of Main Works by Michael McLaverty

NOVELS

Call My Brother Back, New York and London, 1939.
(Poolbeg edition, 1979)

Lost Fields, New York, 1941; London, 1942.
(Poolbeg edition, 1980)

In This Thy Day, New York and London, 1945.
(Poolbeg edition, 1981)

The Three Brothers, New York and London, 1948.
(Poolbeg edition, 1982)

Truth in the Night, New York, 1951; London, 1952.
(Poolbeg edition, 1986)

School for Hope, New York and London, 1954.

The Choice, New York and London, 1958.

The Brightening Day, New York and London, 1965.
(Poolbeg edition, 1987)

SHORT STORY COLLECTIONS

The White Mare and Other Stories, Newcastle, Co. Down, 1943.

The Game Cock and Other Stories, New York, 1947.

The Road to the Shore, Dublin 1976. (Poolbeg edition)

Collection Short Stories, with an introduction by
Séamus Heaney, Dublin, 1978. (Poolbeg edition)

FOR CHILDREN

Billy Boogles and the Brown Cow, Dublin (Poolbeg) 1982.

Index

(* denotes recipient of correspondence from McLaverty)

Works by Michael McLaverty
Published by POOLBEG

NOVELS

Call My Brother Back
Lost Fields
In This Thy Day
The Three Brothers
Truth in the Night
The Brightening Day

OTHER WORKS

The Road to the Shore
Collected Short Stories
Billy Boogles and the Brown Cow
(a book for children)

MICHAEL McLAVERTY

Call My Brother Back

'A Truly great novel, and the best novel out of the North, or for that matter, perhaps out of Ireland, in modern times.'

IRISH NEWS

'Here again we come upon that haunting prose music which is the sole and distinguished property of the Irish writers.'

SATURDAY REVIEW OF LITERATURE

'A book of decided quality.'

THE OBSERVER

'A new milestone on the road of Anglo-Irish literature.'

IRISH INDEPENDENT

POOLBEG

MICHAEL McLAVERTY

Truth in the Night

In *Truth in the Night,* considered by many to be his
finest novel, Michael McLaverty returns to Rathlin
Island, the scene of part of his first book, *Call My
Brother Back.* Whereas in that book the island is seen
with the uncritical eye of a child, here it is viewed more
realistically. Although its beauty is evocatively
portrayed, life on the island is clearly hard — too hard
for some people: the Craigs, who soon abandon it for
Belfast; and Vera Reilly, the sharp -tongued unhappy
mainland woman,widowed with one daughter who
longs to leave. The story of her second marriage to
Martin Gallagher, a native of the island whose return
after a long absence signifies the fulfilment of a
lifelong dream, is told with compassion but
with unflinching realism.

The character of a tightly-knit rural community, with its
concern for its own and suspicion of the stranger, is
magnificently conveyed. Rarely in a novel has the
redemptive power of love been more manifest.

POOLBEG

MICHAEL McLAVERTY

Collected Short Stories

'There is a regional basis to McLaverty's world and a
documentary solidity to his observation, yet the region is
contemplated with a gaze more loving and more lingering
than any fieldworker or folklorist could ever manage.
Those streets and shores and fields have been weathered in
his affections and patient understanding until the contours
of each landscape have become a moulded language, a
prospect of the mind.'

SEAMUS HEANEY

Michael McLaverty is one of Ireland's most
distinguished short story writers. He paints with acute
precision and intensity the landscape of Northern Ireland,
its remote hill farms, rough island terrain and the
terraced back streets of Belfast. His stories evoke
moments of passion, wonder or disenchantment in the
lives of people living in environments that are often
hostile and cruel. He depicts these small dramas with
remarkable compassion and perception, displaying the
breadth of vision and purity of language that are the
marks of a master writer.

POOLBEG

MICHAEL McLAVERTY

The Brightening Day

Michael McLaverty's finely crafted and passionate novel
follows the fortunes of Andrew Wade, a young school-
teacher who finds himself the innocent victim of a
malicious scandal which threatens to ruin his career.
To make a clean break with the past, he flees to a
small village in the West of Ireland where he soon
becomes employed as a tutor to an invalid boy,
Philip Newman. The serenity and beauty of the
Connemara landscape, the kindness extended to him by
the Newman Family and his growing affection for
an attractive young woman all signal the dawn of a new
era for Andrew. But before long the menacing forces of
suspicion and guilt come to cloud this bright horizon..
Told with remarkable depth of feeling and insight,
The Brightening Day is a compelling narrative
of one man's striving for personal
justice and happiness.

POOLBEG